I0608881

BATTLE CRY OF FREEDOM

BATTLE CRY OF FREEDOM

AN ALPHONSO CLAY MYSTERY
OF THE CIVIL WAR

BOOK TWO

Jack Martin

OPEN ROAD
INTEGRATED MEDIA
NEW YORK

All rights reserved, including without limitation the right to reproduce this book or any portion thereof in any form or by any means, whether electronic or mechanical, now known or hereinafter invented, without the express written permission of the publisher.

This is a work of fiction. Names, characters, places, events, and incidents either are the product of the author's imagination or are used fictitiously. Any resemblance to actual persons, living or dead, businesses, companies, events, or locales is entirely coincidental.

Copyright © 2010 by Jack Martin

ISBN: 978-1-5040-7815-3

This edition published in 2022 by Open Road Integrated Media, Inc.
180 Maiden Lane
New York, NY 10038
www.openroadmedia.com

To my parents, Wanda and Jack Martin, the authors of my being. You are forever missed

BATTLE CRY OF FREEDOM

PROLOGUE

THE MEPHISTOPHELES
OF WALL STREET

The thin, bearded man dressed in a black frock coat sat at the ornate wood desk, steadily writing instructions with his new-fangled reservoir pen to a congressman whose vote he had purchased. Wasting time by having to dip his writing implement every few words was not for him.

The room was filled with rich yet subdued decorations and furniture: not the garish clutter that crowded so many upper-class rooms in the mid Nineteenth Century. Suddenly, the clock over his mantelpiece softly chimed, and he carefully placed his pen beside his document as he counted the strokes of the clock. There were twelve of them. Softly, with an economy of movement, he rose from his desk. Closing the door of his study behind him, the tall, dark man quietly entered a room down the hall.

He stood in the doorway, watching the young sleeping woman gently breathe in and out, watching the angelic baby in the cradle by the bed. He shook his head slightly in bemusement. He was a man who believed in money and power, and little else. He had seen numerous times how shallow human relations were when money was involved, what betrayals of the most important trusts were possible. He thought that he perfectly understood the nature of the universe, and was completely free of sentiment and illusions of affection. Yet, little more than two years ago, this woman had entered his life, a woman who, although intelligent, seemed naively unconcerned with his sinister reputation—a woman genuinely unimpressed by his growing wealth and power. She gave him simple, unconditional love, and joined her fate to his without reserve. She heard the rumors of his unsavory activities, the mutterings against the "Mephistopheles of Wall Street," and dismissed them as the products of jealous and disappointed competitors.

With genuine amazement, he had found himself responding with emotions he had felt would never be his. Now, he stared at his angelic wife as she slept, and the perfect little boy she had given him, and wondered briefly if the gods of money and power were all there was. They were almost all there was, he decided. That was why he would go outside just after midnight to meet the woman.

The meeting was the purest business. He would never feel the stirrings for anyone else that he felt for his adored wife. However, he was determined not to allow the smallest shadow from the darker side of his world of business to penetrate the oasis he had created inside the walls of his home. Smiling ruefully, he quietly shut the door.

Silently, he descended the wide stairway to the front door. Glancing about to make sure no servants were up to see him, he went out into the night, softly latching the door behind him. Reaching the sidewalk, he turned to look at the façade of the Italianate mansion he had bought more for his family than himself. The bricks seemed to flicker in and out of existence due to the uncertain fluttering of the gaslights that illuminated the street facing Gramercy Park. He glanced up and down the avenue; aside from the retreating back of a policeman turning into 26th Street, he was quite alone. Hunching his shoulders against the chill of the autumn night, he crossed the street and walked quickly along the sidewalk that bounded the gated park. Turning the corner, he entered a pool of black shadow cast by a large elm tree at the edge of the park.

"You are late, Mr. Gould," came a liquid, seductive murmur from the shadow. "I had almost decided to leave. Had to shoo a soiled dove away. It would not do for there to be a witness to our . . . connection."

"Strumpets on the street where my family lives," muttered Jay Gould. "I will take it up with Mayor Wood. He will see to it that the police discourage them from leaving the parts of New York where they belong."

The woman in the shadow laughed with genuine amusement. "Yes, Mr. Gould. We cannot have common whores near Gramercy Park. There can only be higher class criminals, such as us."

"You forget yourself, Miss Duval," replied Jay Gould coldly. "The fact you have performed many a valuable service for me has not made you any less my employee. Respect is in order."

The woman again laughed softly and stepped from the deepest part of the shadow. Gould's eyes had adjusted somewhat to the dark, and even in the dim illumination from a distant gaslight, he could take an objective pride in the tall, raven-haired beauty that was his creation. Even her very name was his creation. He shook his head with wonder at the transformation.

During one of his nocturnal rambles, the feral guttersnipe whom he had found crouching over the body of a richly dressed man, clutching a billfold in one hand and a bloody knife in the other, had been named Brigid Doyle. In the thickest of brogues, she had hissed threats at Gould, saying she would kill rather than hang, kill rather than go back to the nunnery until she got the pox. Gould did not fear death. He knew the seeds of consumption were already in him, and that death was his lot sooner rather than later. Instead of quaking with fear, he stared directly into the eyes of the cold-blooded murderess and saw the potential for a very useful instrument.

He spoke calm words to Brigid Doyle and made her an offer of a new life if she would perform services of a certain nature for him. She had begun to laugh and had started to respond that she knew what those services would be, but looking into the black, expressionless eyes of Jay Gould, she stopped. She nodded and accompanied him away from the body of the murdered banker.

Brigid Doyle had become Teresa Duval; the brogue replaced by careful diction that gave some indication of the learning she had absorbed like a sponge; the coarse woolen shift gave way to expensive clothes easily worn. With satisfaction in the soundness of his original judgment, Gould found that his creation was a natural actress who could easily pass as coming from any social class, any part of the country. Most importantly, she was perfectly willing to perform tasks of an illegal nature up to and including the removal of inconvenient rivals, provided the price was right. He was immensely proud of his creation, but was aware that she was potentially dangerous to the operator, like all powerful devices. *It is time to remind her who the master is*, he thought to himself decidedly.

"Miss Duval, our relationship has been mutually beneficial, as well you know. However, you are showing a distressing tendency to forget who the master is and who the servant is. Remember who is who, and you can continue to profit from our association. That includes those transactions you have been making on the market for your own account in a false name, thinking I would not learn of them. I care little if you play pilot fish to my shark, so long as you do as you are told, and are discrete."

There was a feline hiss from the woman in the shadows; she had never dreamed Gould would learn of her trading on what she discovered in the course of her assignments. Softly, ominously, she stepped toward Gould out of the shadows. Her hand started to make a movement toward a cunningly concealed pocket in her frock; but she stopped herself. Gould stood calmly, as if engaged in a conversation with an acquaintance in a public place. She smiled, a dangerous, glittering smile.

"Mr. Gould, you really should be careful about surprising me. I tend to react by instinct to . . . the unexpected. Of course, I imagine if something untoward happened to you, documents would find their way to the police. I would have to depart suddenly, with only a portion of what I have gained. I would rather not do that."

"Just so," said Gould, nodding. "You realize, Miss Duval, you have just demonstrated why I value you so highly. You respond quickly, with utter ruthlessness, but you never forget to use your brain. You need not conceal from me the fact you are building your own fortune on the sly and intend to leave my service when complete independence is within your reach. I expected that and have no fear of your . . . retirement. You have performed so many distasteful tasks for me that you will never try to double-cross me with the authorities: that is, not unless you want to go back to the kind of life you led when I found you, fleeing from town to town, living in slums, dreading the policeman's whistle. So much better to become a society lady in a large city, respected and envied by all who know you. A few more years working for me, and that will be within your grasp."

The woman's posture was stiff; it was obvious that she hated being any man's tool. However, she took a couple of deep breaths, an actor's trick she had learned, and found the rage that was always with her, retreating into its inner hiding places. "Very well, Mr. Gould. In any event, I have done some planning, and I am willing to undertake the task we discussed the other night. The only issue is the price."

"Three thousand dollars, Miss Duval."

"I distinctly remember the figure of five thousand being mentioned when last we met."

"It was indeed. Several times, in fact. But not by me."

"There is more risk than is ordinary. Armies will be on the move. In the heat of battle, I will not be able to count on the sanctity of my sex being respected, even by so-called gentlemen of the South. Furthermore, there will be expenses that cannot be anticipated. You will expect them to be met out of my fee."

Gould sighed. "Well, Miss Duval, you do provide a quality product. Four thousand then. Half now, half upon your return. My final offer."

Duval made a show of hesitation, concealing her glee. "Very well," she said with feigned reluctance, "we have a deal."

Gould reached into the side pocket of his frock coat and tossed a thick envelope to the woman, who caught it deftly and made it disappear. "Two thousand in greenbacks," he said.

Duval released one of her liquid, chilling laughs. "Already counted out? You expected me to Jew you up!"

"Of course, Miss Duval. Now, how do you expect to get to Knoxville?"

"Courtesy of the Sanitary Commission, Mr. Gould. They have finally broken down and agreed to accept female nurses, providing they are of good moral character." Her voice suddenly shifted into an unpleasant New England twang. "It seems that when Miss Teresa Duval, a devout Methodist who learned a great deal of practical medicine while on a mission to convert the Modoc, offered her services to the Commission, they were delighted to have her. The letter of recommendation from the Reverend Perry was all that was necessary. Her willingness to go to such an exposed site as

Knoxville made them put aside all chivalrous concerns. Not many want to go to Knoxville just now."

Gould frowned. "I assume the letter is a forgery. Someone might check on that."

Duval threw her head back and laughed heartily, heartlessly. "Oh, let them, Mr. Gould. There was indeed a Reverend Alpheus Perry, heading a mission to the Indians of northern California. However, inquiries will take weeks to cross the plains; and when they do, all that will be found is that the Modoc are quite set in their ways, and resent preachers. The good reverend was separated from his hair early this summer. That would be the end of any inquiries."

"So, your transportation is all arranged?"

"Almost. The Commission has provided me with a ticket as far as Louisville. Thanks to Forrest's cavalry, that's as far as regular trains go towards Knoxville. I was told to go see Mr. Roosevelt, the head of the New York Sanitary Commission; he has some special dispensation to issue passes that will gain me free transport in military convoys to Chattanooga; from there, I will manage somehow to get into Knoxville. I will do that first thing tomorrow, and be on my way. However, I must admit to being curious, Mr. Gould. Why Knoxville?"

Gould stared steadily at his agent, weighing factors, and then shrugged slightly. "I suppose it would be best if you knew the factors driving my decision.

"You know that I expected Grant to come to grief outside Vicksburg this summer, and sold short, counting on a general decline in shares and rise in gold. When he unexpectedly took Pemberton's entire army, I suffered ... considerable losses. Thinking that this was the beginning of the Confederacy's end, I then shifted many of my investments to expect a rise in shares and a fall in gold. I did not anticipate that the timid Meade would allow Lee to escape to Virginia after Gettysburg, or that the bungler Rosecrans would allow his army to be ambushed and nearly destroyed at Chickamauga. Again I suffered . . . considerable losses." Gould stared coldly at Duval for a moment. "Incidentally, I found that you had done exactly the opposite of me and gained considerably over the last few months with your much more modest investments."

Duval smiled sweetly. "Just because I'm a woman does not mean I don't pay attention to the war. The newspapers scream about what a butcher Grant is, but I noticed that heavy as his casualties were, he never lost. Never. The man would take Vicksburg. I also noticed that no matter how much the newspapers praised Rosecrans, he had never truly won a battle on his own. Never. I did not know exactly where or when, but I was certain he would lead the Army of the Cumberland into disaster sooner or later."

Gould was not amused, but he was objective enough to appreciate independent thinking in his subordinates. "Well, well. Live and learn, I suppose. Your . . . insights into such matters makes you even more suitable for what I have in mind. Now it is at least conceivable that the South may fight this war to a standstill and establish independence. It is also conceivable that the bunglers in Washington will finally put their house in order. My sources indicate Grant will shortly be appointed commander of all Union forces in the Mississippi Valley and that Rosecrans will be dismissed from his post at the Army of the Cumberland. However, I cannot get a definitive opinion on how likely it is that Grant will take hold and turn things around; this is a much larger command than he has ever held. Anyone else in American history, for that matter. Your job will be to give me advance knowledge of how the winds are blowing, who will win, who will lose. Having such knowledge ahead of the rest of Wall Street will not only allow me to recoup my losses, it will allow me to ascend to even greater levels of wealth, which of course means greater levels of power."

"Why is Knoxville the key place, Mr. Gould? Why not Chattanooga? That's where the Army of the Cumberland is under siege."

"True, but my . . . usual sources in Washington have indicated that Grant is going to Chattanooga in person. You are quite right in indicating Grant has a history of success; if he is personally present, I believe the Confederates will not succeed in taking Chattanooga, despite the supply situation. Nevertheless, Knoxville remains under the command of Ambrose Burnside and his Army of the Ohio."

"That fool who ordered the insane charge at Fredericksburg, and that comical Mud March, when he commanded the Army of the Potomac? I would have thought Lincoln would have given him the chop a long time ago."

"Abe apparently has something of a soft spot for the man. Must have to do with the fact that he never tries to evade his responsibility for the disasters under his command. Besides, Burnside seems to do well enough in small commands; the Army of the Ohio is nowhere near as large as the Army of the Potomac, and Lincoln's shelves are pretty bare of even mediocre generals. However, it still might be the fatal mistake of the war to put Burnside in Knoxville. All you have to do is look at a map; if the Confederates take Knoxville, they can drive straight north to the Ohio River. Rough country for an army to move through, it's true; but once they are on the Ohio, they will be in the land of milk and honey, all the food, fodder, and horses they could desire. And if they move fast, they can move west, take Cincinnati, and starve out the Armies of the Cumberland and of the Ohio. Or they could move east, take Philadelphia and Baltimore, and starve out Washington and the Army of the Potomac. Either way, such victories would give

England and France the excuse they have been looking for to recognize the Confederacy and break the Union blockade. Confederate independence would be inevitable. So you see, I *must* know what is happening in Knoxville."

"Very well, Mr. Gould. In the unlikely event that I am situated to push events one way or the other, I assume you wish me to push them toward a Union victory."

"Assume no such thing, Miss Duval. I don't care a fig for whether the Union is preserved or the slaves free. Only fools believe in causes; only great fools die for them. I want certainty. If events in Knoxville are so narrowly balanced that you can push them, push them toward certainty, whichever way that tends. Remember to use the code I gave you during that St. Louis assignment. Telegraph something innocuous to me, just putting in the code word for "North" if the Union is certain to win, "South" if otherwise. Is that clear?"

To her surprise, Duval found her anger trying to fight its way out of the place where she usually confined it. Although she liked to think she was as cynical as Gould, she found herself harboring a visceral hatred for the South—and rage at the financier's indifference concerning a Rebel victory. As she fought to control her anger, she suddenly realized the Southern aristocrats reminded her too much of the gilded English landlords and their brutal land agents who had . . . She shook her head slightly, mastered her fury, and simply replied "Very clear, Mr. Gould. You will hear from me only when I have something useful to report." Smiling dangerously, she stepped lightly backward into the deeper shadows cast by the tree.

Jay Gould blinked, stared hard, but could see no sign of Teresa Duval.

Gould stood for a moment, amazed at how quickly his agent had faded from view. Then he turned and walked quickly back to his mansion, forcing himself not to look back. He felt a chill that was not entirely from the cool night air.

Teresa Duval forced her way through the milling confusion of the train station, fighting the exasperation that was rising in her. The next train to Cincinnati was due to leave in half an hour, and if she was not on it, she would lose a whole day. Her railway pass was not the problem; that assured her free passage anywhere there was scheduled service. Unfortunately, she would still need the signed pass from the head of the New York Sanitary Commission that would get her into army-occupied Chattanooga. She had not found him in his office; the clerks finally suggested he might have been called down to the railway station, as there were rumors that an entire trainload of wounded from Chickamauga was arriving, and he might have wanted to organize their care.

Gradually, the distant sounds of screaming became audible. Looking toward the source of the noise, she saw well-dressed men and women moving away from a distant platform, casting uneasy glances over their shoulders. Duval strode toward the platform through the retreating crowd and encountered a hellish scene.

Alongside the platform lay a tired-looking locomotive and about twenty cattle-cars, steam hissing from the engine like the dying gasps of a wounded beast. Pairs of rough-looking men in shirt-sleeves scurried continuously into the cattle cars, only to stagger out carrying stretchers between them, those stretchers containing objects that moaned piteously, screamed in agony, or lay ominously still. The stretcher-bearers would make their way to one of the waiting horse-drawn ambulances, quickly unload their burden, and as the ambulance pulled away to the crack of the driver's whip, they would scurry back to one of the cattle cars to repeat the process.

Presiding over the pandemonium, gesturing like a general on a battlefield, was a tall, fully-bearded man of about thirty, dressed

13

in clothes that obviously came from an exclusive tailor. The man's handsome face seemed distorted with rage as he frantically directed the unloading of the human wreckage of war. Near him stood a small boy of about five who peered at the spectacle, not in horror or fear, but with lively interest. The child stumbled into the way of one of the stretcher-bearers without apparently seeing him. The man accidentally shoved the boy aside roughly, and with a muttered curse continued his grim task without breaking stride. Glaring at the orderly, the tall bearded man drew the child toward him and tried to hug him in a way that would cover the boy's eyes, but the child eagerly shrugged himself away from the man's embrace and peered about with curiosity.

Duval could see that now was not the ideal time to approach the bearded man, but she had little choice; it was now or throw herself at least a day behind schedule. She smoothed her black frock, ran a hand over her head to make sure that her luxuriant hair remained pulled into a tight, unattractive bun, and bustled up to the bearded man. "Mr. Roosevelt, I assume?" she said in a business-like New England twang.

The tall man turned to her with a distracted air. "Ah, yes, miss. And you are?"

"Teresa Duval, of the Methodist Chapel for Christian Propagation. Sir, I know this is a bad time to approach you, but I am going to Chattanooga to tend to the wounded, and I need your counter-signature on the pass they gave me at Sanitary Commission headquarters."

"Miss, can't this wait?" interrupted Roosevelt, in a distracted voice. "They did not tell us that this train of poor souls was on its way—more victims of Rosecrans' criminal incompetence. I did not know until the last moment, and my son was with me. He should not be witness to this. Before I could send him home . . . Teddy? Teddy!"

The child had wandered over where two overworked bearers

had lowered their burden for a moment while they caught their breath. A wild-eyed young man lay on the stretcher, his right arm ending in a bloody wad of bandages somewhere between the shoulder and the elbow. The child leaned over and peered closely at the stump, then looked at the wounded soldier and said, "By golly, you're a hero! You gave an arm for the Union. Bully!"

"A hero!" shouted the wounded man. "You don't know nothin', kid! Do you know what it's like to feel the bone in your arm smashed into a dozen pieces by an ounce of lead? Do you know what it feels like when they saw away your arm, and watch them carry it away while you're screaming with pain? To hell with the Union! How am I goin' work the plow? Who's goin' feed my little ones, and my woman? And all for nothin'! Rosie ran, and me and everyone like me had to pay for the dance. And what does the Union care I'm busted up for life? What does anyone in the Union care? Who will remember in a year what I gave for the Union?"

"I will remember," said the child solemnly, as Roosevelt hurried forward to draw his son away from the unbalanced casualty.

"Ah kid, you'll forget. They'll all forget."

Roosevelt tried to grab his son's hand, but the child shrugged it off angrily. "I promise you I will remember. What's your name?"

The veteran had suddenly calmed and looked at the squinting child with amazement. "Jesse Worth," the wounded man said in a quiet voice.

"Mr. Jesse Worth, I promise you that Teddy Roosevelt will remember what you gave for the Union, for as long as he lives." Then slowly, and with exaggerated care, the five-year old clumsily saluted the wounded soldier.

A strange look in his tear-filled eyes, Worth awkwardly returned the salute with his left hand. The elder Roosevelt gestured toward the bemused stretcher-bearers who carried the wounded man gently to the nearest ambulance. Father looked down at son with an expression of the purest love. Sensing this was her best opportunity to get her precious pass, Duval spoke.

"That was a remarkable performance by your son, sir," she said briskly. "He has a great future ahead of him."

He is a wonderful child, Miss Duval. However, he will have to be content with a more . . . secluded life. His health is not good, and besides, the way he keeps bumping into things and not noticing the obvious . . ." Roosevelt trailed off, and sadly made a vague gesture toward his head with one hand, while with the other, he gave his child a fierce hug.

"Nonsense," she responded in a simulated New England briskness. "Look how he squints. He is nearsighted. Have you tried getting him some spectacles?"

The elder Roosevelt looked startled; it was obvious the idea had not previously occurred to him. "Well, perhaps a visit to the right doctor . . ."

"In any event sir, I know you are distracted by these poor men. However, their brethren in Chattanooga may need medical help very soon, if rumors are true." She reached into her reticule and thrust a piece of paper at the bearded man. "Sign the pass, and I will be on my way to minister, in a Christian way, to their medical needs, and you can continue your duties here."

They were both distracted by an agonized scream from inside one of the cattle cars. Reflexively the elder Roosevelt hugged the child close, as if to protect him from the horror of war, but the younger Roosevelt peered eagerly toward the noise, anything but horrified. Distractedly, the bearded man pulled a pencil from his inner pocket and scrawled a signature on Duval's paper. "Go and do good work, Miss Duval. May God grant this end soon."

Half an hour later, in a crowded second-class compartment of a train pulling out of the station, Teresa Duval smiled grimly at the memory of the elder Roosevelt's prayer. The fool actually prayed to God, she thought as she chuckled. He did not realize that God was gone from this sorry world, and the Devil was now holding sway. The world was filled with chaos, and a woman with no scruples could go far. Very far indeed. She gazed out of the window at the New York cityscape and dreamed of the day when all that would be hers, when she would answer to no man ever again, least of all Jay Gould.

A silvery laugh escaped her lips without her knowing it. The portly commercial traveler sitting on the bench across from her heard the laugh and privately decided he was changing compartments at the next station.

CHAPTER 1

THE CRACKER LINE

General George Thomas scanned the "present for duty" rosters again by the flickering light of an oil lamp, and then he read the quartermaster's report on provisions. He was tempted to crumple the documents into balls and fling them into the corner of the large parlor of the house serving as headquarters, Army of the Cumberland. Still, he controlled the temptation and laid them on the corner of the table where his clerk would find them at dawn. He shifted uneasily in his camp chair; the pain in his back from the silly fall he had taken on a railway platform months ago simply would not go away, and only in the rare moments when he was alone did he permit himself the luxury of groaning.

He stood up and stretched gingerly, a stab of pain shooting through his lower back for a moment. *Need to work out the kinks now, when no one can see,* he thought. *It is vital that a general show no weakness in front of those he commands; if he weakens, his men weaken. Rosecrans surely proved that.*

From his standing position, he glanced at the papers again, although he had no need; he had memorized the figures. 42,175 men present and accounted for, including the wounded and sick.

10,578 horses and mules. About two hundred fifty thousand army crackers, the twice-baked flat squares of iron-hard bread that sometimes would break teeth but without which the army would starve. About eighty thousand pounds of salt beef and pork. No vegetables of any kind, not even the despised dried "desiccated vegetables." *Going to see scurvy soon, thought Thomas grimly.*

At the normal rate of consumption, there was enough to feed the army for no more than five days. He had placed the shattered army on half-rations, so this would last ten days at most. No reserves of forage at all for the animals, nothing but what could be scrounged from the neighborhood of Chattanooga. Soon they would begin to die, and the wagons and the cannon of the Army of the Cumberland would become useless dead weight.

He walked over to the parlor window and looked out moodily. Not much to see; the rain continued its steady fall, the pair of sentries in their India-rubber capes dimly visible to the side by the light of a single oil lamp hanging from the veranda roof. He could not see beyond the dimly-lit front yard. Even if it were daylight, the steady rain would have limited his vision to a few hundred feet. Still, in his mind's eye he could see all too clearly for miles and miles.

He could see Braxton Bragg's victorious Confederate army out there, perched triumphantly on the high ridges that formed a huge semicircle around the besieged city of Chattanooga. He could see the batteries of cannon mounted high on Lookout Mountain, completely dominating the Tennessee River and preventing supplies and reinforcements from flowing easily upriver. He could even see the muddy track that snaked northward out of Chattanooga, mockingly left unguarded by the Confederates: a hundred miles through howling wilderness, devoid of forage for the animals hauling the army's wagons, seas of mud alternating with impossibly steep grades up and down the seemingly endless ridges that stretched northward to Kentucky.

He was trying his best to bring in supplies over that miserable road, but over a quarter of the wagons that set out from Kentucky either broke down on the road or were ambushed by Forrest's cavalry. The ones that did get through were only one-third full, the rest of the space used for the fodder the overworked teams needed just to get to Chattanooga. The Army of the Cumberland had retreated into a trap, he knew. To stay in Chattanooga was to be starved into surrender; to flee across the mountains along that damned road meant to abandon the wagons and cannon and probably see the army disintegrate into undisciplined mobs, easy prey for the lightning-quick Forrest.

The burly Thomas made a sound of disgust, then, surprisingly, he laughed grimly. *Well, here it is George. You always wanted to command a great army; dreamed of it since West Point days. Now you will command it, very possibly as it surrenders. And people will call it treason, call for your head, and say it was your fault. They won't believe or care you begged the fool Rosecrans not to rush ahead at Chickamauga. They won't believe or care it was you that saved the army from complete destruction when Rosecrans lost his nerve and fled. They will say, 'What could you expect, giving a slave-owning Virginian command of a corps. All Southerners are traitors; their word cannot be trusted.'*

Hands clasped behind his back, George Thomas stared out into the darkness, not looking at the black storm but into the memories of what had led him to this place, this time.

He had come to responsibility very early, had learned to deal with death and hard sights sooner than a soul should. He would never forget that long-ago morning in southern Virginia when he had arisen at dawn, and while going to the privy, he suddenly became aware that there were absolutely no noises from the slave quarters. A quick check of the cabins showed them to be completely deserted. This frightened him. There were rumors that some slave named Nat Turner was trying to start an uprising. He had not believed it, but perhaps there was something to it after all.

He hurried to the barn, where his father began his day. In the barn, he found a mound of flesh rendered almost unrecognizable by the slicing and pounding of various farm implements. Only by the curly graying hair could George Thomas be certain it was his father.

Many twelve-year olds would have descended into hysteria or tears, but not George Thomas. He had loved his father, despite the fact that the elder Thomas could be a hard man, especially toward the slaves, but the boy put aside his grief until later. He quickly harnessed the strongest remaining horse to a buckboard and bundled his dazed mother and siblings into it without letting them see into the barn. Balancing a shotgun across his lap, he drove the horse as hard as he dared along the road toward the county seat, where he hoped his family would be safe. On either side of the road, he could see distant pillars of smoke. He feared that he knew what that meant.

He remembered rounding a curve to encounter a band of slaves barring his way, and he drew the horse up short. The mob, eerily silent, was armed with knives, scythes, and the occasional musket. His mother and sisters screamed at the sight; Thomas motioned them to silence, and without a word, he leveled the shotgun at the mob. The silence continued for what seemed to be an eternity. The slaves knew that those in the wagon would be helpless once the shotgun was emptied, but that one or two of them would die in the process of its emptying. Then a large, powerful-looking man advanced from the crowd, a man the boy recognized.

"Well, little George, here we stand."

"Hercules," replied Thomas. "You know they'll hang you for this."

"Maybe. Maybe not. Anyways, no more whippings like your

pa gave me. No more working to make the white folk rich and comfortable-like."

"Enough jabber!" yelled one of the men behind Hercules. "Take 'em now! Cain't kill all of us!"

"You move when I says move, and not before. Ain't no one have more say than me except Nat, an' he ain't here."

The crowd of rebellious slaves muttered, but did not charge the buckboard. Hercules turned back toward Thomas, a small, grim smile on his face.

"You're handlin' yourself like a man, little George, I'll give you that. Well, we're goin' handle the white folk like the niggers handled them down in Haiti, in the '90s. Suppose should handle you the same way. Still, cain't forget how you yelled at your pa to stop beatin' me that time and got slapped across the face for your trouble. 'Sides, someone has to spread the word that whites are done here, an' there'll be no more masters. Run, little George, run. Run and tell the others what you've seen."

Hercules motioned roughly with his hand, and his followers reluctantly cleared the road in front of the wagon. Holding the shotgun in one hand and the reins in the other, refusing to whimper like his mother and sisters, Thomas urged his horse into motion. Nothing else occurred in the two hours it took him to reach the county seat, where the terrified whites were organizing the militia. It was the longest two hours in his short life.

Of course, Nat Turner's rebellion was quickly and viciously snuffed out. Most slaves refused to join, for a variety of reasons, but even if they had, the superior weaponry and organization of the army would have made defeat inevitable. Thomas remembered the day when Hercules' mutilated body was brought to the county seat along with several others. The bodies were set afire in the town square. He quietly watched the body of his father's killer burn with a curious mix of emotions—satisfaction that the killer of his father was dead, sadness at the senseless waste of life, disgust at the glee with which the adults capered around the burning corpses. He reflected that this is what comes of anarchy: death, waste, and barbarism. That was when he made the decision that when old enough, he would try for West Point, become an officer, and help assure that the Government prevented such anarchy from occurring again.

In an unspectacular way, his career had progressed slowly but steadily. After West Point ('... *solemnly swear that I will bear true allegiance to the United States of America, and that I will serve them honestly and faithfully against all their enemies or opposers whatsoever*...' went the oath), there had been Mexico, and endless dreary postings on the frontier. Superiors noted that there was nothing flashy or dramatic about Thomas, but in his stolid, emotionless way, he was absolutely dependable, cool as ice under fire, and devoid of the urge toward petty back-biting that so infected the army. Promotions were rare in the small regular army, but they came to George Thomas sooner rather than later.

He did not hate the Mexicans or the Indians against whom he fought, but neither did he pity them. In his eyes, they had failed to rule the lands they held in an orderly and peaceful manner, and therefore lost their right to them. It was now the duty of the United States to administer them properly, and the duty of the United States Army to perform that administration in the frontier areas.

Well into middle age, he had remained a bachelor, sending most of his inadequate salary to his widowed mother and growing sisters in Virginia, never for a moment feeling that this was in any way a burden on him. It was his duty, and that was the end of it.

Then, improbably, while on temporary assignment in New York, he had met a handsome woman who herself had never married, and was on the verge of spinsterhood. She was from a well-to-do family, prominent in the growing Free Soil movement, and her parents looked askance at the Virginian slave-owner. Surprisingly, both were swept away in a passion that neither had believed themselves capable of, and they married so quickly that they shocked themselves as well as their relations. Although there were no children, their marriage was passionately physical in a way that simply would not have been believed by those who only saw the reserved Victorian couple they presented to the outside world.

Despite furious battles in Mexico and innumerable skirmishes against the Indians, Thomas had been only wounded once, while campaigning against the dreaded Comanche in Texas. His company had been ambushed, and while he was rallying the ill-trained immigrants who made up the most of the enlisted ranks, an arrow embedded itself deeply in his chin. Rolling on the ground in agony, unable to speak rationally, he tried to scream to his men to gather around the battalion commander and retreat to high ground. However, his major suddenly loomed over him. Thomas screamed at the battalion commander to save himself and the men. However, arrows and the occasional stray shot splitting the air around him, Major Robert Lee said, "I will not leave my finest officer to the Comanche."

Swift as lightning, Lee knelt, broke off the shaft of the protruding arrow, grabbed with gauntleted fingers the arrowhead emerging from the opposite side of Thomas' chin, and drew the remainder of the arrow out. Thomas shrieked from the unbelievable agony of these actions and briefly passed out. When he came to, he found himself slung over Lee's shoulder as the major jogged to a rocky hilltop where the sergeants had finally made the frightened men rally. The Comanche quickly desisted in their attack, and after a brief interval, the army column made its way back to the fort, carrying the helpless Thomas, who slipped in and out of consciousness.

Despite a dangerous infection, Thomas eventually made a

complete recovery, with only two lingering effects: a mutilated chin, which he concealed by growing a beard before they had become popular in the country at large, and an admiration of Robert E. Lee that bordered on love. Although Easterners were seldom informed of such details, Thomas was well aware of how the Comanche treated soldiers they took alive; he had seen what they left of soldiers' bodies on several occasions. Lee had been perfectly entitled to leave Thomas to the Comanche; his duty had been to rally the unwounded soldiers. Bravely and honorably, Lee had personally put himself at terrible risk for Thomas ('*I will not leave my finest officer to the Comanche*'); and Thomas could never forget what he owed the elder Virginian.

Years later, on that tragic, terrible day in May 1861, he remembered all too well what he owed Lee. Texas had seceded from the Union, and Thomas and his wife had returned to Washington "for further orders." However, the suspicious glances and sudden silences he encountered as he prowled the halls of the War Department told him how he stood with many in what was left of the United States Army. He was a Virginian, well known to be personally devoted to Robert E. Lee, who had already gone South to receive a general's commission in the Confederate army. Fortunately, General-in-Chief Winfield Scott was himself a Union-loyal Virginian who would ignore those suspicions and give him a command, if he wanted.

If he wanted . . . for in truth, he had not himself decided whether he was going South. There were his sisters, his friends, his home state, and above all, Robert Lee pulling him to the Confederacy. That tragic day in May, General Scott had offered him an important command in Kentucky. To his own surprise, he had asked for a day to consider whether to accept it. The massive old hero had looked put out, but had granted that day. Thomas had gone home to find his wife waiting for him, her face streaked with dried tears, but her voice calm.

"George, this letter arrived for you from Robert," she said, extending a sealed envelope to him. "You will probably want to read it alone." As Thomas reluctantly took the letter, she said with a curious lack of emphasis "George, whatever you decide to do, I want you to know that you are the love of my life, and that my fate is linked to yours. Whatever you do, wherever you go, there I will be." With the dignity of a queen. she swirled out of the parlor.

Still standing, Thomas broke the seal and examined the brief letter, offering him a general's commission in Richmond. He clutched the letter as a jumble of thoughts and voices raced through his head: '. . . *do solemnly swear to bear true allegiance to the United States of America . . .' '. . . run little George, run . . .' '. . . you are the love of my life . . .' '. . . I will not leave my finest office, er to the Comanche . . .'*

Thomas remembered being startled to find he had walked over to the fireplace, where last night's embers still smoldered. He looked at the letter in his hand and caught sight of his blue tunic sleeve—the blue uniform he had worn more years than he had not worn it. Not knowing exactly why, knowing he would never know exactly why, he placed Lee's letter on the glowing embers, where after a few moments, it caught fire.

A knock at the headquarters door jolted Thomas from his reverie. Straightening his aching back, Thomas said, "Enter."

Two men came in the room. One was a stocky, bearded brigadier who dropped his dripping slouch hat to reveal a balding pate, flinging a drenched cape into the corner of the room. He shook himself like a dog emerging from a bath, making exaggerated shivering noises, saluted, and with a grin, said in a heavily accented voice, "Bad night for Americans, yes? My men act as if weather terrible. Better they had been with me in Crimea, to see what bad weather is. Better they fight Turk, so not be so afraid of Johnnie Reb, yes?"

Thomas stared unsmilingly at General John Turchin. Under his original name of Ivan Turchinoff, he had made something of a name for himself in a Russian Cossack regiment ("Ivan the Terrible," which frightened soldiers had called him behind his back) before being dismissed for unspecified acts of brutality and emigrating to America. Originally, Thomas had wondered just what a Cossack officer had to do to be dismissed for brutality in the hard empire that was Russia. However, he no longer wondered. Earlier in the year, Turchin had taken a raiding party into the Alabama town of Athens, where two of his soldiers had been shot by civilians. He announced to his enraged men, "For one hour I close mine eyes," and a small American town found what it was to be a Polish village.

Turchin had been court-martialed and dismissed for his willing refusal to control his men. However, since Turchin was as brave and skilled as he was inhuman—and since Lincoln was short of brave and skilled commanders—Colonel Turchin had been restored to the Army of the Cumberland, freshly promoted to brigadier general. Thomas loathed the man, but he admitted his ruthless bravery, and this night, he needed ruthless bravery. The rest was between Turchin and his God, he reflected.

Thomas turned his attention to his other visitor. In his own way, he was as unusual as the Russian. Lieutenant Ambrose Bierce made no move to remove his wet outer garments; the grin on his face seemed to indicate he positively enjoyed the discomfort of the wild, ominous night. Tall, thin and handsome, Bierce did not look like what Thomas knew him to be: a supremely skilled mapmaker and a scout of near-lunatic bravery. The prudish Thomas was surprised that he rather liked this young lieutenant, around whom rumors of constant drinking and relentless womanizing circled. Whatever his personal vices, Bierce would always have a place in Thomas' heart because of his performance at the battle of Chickamauga. For just a moment, Thomas reflected on that terrible afternoon.

Confederates under the hard-hitting corps commander James Longstreet had split the Union army, pouring through a gap that Rosecrans' poor deployment of his troops had left. Grimly, Thomas rallied his corps, forcing himself to project calm assurance, riding slowly along his wavering line as bullets cut the air all around him, silently cursing the other two corps commanders who had apparently decided to lead their troops in disorganized flight. His men were holding on but were vastly outnumbered by the triumphant Rebels on the left flank. Thomas knew that if his left crumbled, the only practical route of retreat would be lost, and the Army of Cumberland would be effectively destroyed. Up galloped General Rosecrans, accompanied only by his ambitious chief of staff James Garfield and Lieutenant Bierce; Thomas would never forget his shock at the wild-eyed, incoherent appearance of his army commander.

"Thomas, I must lead the army back to Chattanooga and establish a defensive line," blurted Rosecrans without preamble. "Hold the line here as best you can; I leave you in charge of the army in the field." Rosecrans turned his horse and made as to spur it into a gallop but checked himself when he saw that neither Garfield nor Bierce moved to follow.

"General Garfield, aren't you coming with me?"

The ambitious Congressman-elect, a notorious wire-puller who had quickly advanced in the army by relentlessly flattering his superiors, seemed to straighten in the saddle. Speaking slowly and with deliberate emphasis, he said, "General Rosecrans, I believe that under the circumstances, I can be of more use in the field than in . . . preparing Chattanooga. I will place myself at the disposal of General Thomas." He was not asking his superior's permission but stating a fact. Thomas' low opinion of Garfield suddenly was elevated several notches.

Rosecrans looked as if he had been slapped. He turned to the young lieutenant and blurted, "And you Bierce?"

The scout gave Rosecrans a salute that was technically correct but filled with subtle mockery and contempt. "With your permission, sir, I will stay with General Thomas. After all, my permanent berth is in his corps."

"Ah . . . well . . . I must . . . ah . . . carry on!" The commanding general, Army of the Cumberland, put the spurs to his mare and galloped off the field.

Politician-turned-soldier Garfield looked to Thomas. "Where may I be of the most use, sir?"

"The men are nearly out of cartridges. I sent my last aide to the rear to try to locate the supply wagons a quarter of an hour ago. I've heard nothing since. You can be the most use by locating the wagons and seeing the ammunition forwarded equitably to the front line."

Garfield saluted smartly and put the spurs to his mount. As Thomas watched the brigadier gallop on his mission, Bierce asked "Sir, where might I be of service?"

Thomas was peering far into the distance on his left. "General Granger's reserve division was ordered forward this morning, but it had twenty miles to go," he said softly, as if speaking to himself. "Granger would be coming from that direction, and I can just make out a cloud of dust, but it is too much to expect him to march his men such a distance in such a short time. And even if it is him, unless he is led to a precise point on the enemy's flank, our left is going to give before he can get here, and the army be routed."

"Sir, where would you need Granger's men to come in?"

Thomas scanned the left flank, where the men of William Hazen's brigade hung on grimly in the face of continuous Rebel assaults. "If they can get here before Hazen's line breaks, I suppose that stand of four trees there would be the ideal point of contact; it would catch the enemy perfectly on its right flank. However, our lines are bending inward; a messenger telling Granger where to strike would have to make a long loop behind our lines. I don't think . . ."

Without warning, Bierce yelled the slang term for seeing serious combat: "Time to see the elephant!" A wild gleam in his eyes, a manic smile on his face, Bierce put the spurs to his roan gelding, galloping on a straight line toward the distant cloud of dust, placing himself between Union and Confederate lines. By all rights, he should have died in moments, either from Rebel sharpshooters or friendly fire, but most of the troops on both sides ceased firing for a moment, astonished and awed by a lone rider spurring across that field of death. In less than a minute, Bierce was through the worst of the danger and on his way toward the cloud of dust.

It was indeed fortunate that the dust had been from Granger's division, reflected Thomas. Directed by Bierce, the fierce Granger had hit the Rebel flank just as Thomas' line was beginning to crumble. There was more furious fighting until dark, but the line held. After sunset, Thomas skillfully extracted his devastated forces from their positions and set them on the road to the supposed safety of Chattanooga; a safety that now was proving illusory. Once again Lieutenant Bierce may just possibly have pulled a rabbit out of his hat, hoped Thomas.

"Lieutenant Bierce has already briefed me, my general," said Turchin with heavy joviality. "Plan can work, army can be fed, and Rebels can be crushed."

A surge of hope filled Thomas. "I know the outline. After all, I am the one who asked Lieutenant Bierce to scout the ground. Now, bring the map from the desk over there, Lieutenant. I would like to hear you describe what you found with reference to the map."

Bierce had retrieved the map from the roll-top desk in the corner of the parlor. He was in the act of unfolding it on the table, when there was a knock on the door. Without waiting for Thomas to respond, an agitated sentry threw the door open and blurted, "Sir, General Grant and his party have arrived!"

Five drenched, mud-splattered figures filed through the door. First was Ulysses Grant, newly-appointed commander of the Division of the Mississippi, which in effect gave him direct command of all Union forces west of the Appalachians. Grant hobbled into the room using a crutch to support his left leg, a smoldering cigar clenched between his teeth. Thomas had heard that although a superb horseman, Grant was reputed to have badly injured that leg in an accidental fall from his horse. Remembering the prewar gossip about Grant's drinking, Thomas wondered just how "accidental" had been that fall. A disapproving scowl flitted across his face. Behind Grant came Colonel John Rawlins, Grant's pale, haunted-eye chief of staff. Next came Major Ely Parker, a full-blooded Seneca. The old Indian-fighter in Thomas struggled not to glare at him. Finally, behind Parker came two people that Thomas did not recognize. One was a slightly-built blond captain, whose expressionless blue eyes peered out through wire-rimmed spectacles, seeing everything in the room, revealing nothing. The other made Thomas physically start: a light-skinned Negro in a sergeant's uniform: '*run little George.*' Thomas had known the day when blacks would be putting on the blue uniform was coming, and now it was here.

Standing formally at attention, Thomas saluted his commander. "General Grant, sir, my apologies for not having a formal guard of honor ready. I, of course, knew that you were coming, but assumed you would delay the trip due to the inclement weather."

Grant absently touched the rim of his soaking wide-brimmed

hat; then he removed the drenched piece of headgear and collapsed wearily into a chair, letting the crutch clatter to the floor. "I don't care about such doggone nonsense, General Thomas. Needed to see what that road was like, especially in bad weather. Darn thing shouldn't even be called a road, more like a hundred-mile-long hog wallow. They told me you couldn't keep this army supplied along that road, and now I believe it. Anyway, you know Rawlins and Parker. These other two . . ."

"Are Captain Alphonso Clay, late of Louisville, New Orleans, and Vicksburg, and Sergeant Jeremiah Lot," interrupted Lieutenant Bierce insolently as he turned toward Thomas. "They perform, ah, special staff duties for General Grant. I had the privilege of seeing them at close hand during the siege of Vicksburg." Bierce turned to his old acquaintances and bowed ironically. "Sergeant, always a genuine pleasure. And Captain, I look forward to an entertaining renewal of our acquaintance; seldom a dull moment when you are around." Sergeant Lot saluted, smiling; Captain Clay merely nodded his head, not smiling.

"Lieutenant Bierce, you will pay attention to military etiquette," said Thomas ponderously. Ignoring the black sergeant, Thomas turned to the young officer and said, "Your name is familiar to me, Captain Clay, although I am certain we have not met before. Perhaps . . ." Thomas trailed off; his eyes hardened. "New Orleans: the Deveraux family! Sir, what are you doing free, much less wearing the uniform of the United States? You killed a civilian couple in front of their children, along with an overseer and an infant child."

"Lots of hard things are done in war," said Grant from his chair, producing a relatively dry cigar from an inner pocket and proceeding to light it. "All charges against Captain Clay have been dismissed. He has rendered services to the country that far outweigh the . . . unpleasantness in New Orleans, and he has my complete confidence."

"General Thomas, sir, the matter to which you allude is indeed a stain on my personal honor; I have never denied that," said Clay in a soft, emotionless voice. "I will endeavor to balance the books on that matter in serving my country however General Grant directs."

Turchin laughed heartily. "I remember now! You Kentucky officer who make example of the traitor family and one of servants. Nothing to regret, Captain. Traitors must be dealt with so those who survive will sweat blood at thought of treason. I teach Poles that lesson, but does Tsar say thank you Turchin? No, he turn back on man who left him loyal district where revolt had once brewed. Tsar soft man, like so many in this so new, so rich country. I am glad to meet American like you, who knows what needs be done. We be alike, I think."

Clay focused his pale blue eyes on the jovial Russian. "You are General Turchin?" he inquired mildly. Behind him, Sergeant Lot looked apprehensive. Lieutenant Bierce grinned from ear to ear.

"I be Turchin. More officers like me and you, and we put boyars of the South in their place, and Lincoln's foot on their necks."

"And so, sir, you believe we are alike?" replied Clay quietly, a hint of weird amusement in his voice.

"Yes, well, enough of such chatter," interrupted Grant smoothly. "There is not a moment to be wasted on determining a plan of action. Washington was glad to hear that you wouldn't consider retreating. They're already calling you the Rock of Chickamauga back East."

"Retreat is not an option, sir," replied Thomas, easing himself back into his own chair, careful not to let the pain in his back become obvious to his visitors. "If we started to retreat, there is no good place to make a stand short of the Ohio. And if a Confederate army gets that far, I will guarantee you that John Bull and Mr. France will recognize Confederate independence.

Besides, you've seen the road for yourself, sir. The army would simply disintegrate if it were forced to retreat. It would be worse than Napoleon's withdrawal from Moscow."

Grant took a long pull on his cigar and slowly expelled the smoke. "I've already got Sherman driving the Army of the Tennessee overland with thirty thousand or so men. Stanton is scraping up another twenty thousand or so and sending them out under the command of Joe Hooker. But it does no good to double the size of your army when you can't feed what you've got."

"My army?" Thomas blurted with surprise. "Sir, I had assumed that you would place Sherman or McPherson in command, and I would resume command of my corps."

"Those would be good choices to command any army," replied Grant, looking levelly at Thomas. "However, they are needed where they are. You proved at Chickamauga you have what it takes to command an army. The Army of the Cumberland is yours, General Thomas. Now, of course you see that the first step is to regain control of the Tennessee River all the way into Chattanooga. That way we can bring up the supplies your men need with ease by boat, as well as feed Sherman and Hooker when they get here. What plans do you have to regain that control?"

"Sir, with the forces now at my disposal, it is really not feasible. However, I think that there is a way to secure our supplies that does not involve completely retaking the river. My chief engineer has provided the details of how to go about it, but the feasibility depends on the exact nature of the land. I sent Lieutenant Bierce out to scout the path in question, and he was about to brief me when you arrived. With your permission, let him show you on this map. Lieutenant Bierce, if you will proceed."

The assembled soldiers moved to surround the table, on which Bierce had already unfolded the map. Grant struggled with difficulty to get to his feet. Smoothly, Major Parker steadied him with one hand while scooping up the crutch and deftly slipping it under Grant's armpit.

Bierce took a pencil to act as a pointer, and with a smile, he took on the air of a schoolmaster; it was obvious he enjoyed being the center of attention. "Gentlemen, here you see Chattanooga," he said, pointing to a town on the east bank of the Tennessee. "You can see the river runs south for about two miles from the town and then makes a sharp turn to run north, eventually into territory firmly held by Federal forces. The locals call the peninsula between the two stretches of the Tennessee, Moccasin Point. Moccasin Point is occupied by Reb forces, but lightly. My reconnaissance leads me to believe there are only three regiments actually on the peninsula. Now, about three miles north of where the river makes its turn is a crossing called Brown's Ferry, lightly held by one regiment of Confederates. The west bank of Brown's Ferry connects directly with the only truly good road in these parts, which must be the one that General Sherman is using to come to Chattanooga."

"Why are the Confederates leaving Moccasin Point and Brown's Ferry so lightly occupied?" asked the pale Rawlins. "It's obvious that this peninsula must be held to cut off Chattanooga from resupply by river."

"Because of this," replied Bierce, tapping a point on the map just opposite of Moccasin Point. "You can't tell it from a map as crude as this, but here lies Lookout Mountain: over a thousand feet high and with unobstructed command of the river for a mile in both directions. The Rebs have moved at least half a dozen batteries of cannon up there. It would be suicide for a boat to attempt to run past them to Chattanooga, night or day. General Bragg must feel no need to waste troops on the lowlands on the other side of the river."

"Then I really do not understand why you were scouting Moccasin Point," commented Parker, his college-accented English contrasting weirdly with his pure Indian appearance.

"Ah, because of something General Thomas suspected must be there, but needed to confirm," replied Bierce smugly. He drew a straight line between Brown's Ferry and the bridge at Chattanooga across the base of the peninsula. "The map does not show a road, but there had to be one; else there would be no point in having a crossing at Brown's Ferry. I played hide-and-seek with the Confederate pickets and outposts tonight, and confirmed that there is indeed a damn fine road covering the half-mile between Brown's Ferry and the bridge into Chattanooga; a short-cut well out of range of the cannon on Lookout Mountain."

"I see," said Parker, nodding slightly. "If both ends of this road can be secured, boats can safely come up as far as Brown's Ferry, unload their cargoes, and their cargos safely hauled the short distance into Chattanooga."

"Exactly," replied General Thomas. "Tomorrow night I propose to place afloat the brigades of Hazen and Turchin in boats. They will drift silently downriver; Hazen will secure the west bank and prepare to receive any Rebel counterattacks, while Turchin will land on Moccasin Point itself and clear away all the Confederates that are on the peninsula. Silence and surprise are vital. If the artillery on Lookout Mountain notices the boats, it will be a massacre."

Grant puffed thoughtfully on his cigar. "An excellent plan, General. I want to order trusted couriers this very night to contact Sherman and Hooker. They have to redouble their pace and get here in time to give us overwhelming odds against any Confederate attempt to retake Brown's Ferry. Also, I need to let them know to send out instructions to load up every riverboat they can find with supplies and fodder. By the time the boats actually get here, we will have secured the line."

Thomas nodded grimly. He could already see that Grant would receive full credit for the plan. The fact that Grant was not pressing to take such credit would make it no less painful to his self-esteem. Thomas then turned to Bierce. "Lieutenant, you have performed magnificently. I do not feel right in asking after what you have already risked, but I need you to guide Turchin's men tomorrow night."

Smiling, Bierce replied, "I would not miss this for the world, sir."

Unexpectedly, Clay said to Grant "With your permission, sir, I would like to accompany Lieutenant Bierce. The experience could be highly instructive; and besides, you should have a member of your staff present during an action so vital to the future of this army."

Grant thought for a moment and then nodded. "That will be all right I guess." He did not notice Sergeant Lot grimace. The black knew that he had no choice but to accompany Clay on this adventure, for reasons that had nothing to do with line of command.

Bierce laughed, "Just like old times, Clay. I expect things will be even more entertaining with you along."

Turchin burst in a hearty laugh. "I said it! You like me Captain Clay. Like to see the blood of your enemies. Only greater pleasure is that of a woman, yes?"

Clay stared at the Russian, his face an expressionless mask.

Two thousand men floated in silence down the Tennessee River, crammed into small boats and skiffs to the point where water was just inches from the gunwales. Tonight it was not raining, but it remained cloudy. This was additional luck for the Federals, as otherwise, the quarter-moon would have raised the chances of their detection significantly. They had loaded the boats in silence, leaving behind everything that might rattle and clink, ordered to maintain absolute silence until the moment of attack, instructed to use the muffled oars only to avoid drifting into the banks.

Clay, Lot, and Bierce were in the lead boat with Turchin. Turchin removed a flask from his side pocket and took a long pull, grunting softly in satisfaction. Bierce stared about him, obviously enjoying the experience. Clay could observe both more clearly than either would have imagined in the near-total darkness. He frowned. It would be hard to tell who he disapproved of the most. As the current carried the boats silently around the tip of Moccasin Point, Clay looked to his left and saw twinkling lights seemingly suspended high in the sky. He realized that those must be the campfires of the Confederate artillerymen, camped high atop Lookout Mountain.

Clay felt Lot tug at his sleeve and saw his friend point urgently to the right. On the shore of Moccasin Point was a bright, cheery campfire. Several gray-clad soldiers gathered about it; none of them looked particularly alert. As the lead boat drew abreast of the campfire, one of the soldiers got up, stretched lazily, and ambled to the shore. A single noise could have been fatal at this point; scarcely twenty yards separated the drifting boats from the bored young soldier, who would have inevitably seen them, had not his night vision been temporarily destroyed by staring so long into the fire. Clay was amused to watch the man casually unbutton his trousers and begin to piss into the river; the sound of the stream striking the water reached the Union soldiers clearly, as did the soldier's tuneless whistling of "*The Bonnie Blue Flag*" as he relieved his bladder. Clay felt Turchin tremble next to him in the crowded boat and was puzzled until he realized that the Russian was struggling to keep from laughing aloud. Turchin, and undoubtedly many others in the boats, managed to keep their mirth silent. The young Confederate casually rebuttoned his trousers and rejoined his comrades at the fire. Clay was astounded that he could get close enough to the young man to clearly make out his features, and yet the soldier had no inkling of the water-borne Union forces.

The tiny armada continued floating downriver until those in

the lead boats could make out several campfires on each shore of the river up ahead. Clearly, the fires belonged to the Confederate forces, lazily guarding both ends of Brown's Ferry. Turchin hissed instructions to the boats behind his own, with orders to pass them along. The soldiers with oars began to row the boats to the right bank. Meanwhile, about halfway back in the line, the convoy split, the boats to the rear heading toward the left bank; General Hazen and his men were on their own mission to secure the western approach to Brown's Ferry.

The lead boats began to bump into the bank. In a low but penetrating voice, Turchin hissed his orders. "Cold steel, boys! Bayonet, but not fire until cannot be helped! Pass it back!" With that, Turchin jumped into the shallow water and slogged quickly to shore, drawing his heavy saber as he ran straight to the first campfire.

A grizzled old sergeant heard Turchin coming but had been too long near the comfortable fire to see well in the dark. "Who goes there! Give the sign!" he shouted just as the Russian surged out of the dark at him, gleefully screaming something in his native tongue. The Confederate tried to level his rifle, but Turchin swung his saber with terrific force, and the man's head went flying away from his body.

In a moment, utter confusion ensued as hundreds of attackers overwhelmed the unprepared rebels. Many sleeping soldiers stumbled bleary-eyed out of their tents only to be bayoneted before they had any idea what was happening. There were shouts, pleas and screams, but few gunshots, almost all of them from Confederates firing wildly into the dark, harming nothing.

Then, in a moment, it was over. Hundreds of gray-clad soldiers stood prisoner, terror on their faces; scores more lay dead and dying. Triumphant shouts from across the river indicated Hazen's troops had met with similar success. Only a few Union soldiers were wounded or dead, hardly worth mentioning after all the massacres of the first two years of the war.

Spattered with gore, Turchin bellowed for his men to join him near the largest of the campfires. "Boys, you make me proud. Today you show you could make a Turk shit his pants! Now, we finish job. All right to shoot, for they know now Turchin's boys come! But more fun to use bayonet, to see light in Johnnie Reb's eyes go out as you kill traitor! Those who not guarding prisoners, follow me; we clear path back to Chattanooga!"

Lot was unnerved by the viciousness of the speech, but he could tell that the men were not; they were roaring their approval. Lot looked around for Clay and saw him standing near Turchin, his own sword stained with blood halfway to the hilt. It disturbed Lot even more that Clay's blue eyes seemed to dance with joy behind the spectacles. He then noticed Lieutenant Bierce standing alongside Turchin, arms crossed on his chest, a sardonic smile on his face, seemingly amused by the spectacle. That disturbed the black sergeant even more.

Setting off at a brisk walk, Turchin led his forces along the road to Chattanooga, a mere half mile away. Periodically, he would shout orders to a particular company to peel off to the left or to the right, to round up Confederate pickets and stragglers. Occasional shots and screams came from the darkness, but they were rare and signified little in the grand scale of war. Bierce jogged to the front and went to the lead. Clearly, the young Lieutenant felt obligated to make sure that the advance did not get lost in the darkness. Clay moved up to accompany him. Lot cursed to himself, feeling that Clay put them both at risk in some obscure desire to prove his courage the equal of Bierce's.

Suddenly a shot erupted from the brush to the side of the road. Bierce stopped and clapped a hand to the side of his neck; in the dim light of the coming dawn, a look of surprise came to his face.

He brought his hand to his face and looked with amazement at a dark smear. At that moment, a shadowy figure leaped, screaming from the brush, running at Bierce with a bayonet-tipped musket.

In a blur of motion, Clay whipped his German-made saber from its scabbard and lunged at the Rebel. The man started to turn, but Clay batted the bayoneted musket away with the flat of his saber. Then he thrust his sword deep into the man's bowels. The Confederate soldier dropped his weapon and made as to grab the sword and remove it from his vitals. He then looked directly at Clay, who hissed in surprise as he recognized the young soldier whose artless relief of his bladder had given such amusement a quarter of an hour ago. Clay drew out the sword and the man fell to the ground, beginning a keening series of low cries. Clay stood stock still, bloody sword in hand, looking at the man he had just stabbed. Up trotted General Turchin, who saw the blood on Bierce's hand.

"Lieutenant, what happen here?"

"Some fool shot at me," Bierce replied in wonderment. "I don't believe it is serious; just grazed the side of my neck. He would have finished me off but for Captain Clay. I suppose that I owe him my life."

"Good job, Captain," said Turchin. "Not many like Bierce; should not lose him in silly skirmish. You think quick."

Clay said nothing but continued to stare expressionlessly at the young man on the ground, whose cries were getting louder and more pathetic.

Turchin bent over, and inspected the Rebel in the strengthening light of the dawn. "Man will not survive this; no point in taking to hospital." In a smooth motion, Turchin drew his saber and plunged it into the chest of the young Confederate, who shuddered and died.

Clay started. "General Turchin, was that really necessary?" he asked in a quiet voice.

The Russian shrugged as he wiped his blade clean and restored it to its scabbard. "Man was dead, Captain. Better it be quick and now, rather than later of infection. This is war. Come, Chattanooga Bridge just around bend." Without waiting, Turchin began jogging along with his men, who were advancing up the road in greater and greater numbers. Bierce stood looking at Clay in puzzlement, Clay looked at the body of the young soldier with no expression at all, and Lot looked at Clay with pity.

"Huzzah for the cracker line, boys! Huzzah for the cracker line!" Soldiers along the riverfront kept repeating the cheer as the first wagons from the new wharfs at Brown's Ferry made their way into Chattanooga. Generals Grant and Thomas stood together on a hilltop overlooking the riverfront, with Rawlins, Parker, Clay, Lot, and Bierce at a respectful distance.

"Strange how the soldiers have taken to calling the route across Moccasin Point 'the cracker line,'" muttered Grant, lighting another of his ever-present cigars. "Crackers aren't the most important thing. Fodder for the animals, fresh vegetables and meat for the men, ammunition, and medicine—all of those are as important, if not more so."

Thomas stared moodily at the waterfront, while the distant cries of 'Huzzah for the cracker line' continued. "I expect it's the symbolism of the humble army cracker, sir. All of the things you mention are critical, and we're short of them all, but the cracker is the most basic of the rations. When it starts coming through, the soldiers know that everything else will follow."

"I expect you're right, General. Anyway, now we can not only supply your men, but bring in Sherman and Hooker. With their fifty thousand extra men, we can go on the offensive, and finally whip Bragg and Longstreet."

"Sir, I meant to tell you something of importance," replied

Thomas. "My staff has interrogated several prisoners and confirmed that Bragg is detaching Longstreet to go attack Burnside in Knoxville."

Grant stared at Thomas in amazement. "Why would Bragg do such a doggone foolish thing? Longstreet's corps is one-third of his army, and the best third at that."

Thomas shrugged. "The prisoners are not entirely sure, but they feel that Bragg fears he will be kicked out of his command, and Longstreet named his replacement. You know Bragg's reputation in the old army: the most contrary, mean, ornery, and high-handed officer you could meet in a month of Sundays. He's hated by his officers and despised by his men, who are kept in line only by vicious punishment. Do you know, he actually executed a man for shooting a chicken! I am more against looting civilians than most and certainly believe in discipline, but that kind of harshness can only impact the morale of an army adversely. Anyway, it sounds like Bragg is actually willing to weaken his army in order to get rid of a potential replacement."

Grant stared moodily at his smoldering cigar. "Well, that will make it easier for us here. However, if Burnside is destroyed and Longstreet drives north from Knoxville to the Ohio, it won't matter what we do. I need to know more of what's going on in Knoxville." Grant turned to the knot of soldiers standing behind the two generals, and motioned for them to come forward. "Rawlins, tell General Thomas of that telegram you decoded."

The gaunt chief of staff nodded. "When we finally got the telegraph working day before yesterday, one of the first things to come through was a coded message from Major Joachim von Lindau, a signals officer on the staff of Burnside's Army of the Ohio. It said that he had irrefutable proof that the Rebels were obtaining advance knowledge of Burnside's movements and dispositions, and that the information could only have come from within Burnside's immediate staff. He apologized for not respecting the chain of command. However, he felt that he dare not alert the traitor that he is suspect. He appeals to you to send experienced officers to root out the exact identity of the traitor."

"This could make a more rational reason for sending Longstreet to attack Burnside," commented Grant. "Burnside is not the most . . . shall we say . . . quick witted of our generals, and Longstreet is one of their very best. If Longstreet had inside knowledge, he could very well destroy Burnside and his command before we could do anything about it."

"Who is this von Lindau?" asked Parker. "Is he reliable, trustworthy?"

"I know him by reputation, sir," responded Clay unexpectedly. "A Prussian lawyer who had some role in the revolution of '48. He fled Berlin one-step ahead of the hangman and settled in the German community in St. Louis, where he became a prosecutor with an excellent record of obtaining convictions. He is said to be highly intelligent and fiercely devoted to abolitionism. He is also well connected with the Republican Party in Missouri and is a personal friend of both Generals Schurz and Sigel. I would consider him as reliable as anyone who I have not had the pleasure of actually meeting."

"Well, maybe we can kill two birds with one stone," said Grant. "Captain Clay, you and Sergeant Lot are to go overland to Knoxville, establish contact with Major von Lindau, and investigate whether there is merit to his charges. I sincerely hope that there is not, but we dare not take the chance, especially after . . . well, we dare not take the chance.

"Officially, you are to be my observer at Burnside's headquarters, Clay, and in fact, if you feel he is getting overwhelmed, you let me know. We can't have him losing control again, like he did at Fredericksburg. General Thomas, with your permission, I'd like to send Lieutenant Bierce with Clay. It may be necessary to move reinforcements directly from Chattanooga to Knoxville, and it is vital that I have a better idea of the roads and terrain than is given by the sorry excuses for maps that we have."

Thomas nodded. "Lieutenant Bierce, please accompany Captain Clay to Knoxville, starting dawn tomorrow. I will have official orders drafted, and the best horses ready for all three of you."

Bierce saluted Thomas then grinned sardonically at Clay. "Ah, just like old times, Clay. What times we had before Vicksburg! Still, it's bound to be disappointing, not having a personal murder to look into—just masses of bodies from state-sanctioned slaughter."

"Remember, Clay, I want certainty," said Grant. "No rumors or guesses. Let me have the unvarnished truth about Burnside and whether there's a traitor in his headquarters. I don't care which way the answer goes, so long as it is certain."

"Of course, sir," said Clay saluting, nonetheless thinking to himself that even if certainty was possible, few men were able to endure it. Of all people, Ulysses Grant was probably one of those very few.

CHAPTER 2

"SO WE'RE SPRINGING TO THE CALL FROM THE EAST FROM THE WEST"

It had not rained at all that day, but this fact pleased the three riders less than it should. They had been picking their way along a road little better than a game trail through countryside that had been hardscrabble in the best of times. The soil was poor and the drainage so bad that mud was everywhere, even when it had not been raining. Thinly settled as the land must have been in peacetime, it was virtually deserted now. Like most highland people in Tennessee, the inhabitants of this area were largely Union loyal. Confederate militia had been through a number of times, leaving untended fields and blackened chimneys as testimony to their opinion of those who clung to old allegiances.

The muddy trail was so narrow that the three soldiers had to ride single-file. Bierce was in front, as befitted his status as a scout. His restless eyes never ceased darting about: first the ground in front of them, then the woods and fields to either side, then the distant ridgeline ahead, then back to the ground in front of them. Next came Clay, frowning slightly as he took in the surroundings;

the poor, untended land offended the sensibilities of a planter's son who had grown up in Kentucky bluegrass. Last rode Lot, his constant vigilance as to their flanks and rear giving him a worried expression.

"This detour of yours will add at least two days to our journey," said Clay to Bierce, breaking a long silence. "Yes, I know you were concerned that taking the direct route through Loudon County might cause us to run into Longstreet's advance guard, but we could avoid contact if reasonably careful, and the roads would be much better."

"I don't quite share your optimism about avoiding capture if we come across the Reb main body. I would take the chance if it was Bragg. He's sloppy, and his men don't give their best. But Longstreet? Longstreet has a pretty smart outfit, and his men really stir themselves to give an extra ten percent. No, I do not want to be taking the long way any more than you, Clay, but have faith in my skills as a scout. Up here in Roane County, the roads are so bad, and the few sources of forage have been so picked over, that Longstreet's Corps would never dream of coming this way. Even Forrest, light as he travels, wouldn't risk more than a few companies of his horsemen up here, and we are unlikely to . . ."

Clay held up his hand and hissed, "Listen."

All three horsemen drew up their mounts. Bierce wore a puzzled expression; he obviously heard nothing.

Clay said, "Somewhere up ahead and to our left. Crying or moaning."

"I hear pretty damn good, Clay, but I don't hear a thing," replied Bierce.

Clay did not answer, but just spurred his horse into a gallop, heading at an angle across a muddy, uncultivated field. Wordlessly, Lot followed suit. Muttering curses under his breath, Bierce brought up the rear.

Clay galloped toward a ramshackle farmhouse, with an even

more decrepit barn to its left. As he approached the farmhouse, Clay suddenly veered toward the barn and galloped around its corner. Bierce and Lot could now hear the sound that had attracted Clay's attention, half moan, half sob, repeating over and over.

"How in the hell could he hear that from the road?" asked Bierce of Lot as he slewed his mount to follow Clay.

"He always could hear things no one else could," responded Lot, just in front of Bierce. The two soldiers rounded the corner and reined their mounts in sharply. Later, both would recall that their eyes took some moments to acknowledge what was before them.

Clay had already dismounted and was standing beside a man in shapeless farmer's clothing who was huddled on the ground, his back to the newest arrivals; from this man came the continuous moaning, weeping sounds. Clay was not looking at the man, but at an object that was in front of the moaning farmer. The object was a cross. On the cross, a naked boy of about ten had been nailed upside down in an obscene mockery of the Crucifixion. Lot cried out when he saw the gaping hole where the child's heart should be. He was a believing Christian, and the sight was horrible to him on more than one level. Clay stood mesmerized at the sight of the child.

"Dear God," whispered the black sergeant. "Dear, sweet Jesus."

"You can look at this and believe in a God of mercy?" asked Bierce angrily, not taking his eyes off the sight. "Look at that! Someone took time with that child. Only thing I ever heard like this is what the newspapers said was found in the basement of the Starry Wisdom church in Rhode Island, back in '61. Besides all those bodies under the basement floor, they said there had been some sort of human sacrifice. I thought it was something the newspapers made up to thrill the ignorant rabble and sell papers. Maybe not."

"Where is the blood?" asked Lot suddenly. "A wound like that, blood should be splattered around all over. Where is the blood?"

Bierce had no answer, but continued to stare at the somber scene.

Without taking his eyes from the slaughtered child, Clay suddenly said "Sir, what happened here?"

The huddled farmer ceased his moaning. "Who's there?" he asked in a cracked voice.

"Captain Clay, United States Volunteers, sir. I know this is hard on you, but I must know what took place here. I must."

"Should've gone to Lenoir City, or to Knoxville," came a low response from the huddled farmer. "Most folks hereabouts refugeed to them places when they heard Forrest's boys were coming. Most of 'em don't hold with the slavocracy or with Richmond. Never was political myself; didn't feel I had a dog in this fight, and figured that if I didn't bother nobody, nobody would bother me. Had a farm to run. With my woman passed on and with my daughter Celia and son Jethro to raise, no time for getting mixed up in foolishness." The man stopped talking, and began rocking gently back and forth.

Clay tore his gaze away from the obscenely slaughtered youth and grabbed the farmer's shoulder, shaking him. "I must know, sir. Did General Forrest do this?"

"It were his men, I guess. 'Bout thirty of them, with this big major calling himself Solomon Ward. Came outta nowhere and started ransacking the feed and the smokehouse. Went up to Major Ward and told him to git. He laughs and asks what a healthy man like me is doing out of uniform, with the Conscript Act and all. Told him I didn't hold with either Richmond or Washington, and he should mind his business and I would mind mine. He laughs again, and said General Forrest had told him to burn loyalty into eastern Tennessee. Said the general was tired of all the nigger-lovers between Nashville and Knoxville and had left it to him and some others to make examples to show folks their proper loyalties. Told his men to bring Celia and Jethro in front of me. Celia was bawling. For the love of Jesus, she's only sixteen! Ward laughs while she cries. I tells him let my kids go, and I'll join up. He laughs again and says it's too late for that, but I should be honored, for Celia was going to be given a chance for glory, while Jethro would be used to prepare the way while providing an example to Lincoln Republicans hereabouts. Don't rightly know what he meant, but they takes Jethro, cuts his clothes off, and . . . and . . . He tells me they were going to let me live, to be an example to nigger lovers, and that the last thing I would ever see . . ."

The farmer choked up and began to cry. He turned his face toward Clay. Bierce and Lot could now see the ruined bloody holes where the man's eyes had been. Lot cried out in horror; Bierce spat an obscenity.

"Sir, can you tell me what became of Celia?" came the pleading voice. "It was . . . I mean, they held me while they took Jethro and . . . then my eyes . . . but I need to know what happened to Celia."

"I believe they had their way with her, but afterwards there would be no cause to harm her," said Clay gently. "My friends will search for her while I help you. You have been through hell, sir, but you will be reunited with your daughter. Lieutenant, Sergeant, search the farmhouse. They undoubtedly left her in there."

Bierce and Lot dismounted, tied their horses to a hitching-post, and hurried in the direction of the farmhouse. As they walked, Lot said quietly to Bierce "I know Alphonso Clay better than anyone, but I can't understand why he would hold out hope to that poor soul. The monsters that would do what we just saw would never leave a witness . . ."

Suddenly Lot stopped and looked wide-eyed at Bierce, who

only smiled grimly. The black sergeant whirled around and ran for the barn, but halfway there, a pistol shot rang out. He rounded the corner of the barn to find the farmer lying in a heap. Clay had broken open his new-fangled Smith & Wesson and was replacing one of the shiny cartridges in the cylinder, his face utterly devoid of expression.

Without looking at his friend, Clay spoke. "Of course, we will not be finding the girl, at least alive. She was taken for . . . well, purposes beyond the obvious, purposes for which I hope you cannot imagine. This was for the best. The last thing I told him was that Forrest would pay for this." He closed his revolver and inserted it into his holster as Bierce walked up, a thoughtful look on his face.

"I understand why you did this, Clay," said Bierce. "Still, the law might take a different view than we three would."

"Report it if you like," responded Clay, eyes fixed now on the slaughtered child.

"I would not do so. You have saved my life. And besides, you behaved with greater kindness to this fellow than I would have done. Still, this puzzles me. The boy's wound should have left blood everywhere. What became of the blood?"

Clay did not respond. Bierce had the impression that Clay knew, but suddenly, he decided that he did not want to know what Clay knew.

"Although I fear what we may find, we must now inspect the farmhouse," murmured Clay softly. Without another word, he marched toward the ramshackle home. Pausing only a few moments, Bierce and Lot fell in behind him.

The three soldiers went through the open back door that swung listlessly in the breeze and found themselves in a disheveled kitchen; broken dishes and scraps of food were everywhere, the sheer quantity making it obvious the Confederate raiding party had caused the damage.

Lips curled into a faint look of disgust, Clay paused only briefly before passing into the parlor. Bierce and Lot had paused to inspect the damage more closely when they heard from the next room an agonized roar, like the death-cry of a wounded beast. It obviously could not be the soft-spoken, high-voiced Clay, so Bierce and Lot drew their pistols, rushed into the parlor, and found that the inhuman sound indeed came from the small captain, who had fallen to his knees before the obscenely defaced, naked body of a teenage girl.

"Alphonso!" Lot cried out.

Clay's entire body seemed to quiver, while the unearthly roar died away to nothing. The quivering slowly stopped, and Clay rose to face his two friends. Lot noticed that tears streamed from his eyes.

"I am sorry that you must witness this . . . abomination," said Clay in his normal, emotionless voice, taking a handkerchief from his pocket and neatly wiping away his tears; calm was restored. He pointed to a mass of bloody flesh spread on the floor, barely recognizable as a young woman. "Even though I suspected we would find a scene such as this, to see it . . . overcame me for a moment. You will note the bruising and scratching on the inner . . . legs . . . indicates that the child was . . . used—repeatedly and with violence. You will note that this outrage continued with the heart of the girl being removed." Behind his spectacles Clay's ice-blue eyes flicked over to the fireplace, where something smoldered behind the grate. "I believe you will find the remains of the girl's heart over there, probably with her brother's."

Bierce let fly with a stream of obscenities that nonetheless seemed to be inadequate to express his rage. Lot's eyes filled with tears; he asked Clay "What in the name of the Lord Our Savior were they doing?"

"Sacrifice, Sergeant. Sacrifice in propitiation of an entity that has little to do with the Christian God."

"Don't tell me the sick bastards actually believe that!" Bierce almost shouted. "There's nothing that would want to respond to this sick atrocity!"

Clay retained his recovered calm. "It matters not whether the . . . entity . . . to which they sacrificed exists; the monsters who committed this act believe it and acted accordingly." Suddenly, Clay's head jerked slightly to the side. "Horses are approaching. It might be Forrest's men, coming back for something they have forgotten." Clay dashed back into the kitchen, looked through the grimy window, and snarled a rare curse. "There are four riders, and they have already spotted our horses. Butternut jackets; Rebels to be sure. They are dismounting far short of the barn and drawing carbines and revolvers from their saddles." Clay turned to face his companions. "Even if we drive them away, they would just return to hound us with more men. You two keep their attention on this house, without exposing yourselves unnecessarily. I can get out the front and into the scrub before they are in a position to see me." And Clay was gone in a blur of motion.

"What the hell?" exclaimed Bierce. Meanwhile, Lot was peering out the kitchen window.

"Ambrose, two are taking up positions inside the barn, a third behind a tree to the right, the fourth behind a shed to the left. The latter two should have a clear view of the sides and front of the house; they haven't opened fire, so Alphonso must have gotten clear undetected."

"Hey, Yanks, come on out with your hands up!" came a shout from the barn. "Make us come in there, an' we'll kill you fer sure!"

Bierce had joined Lot at the window. "I think those are Sharp's breechloaders those Rebs have. Damnation! Long range and fairly quick to reload. Where in the hell did they get guns like that? They can just start potting away at us, the bullets going through the boards of this house like they were made of newspaper. And all we have are a couple of goddamn Colts."

"All right, Billy Yanks, we ain't asking twice! Let 'em have it boys!" Four loud shots rang out; the two kitchen windows exploded with a shower of glass. Bierce and Lot hit the floor, drawing their Colts uselessly. After about fifteen seconds, another four shots rang out in rapid succession; the aim had been below the windows, and the bullets criss-crossed the kitchen just inches above their heads.

"Got to give them something to think about and distract them from what Alphonso's doing," said Lot. "Rise up, fire twice at the barn, then hit the floor." Bierce nodded, and they leaped to opposite corners of one window, fired twice each, then fell back to the floor just as they heard an angry shout, followed by four more vengeful rifle bullets raking the house.

"Can't keep this up for long," muttered Bierce. "Our little captain better do something quick.

The Reb stationed behind the shed grinned at the sound of the four pistol shots from the farmhouse. *Popguns,* he thought to himself. *With the Sharp's rifles, we'll take that building apart and cut up anything left inside. Just like the girl.* He grinned as he took aim low underneath the windows of the house where he figured the Yanks were cowering. He only heard Clay's soft, light footsteps coming up directly behind him at the very last moment; the firing of the heavy bullets had left a ringing in his ears. When he did hear the footsteps, he turned just in time to see Alphonso Clay leap into the air. He froze more at the sight of the monstrous look of hatred in a face that scarcely seemed human and the eerily blazing blue eyes behind steel-rimmed spectacles, rather than the huge Bowie knife in the apparition's right hand. As Clay slammed into the Rebel, the blade of the knife went in under the ribs and found the heart; Clay's opponent was dead before the pair hit the ground. Clay jerked the blade out of the man's body and cut his throat to the bone, to assure silence; the feeble spurts from the severed blood vessels showed the last act had not been necessary.

Crouched low, Clay quickly examined the barn and the tree beyond it; it appeared that none of the other three attackers had seen what had happened and were still concentrating their attention on the farmhouse. Nevertheless, he knew they would soon realize that their four guns had been reduced to three. He took the dead man's Sharp's, grabbed several cartridges from the raiders belt pouch, and began a swift, silent run to the rear of the barn, so low to the ground that one would have sworn he was running on all fours. Clay achieved the rear of the barn without being spotted, broke open the breach of the gun, and inserted one of the large cartridges. Creeping noiselessly to the far side, he peeked around the corner and spotted a second Rebel behind a tree, concentrating on killing his two friends. In one smooth motion, he raised and sighted the rifle, then touched the trigger. The second raider's head shattered in an explosion of blood and bone. Permitting himself a brief smile of satisfaction, Clay wasted no time in breaking open the carbine and inserting another cartridge.

Meanwhile, from the front of the barn, Clay heard a rough voice shout "Jed? Zach? What's wrong? Answer me!"

The smile disappeared from Clay's face. The two surviving raiders knew something was wrong and might be thinking of a retreat. Clay was determined not to allow it. There was no door at the rear of the barn, but there was a very wide, very loose board. With a wrench that was surprisingly strong for such a slightly-built man, he tore the board off and squirmed through the gap. He immediately saw a figure crouching in the shadow to the left side of the open door. Clay advanced several steps to get a better view, aimed, and fired; the figure at the door cried out, fell backwards, and was still.

Eyes darting about the dark interior of the barn, searching out the remaining raider, Clay reloaded the carbine by feel.

He heard a noise above him, and swiveled around—just in time to get a heavy bale of hay in the face. His carbine was knocked away into the darkness by the fall, and the stunned Clay looked up to see a bearded, hate-filled face staring at him over the sights of the owner's own carbine from the hayloft. Even as Clay scrabbled for the revolver in his holster, he knew that it was probably too late. Then two pistol shots rang out; the raider coughed, dropped his weapon, and looked with surprise at two bullet holes, one low in his stomach, one in his upper chest. He pitched forward and fell heavily, ten feet to the barn floor where he landed with a sickening thud and where he gave out low, piteous moans.

Clay got up and looked to the barn door, where stood Lot and Bierce, smoking Colt .44s in their hands.

"Alphonso, you damn fool!" said Lot shakily. "You took on the whole raiding party yourself. Do you think we are useless?"

"Hardly useless," replied Clay brushing hay and dirt from his uniform; he was vain about his appearance. "You kept their attention focused, giving me the opportunity to take them from the rear."

"And you would have died if we hadn't figured out that you were inside the barn and needed help," responded Bierce with an ironic grin.

After a moment's hesitation, Clay replied, "I suppose I did miscalculate the odds. I thank you gentlemen for saving me from my miscalculation."

Lot had been examining the wounded raider. "We at least have a prisoner, although I don't know how long he will live with these wounds."

Clay drew his revolver, walked over to the Rebel, and fired five shots into the man's head. "We have no prisoner," responded Clay emotionlessly.

* * *

"So this must be why those four came back," said Clay, showing his friends the small leather bag he had found under a cushion in the parlor where a horror had been perpetrated. He opened it; the distinctive gleam of gold showed in the dim light.

"How much do you suppose it is?" asked Lot.

"Difficult to say," responded Bierce, who had taken one of the coins and was examining it closely. "This isn't American; looks like Spanish, and the date is over two centuries ago."

"The bag weighs about four pounds," reflected Clay. "There's about one ounce of gold in an American $20 piece. Make it about $1200 or so—an army captain's salary for a year. They must have lost track of it while they were doing . . . what they did. Given how much money was at stake, their commander must have given them permission to come back and search for it. We should be gone before he realizes they aren't coming back—and before he sends a search party after them."

"What are hard cases like them doing with so much money?" asked Lot.

"I do not know," responded Clay. "And that bothers me." He sighed. "In any event, we should give the remains of the farmer and his children a Christian burial."

"We don't have time for that," responded Bierce. "Forrest's men may still be in the neighborhood."

"If we do not make time for that, then we are little better than the . . . the animals who committed this obscenity," said Clay turning his gaze on Bierce. Behind his spectacles, the blue eyes flickered with unearthly light.

Bierce hesitated, then said, "I imagine there are picks and shovels in the barn. It should not take long with the three of us working together. But what should we do with the four Rebs?"

"Leave them for the crows," responded Clay indifferently

* * *

The three exhausted riders topped a ridge and suddenly saw the grandly-named Lenoir City, a few hundred ramshackle buildings on the banks of the Tennessee. They paused, and Bierce laughed harshly.

"So that is Lenoir City," said the lieutenant. "Good God, what a sense of humor the huckster who christened that little hamlet must have had."

Suddenly, four blue-clad cavalrymen galloped out of a nearby copse of trees. Their leader, wearing a corporal's stripes, leveled a shiny-looking Spencer carbine at the new arrivals and addressed himself to Clay as the ranking officer. "Beg your pardon, sir, but some of Forrest's scouts have been wearin' uniforms they've taken off dead Yanks, and you're coming from the direction we know Forrest's boys own. So beggin' your pardon in advance, would you be so good as to identify yourselves and present some proof you're who you say you are?"

Clay favored the apologetic corporal with a tight smile. "Certainly, Corporal. In your position, I would take the same precautions. I am Captain Clay, of General Grant's staff. This is my orderly, Sergeant Lot. The lieutenant is Bierce, a scout seconded to me from the Army of the Cumberland." Careful to make no sudden moves, Clay withdrew a document from an inner tunic pocket, trotted his horse over to the corporal, and handed the paper to him.

"Boys, keep an eye on the officers while I look at this here," said the corporal. While his three soldiers leveled their carbines at the newcomers, their leader slid his own into the scabbard behind his saddle and read the paper. It was apparently a chore; the corporal frowned and moved his lips silently. After a long time, he finally completed reading the short document, folded it up, and handed it back to Clay. "Well, Captain, everything seems to be all right.

My boys will stay here and watch the road while I take you down to talk to General Burnside."

"General Burnside is here?" asked Clay in a surprised voice. "I would have thought he would be in Knoxville."

"Just between us, most of the boys were surprised too. Burnside has the reputation of being a headquarters general. Still, when the patrols said Longstreet was comin' up the road that goes through Lenoir City, he came a runnin' with the Ninth Corps and most of his headquarters staff. Got to give him credit. Anyways, if you'all don't mind, let's take you to the General." The corporal led the three new arrivals down the steep path to the rural hamlet that hopefully called itself Lenoir City.

They stopped in front of a three-story brick building on the main street, obviously the best, possibly the only, hotel in town. The two soldiers at the entrance had the faint arrogance that always seemed to infect headquarter guards, but they recognized the corporal and waived the new arrivals through the entrance. In what had been the hotel's small parlor, a number of desks and tables had been scattered at random. Officers and enlisted men bustled about the room, while four generals, a major, and a captain stood around the largest table engrossed in a large, spread-out map.

The corporal was not overawed with rank; he easily approached a tall, balding general with elaborate muttonchops whiskers, saluted, and said, "Beggin' your pardon, General, but these officers come from General Grant. I figured you would want to see them as soon as may be."

The tall general looked at the corporal with an expression that he must have thought was fierce but only managed petulance. "Yes, well corporal . . . yes. You are dismissed." The corporal easily saluted and left the parlor, while the general turned his attention to the new arrivals.

Major General Ambrose Burnside was well over six feet in height, with broad shoulders and a narrow waist. Somehow, his balding head and flaring side-whiskers seemed to enhance his handsome features, rather than detract from them. Burnside studied the new arrivals silently for an unaccountably long time. This puzzled Clay until he remembered how Burnside's brief tenure as head of the Army of the Potomac had been a disaster more from petty backbiting and jealous intrigues among his own officers rather than his somewhat limited military abilities. With a flash of insight, Clay realized that the commander of the Army of the Ohio was suspicious and afraid of staff officers sent by his division commander, Grant. Although not normally a warm character, Clay felt a stab of sympathy for the general and sought to break the ice.

"General, I have been sent by General Grant to act as liaison between his headquarters and the Army of the Ohio. He is with the Army of the Cumberland, which as you know is in a very delicate situation just now. He believes it is essential that there be someone at your headquarters with a good appreciation of the situation."

"A spy!" exclaimed the short, thin brigadier immediately to Burnside's right, sporting an exact replica of the commanding general's facial hair. "Damn, you sir! I saw what your type did to General Burnside back in the Army of the Potomac. Your kind pulled him down, sir. Why, I will . . ."

"That is enough of that, John," said Burnside quietly but firmly, laying a hand on his furious subordinate's shoulder. "General Grant is well within his rights. In fact, coordination of our forces is vital. Hang together or hang separately, you know." He turned to the new arrivals and said, "This is General John Parke, my chief of staff. Forgive his outburst. We have all been under strain, and his personal loyalty led him to some intemperance of speech. And who might you be?"

"Captain Alphonso Clay, of Grant's staff. This is my orderly, Sergeant Lot, and Lieutenant Bierce, a cartographer and scout with the Army of the Cumberland."

"Well, Clay, in addition to my invaluable Chief of Staff, here we have General Robert Potter, acting commander of the Ninth Corps," said Burnside, indicating a small, mild-looking man who responded, "Pleasure to meet you," in a curt New York accent. Nodding to the remaining general, Burnside said, "And this is my invaluable cavalry commander, General William Sanders," indicating a tall, solemn, fully-bearded young man, who responded, "Pleasure to make your acquaintance," in the syrupy accents of the South.

Gesturing to the stiff-backed, fierce-looking captain, Burnside said, "This is Orlando Poe, my chief engineer." The dark, unsmiling Poe merely inclined his head, saying nothing.

Burnside turned to the last of the officers gathered around the table. "And this is the most recent addition to my official family, Major Joachim von Lindau, an excellent signals officer. In addition to everything else, he has undertaken to personally question the prisoners we collect, and he has proven able in extracting useful information from them." Von Lindau, a tall, portly man of about fifty with heavy side-whiskers and sad brown eyes, stared intently at Clay.

"I know of Hauptmann . . . ach . . . Captain Clay," said von Lindau in careful but heavily accented English. "Read of his . . . exploits in Louisiana. Read of his grandfather, Friedrich von Juntz, back in Germany, before I had to flee Prussian police in '48."

It was painfully obvious that von Lindau disapproved of Clay. However, as his words gave no overt offense, Clay chose to ignore the hostile overtone.

"And I know of you sir," responded Clay. "Your fight for democracy in Germany was admirable, if ahead of its time; your fearless prosecution of politically well-connected criminals in St. Louis is an example to all district attorneys. In fact, when you have the time, I would like to discuss certain individuals in the St. Louis city government with you. You may not know it, but General Grant lived there for some years and has suspicions that certain individuals may be secret Confederate sympathizers. He undoubtedly would wish me to get your opinion on those people, whom you must know. I am sure that you will agree that there is nothing worse than a secret traitor."

Von Lindau focused his sad brown eyes on Clay with some surprise but recovered quickly, "That would indeed be interesting, Captain. Matters are quite intense right now. Still, I should be able to spare some time, if General Burnside can spare me, after eleven o'clock tonight. Room 3E upstairs."

"That will be fine, Major," responded the army commander, who turned his undivided attention to the new arrivals. "Now gentlemen, you could help us by telling what you learned about the enemy on your trip from Chattanooga."

"Certainly," responded Bierce without prompting; the young lieutenant certainly did enjoy his area of expertise. "We did not take the direct road to here, as without doubt, Longstreet and his corps are using it to advance upon Knoxville. We took a wide swing through Lenoir County, using the miserable trails that pass for roads in those parts," indicating the path on the map with his forefinger. "We had no actual contact with Confederate forces up there, although we ran across indications that elements of Forrest's cavalry have been active in oppressing loyal citizens." Bierce suddenly stopped, a dark cloud passing across his handsome features. He slightly shook his head, evidently deciding that the horror at the farm was of no practical interest to his audience, and continued. "In any event, no forces of military significance are coming here from the northwest, and all accounts are that the road network to the southwest is even worse. Therefore, you can count on Longstreet using the main road through here to Knoxville. It is the only hope he has of moving fifteen thousand troops and their supplies and equipment."

"General Burnside, I am empowered by General Grant to tell you that the supply situation in Chattanooga is well on its way to being solved," said Clay. "However, he must still dislodge Bragg's army from its stranglehold on the town before he can think of aiding you here. In fact, he is as much in need of your help as you are of his."

"That much was obvious," replied General Parke. "That is why General Burnside ordered the Ninth Corps forward to either frighten Bragg into inaction or to tempt him into detaching part of his army to gobble up the bait posed by the Ninth. Bragg went for the latter alternative."

"Very prompt, very intelligent," said Clay. "Grant will appreciate that, General Burnside."

"Now, now, General Parke is modest," replied the bewhiskered Burnside. "It was his plan entirely. I simply endorsed it."

"With respect sir, it was your basic idea," General Parke said. "I only translated it into specific orders."

"Well, let's say we came up with it together and have done with it," replied Burnside, smiling indulgently at his chief of staff. "Be that as it may, now that Bragg is taking the bait, we have a narrow path to walk. We will be falling back on Knoxville; however, we cannot do that so quickly that Longstreet tires of the chase or entrench so thoroughly at Knoxville that he regards an assault as hopeless. We do not want Pete Longstreet returning to Bragg before Grant and Thomas have had a chance to chase the Confederates away."

"So what will be your plan of operation, if I may ask?" asked Clay.

General Parke answered for his chief, leaning over the map

on the table and pointing with the stub of a pencil as he spoke. "The road from Chattanooga crosses the Tennessee here at Huff's Ferry, a natural ford. Crossing a large body of men is not feasible for many miles in either direction, so Longstreet must come that way. General Potter will move his forces to the ford, supported by General Sanders' cavalry."

"Could you not hold Longstreet indefinitely at the ford?" asked Bierce.

"Such an attempt would be unwise," responded Burnside. "The Ninth was sadly depleted by illness and casualties during the Vicksburg campaign. What with garrisons I've had to leave at various points, Potter has barely eight thousand men, many of them untrained, green replacements. Sanders' cavalry is as good as there is, man for man, but he can count on less than twelve hundred sabers. Longstreet's corps has at least fifteen thousand well-trained veterans, and if I remember Pete Longstreet aright, you can count on him using them very well."

"We must count on a fighting retreat," continued Parke. "It will be tricky, very tricky. If the engagement becomes general, Longstreet will pin us in place and grind us up with superior numbers. I am especially concerned about our supply train. The one advantage to the limited supplies possessed by Johnny Reb is he is not slowed down by their weight. The officers and men must be told to discard or destroy everything not immediately necessary to fighting. Meanwhile, we wait for the pickets at Huff's Ferry to alert us to the main body."

"You should not forget Forrest," said Clay quietly. "The man is moving east with Longstreet. There is a tendency for both sides to dismiss cavalry patrols as irrelevant in the grand scheme of things. I assure you, anyone who dismisses Forrest will be fortunate to live to regret that assumption."

Parke looked at Clay carefully, appearing to try to determine if he was an alarmist. After a moment, he said "We'll keep that in mind, Captain."

The genial Burnside intervened, "Well, gentleman, my staff and I have much to do to prepare the army for this fighting retreat. There is little you can do to aid us, and you look exhausted from the road. Best get some grub from the commissary wagon out back. Then if you don't mind being cramped, the three of you can share room 3G upstairs. It is set aside for visiting generals, but we don't have any right now, and it's yours, at least for tonight."

The three new arrivals saluted Burnside and his officers and exited through the front door. They found the commissary wagon immediately, a broken-down affair serving an indescribable substance that was allegedly stew. Each took a tin plate of the gruel, which had the sole virtue of being hot, served by a dirty private who seemed to be largely unacquainted with soap. All three were famished from the road and sat down on empty cracker boxes to eat. Lot was only able to finish his plate with difficulty, and the fastidious Clay took one spoonful, grimaced, and left the rest untouched.

With loud approving grunts, Bierce finished his entire meal, and to the surprise of Lot and the disgust of Clay, he licked his tin plate clean. He sighed contentedly, belched, then stood up and strolled over to the filthy cook who was pretending to clean his pots. "Private, an excellent meal. Now all I need for perfect contentment is refreshment of both the liquid and horizontal kind. Any establishment in this thriving metropolis that can answer that need?"

The private seemed to consider, then he spat on the ground and said, "Well, the only fancy house hereabouts is Rosie's place, the two-story frame building about halfway down the main street on the right. Hear tell they got some damn good whiskey, and even a couple of fresh Dutch girls. Don't know from personal experience."

"Ah, a good Christian?" asked Bierce.

"No, sir, just can't afford the tariff. Only officers and sutlers seem to have that kind of money. Get what you pay for, I suppose."

"Well, I've been saving my allowance," said Bierce with a smirk. "Thank you, private." He strode over to Clay and Lot, saying, "Care to join me in exploring the mysteries of Rosie's? It will be my treat; I am feeling generous for some reason."

"Intimacy without love is fit only for animals," said Clay with sneering contempt in his voice. "I do believe I will find more elevated ways to spend the evening."

"Lieutenant, please think twice," said Lot, genuine concern in his voice. "You are an intelligent man; surely you know the . . . risks to your health in such establishments."

Bierce threw his head back and laughed his harsh, barking laugh, a laugh devoid of genuine amusement. "Risks to health, Sergeant? What risks, sir? The risks of distilled liquor destroying my liver and kidneys? What are the chances of any of us making old bones? The risk of unmentionable diseases? The clap passes with time, and as for the pox, it only kills you after many years, and then does the mercy of extinguishing your mind before ending your life. The risk of having my heart broken? No heart to break, sir, no faith in humanity to destroy sir, not after . . . never mind. To lose oneself in sensation, to have one's conscious mind overwhelmed by pleasure—now, that is true entertainment, sir."

Lot averted his eyes; his mouth set in sad lines.

Suddenly serious, Bierce placed his hand on the black sergeant's shoulder. "Do not be disappointed in me, Jeremiah. I never pretended to be better than I am. Part of me wishes I wasn't this way. It is hard to explain. All I can say is that I need the release of dissipation from time to time, need it desperately."

"Ambrose, you are capable of being so much more than what

you pretend to be," blurted Lot suddenly. "You do dishonor to the gifts that God gave you."

"Let us agree to disagree on the superstitions that some people hold," said Bierce, his expression darkening. "Perhaps, if I survive this war I will try to do something in literature. However, I will not deceive you. My character will always be what it is now; accept me as I am. I did not entirely create what I am, but I accept it despite . . . ah, well. In any event, do not wait up for me, gentlemen." With a mocking salute, Bierce strolled off down the main street, whistling "*The Yellow Rose of Texas*."

That evening, Clay and Lot were in the cramped Room 3G; Lot sat on the rickety bed, while Clay sat stiff-backed on the room's single stool. Clay removed his new pocket watch, the inadequate replacement for the precious one he lost the day Vicksburg had fallen, the one that contained the portrait of the only woman he had ever loved. "It is a quarter until eleven," commented Clay, snapping the watch shut and restoring it to its pocket. "We will go to von Lindau's room soon. I believe he took the hint and knows we are here to receive his information on the traitor."

"It appears that Bierce will not be back for this interview," said Lot, a disillusioned tone to his voice. "He may be gone all night."

"He prefers his whores to saving the Union," muttered Clay darkly. "Just as well, this room is crowded enough with two people; with three, it would be intolerable."

"You are being unfair to Bierce. Whenever needed, he has done service that few of his rank can equal, and none exceed."

Clay sighed. "I suppose I am being unfair. After all, he did help you save General Sherman outside Vicksburg, and in the process save you from almost certain death. I owe him much for that. It is just that I am so irritated to see him not living up to his considerable potential."

"We both know that something horrible must have happened in his youth, something that twisted him. He has started to talk about it several times, only to stop himself. Whatever it was, it has warped his character. He chooses to battle his demons privately. Perhaps we should pity him rather than despise him."

"Perhaps."

Lot hesitated, then said, "I hope you will forgive me. I know the issue of your German grandparents is a sensitive one, one that you prefer to keep private. However, Major von Lindau alluded to it today. In private, let me be blunt. We are cousins— our fathers were brothers. That is not uncommon with the so-called gentry of the South, who usually act as if the relations of blood do not exist when offspring results from their lusts with slaves. You have never acted that way. You have always treated me not only as a friend, not only as the cousin I am, but as a brother. That means more to me than I can say. So it pains me that you do not share whatever it is that concerns you, something that even complete strangers like von Lindau seem to know. I cannot demand, but I do ask, as family, what von Lindau was hinting at."

Clay stared into space for such a long time that Lot had almost decided the captain had chosen to ignore him when Clay suddenly started to speak.

"You must understand that the Starry Wisdom cult is older and more widespread than people dream. When Professor Slaughter and his henchmen were captured and hanged two years ago, the discovery of all the mutilated children's bodies made people think they were degenerate monsters with unnatural tastes. Revolting, but a one-time horror, gradually being forgotten as this war releases seas of blood. Perhaps that is just as well; the public would not bear the truth. Starry Wisdom was simply the name the local practitioners used of a cult so old that it has no proper name. My grandfather, Friedrich von Juntz, described it, albeit imperfectly, in his little-known book *Unaussprechlichen Kulten*, published in 1827 in Weimar. The followers of the cult, who spread throughout Europe and even the Americas, had many goals, my grandfather reported. The indulgence of unnatural desires and opposition to the principles underlying the Christian and Judaic philosophies were the more prosaic. However, there were rumors of attempts to obtain powers and dominion through . . . unusual paths."

"Surely he didn't believe such superstitious nonsense," exclaimed Lot. "He was a professor of natural philosophy at the University of Jena, I understand. The Germans take the quality of their academics very seriously."

Clay laughed mirthlessly. "Remember when I went to Germany in the summer of '61? For reasons that are not relevant right now, I had acquired an urgent need to learn more about Grandfather. It was there that I was finally able to get a copy of *Unaussprechlichen Kulten*, which was never widely circulated. The book talked of wild, incredible things. He certainly wrote as if he believed all of it. In fact, a sense of excitement seemed to leap out of the pages, as if the author could barely contain his eagerness to try . . . certain things, things only hinted at in the book. It was a disturbing read. I then better understood the stories about his colleagues and friends dropping away from him, leaving him an isolated, even feared figure. Then, in 1829, my mother was born. Friedrich von Juntz was never married, and there is no clear record of upon whom he sired my mother."

Speaking gently, Lot said, "I suspected that your mother was a natural child. That only strengthens our bond. I am also a natural child."

Clay threw his head back and laughed again, a hysterical note creeping into his voice. "Yes, you are natural, Jeremiah, which is all to your credit, whereas I . . . Anyway, you know much of the rest—about how von Juntz was found in 1845 in his locked room, literally torn to pieces, with no sign of how the murderer entered or left, and of how my father rescued von Juntz's daughter, the product of his liaison, as a mob was about to stone her to death. What I had learned, the knowledge from which I wished to spare you, is that my father's presence in Weimar was no accident. For years, he had been on the edges of Starry Wisdom, too honorable to commit himself to their atrocities, too greedy for knowledge and power to stay away entirely. He had come specifically to find von Juntz's daughter because he had learned . . ."

A muffled boom rang out. Both Clay and Lot leaped to their feet.

"That was a pistol-shot, a .44 revolver," said Clay. Closest to the door, he flung it open just as another door slammed somewhere out in the hall.

The two friends lunged into the hall. All doors were shut, and the stairs were behind them. One by one, the doors opened in the hall, disgorging their occupants. General Burnside was the first to come into the darkened hallway, holding a guttering candle. He was still in uniform, as was General Parke; Generals Potter and Sanders and Captain Poe were in their drawers.

"What, what . . ." exclaimed the commanding general in a bewildered voice.

"Who's the damn fool letting off a pistol in the hotel?" demanded Parke angrily. "General Burnside could have been killed!"

"Where is von Lindau?" asked Sanders. "That noise would've awakened the dead. Certainly woke me up!"

Suddenly the group became aware of heavy footsteps coming up the stairs—and a voice singing "*Dixie*" in a singularly unmelodious manner. Bierce appeared at the top of the stairs, a silly grin on his face, tunic buttons askew. He stopped short when he saw the crowd in the corridor and nearly fell backwards down the stairs he had just ascended. "Whoa, quite a crowd for this time of night. Who died?"

"There was a shot fired up here, and we want to find out why," said Clay. "Did you pass anyone on the stairs?"

"Not a soul, Captain. There was just that brace of guards at the front door, no one else."

"Where is von Lindau?" asked Sanders again, urgency in his voice.

"Let us find out," said Clay grimly. He strode to the door of 3E and knocked. "Major von Lindau, are you there?" Clay said loudly. "I must speak with you!" There was no response. Clay tried the door; finding it unlocked, he pushed it open. Light from an oil lamp inside the room fell on his face. In that light, the others could see the captain nod grimly, then virtually leap into the room. The others crowded in, as the acrid smell of burned gunpowder assailed their nostrils.

Inside the room, lying crookedly face-up on the narrow bed, was Joachim von Lindau, a jagged hole in his tightly-buttoned tunic oozing blood, a large Colt revolver clutched loosely in his right hand.

"Good God, the poor devil has killed himself!" exclaimed Burnside.

Ignoring the general's comment and the murmurs from the others, Clay gently touched the area around the hole in the tunic. Suddenly, von Lindau's eyes flew open. With sad brown eyes focusing on vacancy, he whispered "*Wasser, bitte . . . wasser.*"

Clay quickly looked at the table that held the lamp. It also supported a pitcher and a small glass. He quickly filled the glass, and placing his arm to support the dying man's head, he prepared to give him a drink.

"Captain, are you sure you should do that?" asked Lot quietly. "It's bad to give water to gut-shot men."

Turning his head toward the black sergeant, Clay hissed, "This wound will be quickly mortal. Water may give him the strength to tell us what happened before he expires." Turning back to von Lindau, he allowed the wounded man to take several sips. Von Lindau coughed and blinked repeatedly.

"Major, tell me what happened here," said Clay urgently into the dying man's ear.

"*Ach, meine Lieber, er kennt nicht diese verdamte Welt,*" muttered von Lindau in his native tongue. Then in English, "My love . . . the shame . . . Delilah . . . Samson . . ." The sad brown eyes glazed, and the labored breathing stopped.

Clay felt for a pulse at the neck but found none. "Major von Lindau is dead," he announced to the room.

"Shameful, an absolute disgrace!" exclaimed General Potter, the son of an Episcopal bishop. Suicide was grievous sin in his faith.

In a mournful voice, Burnside spoke. "Poor, poor devil. If he was troubled, why didn't he come to me? We all have low times in our lives. I would have done what I could to see him through whatever his troubles were."

"Gentlemen, you all have important duties with tomorrow's movements that Lieutenant Bierce, Sergeant Lot, and myself do not," announced Clay smoothly. "It may be best if we three handle the disposition of his remains and effects while you get what little rest you can after such an event."

"Very kind of you, Captain, very kind," said Burnside. "I'm sure we all appreciate your consideration in this matter." With a final look at the corpse on the bed and a muttered, "So sad, so sad," General Burnside led the other officers from the room.

When they were all gone, Clay went softly to the door, closing and locking it. Then going back to the corpse, he said "Help me with this. We must make a very careful examination of the body and of the contents of this room. Then I want to have a post-mortem performed at the nearest hospital. However, this all must be done with utmost discretion; the walls are so thin that we must take care to keep our voices low."

"Why is that? I mean, suicide is a disgrace, but that can hardly be kept secret under the circumstances," said Bierce, who was now considerably less drunk than when he had arrived.

"Lieutenant, try to recover your wits from wherever cheap whiskey has sent them," whispered Clay impatiently. "Look at the bullet-hole in his tunic. There is almost no scorching around it; the gun was fired from a distance of at least three feet. Joachim von Lindau's last visitor was undoubtedly the traitor, who murdered him to preserve his secret, and the murderer can only be one of the officers on this floor."

CHAPTER 3

THAT DEVIL FORREST

"Are you certain, Alphonso?" asked Lot urgently in a low voice. "These are all important, well-connected people on this floor. A mistaken accusation could result in great trouble for you."

"Clay is right," responded Bierce slowly. "I've seen the results of close-in gunshot wounds, at Shiloh and Chickamauga. There is always at least some scorching of the clothes unless the gun was fired from more than a yard away."

Clay looked thoughtfully at the murdered body. "You remember my telling you of how some European scientists hold that certain human patterns are unique to the individual, the pattern of the cartilage in the ear, for instance. The same authorities believe the ridges of the human fingers are equally complicated; in fact, for centuries, Chinese officials have signed documents by smearing ink on their thumbs and lightly pressing them to documents, creating a signature more unique than any writing."

"Very interesting, Clay," drawled Bierce. "However, of what possible use is that to us now?"

"I suspect the killer may have shot von Lindau with his own pistol and quickly thrust it into the dying man's hand before fleeing the room. Murder will be confirmed if the mark of someone else's finger mark can be found on the Colt—and could even allow us to prove who the killer is."

"Come sir," scoffed Bierce. "Even if what you say about the Chinks is true, I seriously doubt a killer would be so thoughtful as to dip his thumb in ink before doing the deed. And how can you compare the killer's thumb before you have identified the killer?"

"I think I see part of what you are driving at, Captain," said Lot slowly. "You will be wanting photographic equipment, will you not?"

Clay nodded. "Of course, difficult to locate in such a primitive area."

"Perhaps not," replied the black noncom. "Early this evening, I heard some headquarters aides laughing about a reporter who had come from back East. I really was not paying attention, but if I remember aright, they said he had come out here to photograph battle wounds, for some New York exhibition. The guards found it amusing that the reporter died in a fit of delirium tremens shortly after he got here. In any event, it is possible that the dead man's equipment is still at the hospital."

Clay nodded approvingly. "Very good, Sergeant. Go to the hospital area and see if you can locate the deceased alcoholic's possessions. There will undoubtedly be staff to guide you, despite the hour. Sad to say, hospitals of armies in the field are never closed. Lieutenant Bierce and I will examine the room here and transport the body to the hospital. We'll meet you there."

Lot saluted and left the room, closing the door softly behind him.

Clay turned to Bierce. "Lieutenant, find me some kind of bag or container."

Bierce glanced about the sparsely furnished room and quickly spotted a large cloth bag with a drawstring at the opening. He quickly emptied the contents onto the floor; mainly they were shaving gear and other toiletries, including a package of talcum powder. Bierce laughed softly at the last item. "Talcum. It would seem that our departed Dutchman was something of a nancy-boy."

"I see nothing effeminate in using such a powder in the heat and humidity of the South," replied Clay coldly. "In fact, I use it myself. Be that as it may, pocket that, as it will prove useful for what I have in mind, and bring the bag here and hold it open for me."

Bierce did as he was told. Holding the revolver carefully by the end of its seven-inch barrel, Clay lowered it gently into the open bag. Taking the container from the lieutenant, Clay gently drew the top closed and carefully placed the bag into the large side-pocket of his tunic.

"Now, let us carefully examine the body; we will be witnesses for each other as to what is found."

While Bierce watched, Clay unbuttoned the dead major's double-breasted tunic, to reveal a surprisingly clean shirt, and an irregular red stain surrounding a rent just below the sternum. "Unusually little bleeding, given that he did not die immediately," commented Clay absently. "Most of the hemorrhaging must have been internal. Surprising that he lived as long as he did. The bullet cannot have missed the heart by half an inch."

Clay began the search as the still somewhat tipsy Bierce looked on. Trouser pockets disgorged only an odd assortment of loose change, stamps, pencil-stubs and such. One of the dead major's inner tunic pockets revealed a billfold and a small portrait case. The other inner pocket contained a somewhat dog-eared notebook and a soiled letter. Clay opened the portrait case; it contained a picture of a man and a handsome woman, the thin, smiling young man barely recognizable as the dour, flabby von Lindau. Between them was a small, well-formed girl of about eight, who stared into the camera with arrogant disdain. The billfold contained $165 in Federal banknotes. Clay unfolded the creased letter to find it written in German.

Looking over Clay's shoulder, Bierce frowned. "Never learned Dutch. Can you make that out?"

Clay could. He swiftly read the letter, its bold strokes indicating the writer was unlikely to lack confidence or energy.

"It is from a man named Bismarck," he informed Bierce. "If he is the man I am thinking of, he is the new chief minister to the King of Prussia. Curious that he should be in communication with von Lindau, who was involved in the anti-monarchical uprising in 1848."

"Well, what does the Prussian say?"

Clay considered his answer. "German does not lend itself to direct translation into English. Let me paraphrase. *'It is with regret I inform you that his Highness will not consider allowing your grandson Paul to undertake a military career, as your daughter has petitioned. Nor does his Highness accept your offer to return to Prussia for punishment in return for allowing your daughter's request. He issued an amnesty for the surviving rebels such as you, and a Hohenzollern does not go back on his oath. At the same time, he swore that no blood descendent of an amnestied traitor would be admitted to the officer corps; and a Hohenzollern does not go back on his oath. It is true that your daughter utterly repudiated her mother and yourself, and fled to loyal relatives rather than accompany you in your flight to America. However, I must remind you that your wife Else was found dead with a musket in her hands by a barricade when his Highness' loyal troops retook the streets of Berlin. I am sincerely touched by your desire to be of service to a daughter who disowned you, and to a grandson you have never seen. If it were up to me, I would grant your daughter's petition; your grandson Paul has his mother's blood as well as your own, and she demonstrated unswerving loyalty to the Fatherland and the dynasty while still a child. By all accounts, Paul is becoming an upstanding young man, who would be of great use in the years to come. Perhaps with difficulty I could persuade his Majesty to change his mind. Unfortunately, there are many things to do in the next few years, some of which will require the use of much persuasion on my part. I only have so much political capital, and cannot expend any of it on a request such as yours. Of course, if you could persuade some prominent American to write on Paul's behalf, it might change his Majesty's mind; he is much in favor of national unity in general and speaks favorably of Mr. Lincoln and his efforts. Until you can produce some American official to speak on your behalf, the matter is closed. —Bismarck."'*

"This Bismarck sounds like a bastard of the first water," commented Bierce grimly.

"I have heard similar opinions. In any event, it probably has no relation to what has transpired. Still, we will retain this letter with his personal effects, in case a connection is discovered later."

Clay placed the letter and all the other contents of von Lindau's uniform except the notebook in his other side pocket. Finally, he turned his attention to the notebook itself.

"As well you know, Lieutenant, educated men feel an irresistible need to write, even about things that should not be in writing. Major von Lindau was an educated man. Let's see if he holds true to form."

Clay opened the dog-eared notebook and began leafing through it. "In German, and very well written and organized for informal jottings. Von Lindau seems to have had an orderly mind."

Bierce watched Clay flip rapidly through the pages; despite appearances, Bierce found himself doubting that the slight young captain was merely glancing at their contents.

"Records of interrogations . . . observations on the failings of General Burnside . . . informal account of the hanging of a spy on a bridge over Owl Creek . . . nothing terribly out of the ordinary, given the position the major held," muttered Clay to himself. "Ah, here there is a gap of several blank pages, followed by a page and a half of jottings, much less complete and clear than what has preceded. Even the writing seems shaky. Curious, like he had undergone an emotional shock. Many of the comments simply do not make sense."

"Like what?" asked the inquisitive Bierce.

"Several times he simply writes 'Delila' once, as he does 'It was always thus with Samson,' and two times that phrase '*Ach, mein lieber, er kennt nicht diese verdamnte Welt.*' That was what he muttered as he died."

"What the hell does that mean in English?"

Clay paused to consider. "Well, loosely translated, it is something like "*My friend, this damn world is unbelievable.*" Words to that effect, anyway; there is an element of despair that does not translate easily into English."

"Anything else of interest?"

"Other obscure jottings that do not immediately make sense. Very strange, given how orderly and precise the previous entries showed him to be. We will have to consider it at greater length later. Right now, let us transport the major's mortal remains to the hospital. Go ask one of the sentries downstairs if there is an army cot that can be spared for an unpleasant duty."

Teresa Duval stood in the center of the large barn that served as a makeshift hospital, looking down curiously at the young lieutenant who had just died. A festering belly wound had been the youth's death sentence. Of course, he might have lived a few more days, but once Duval had decided he could not recover, she had selected him for one of her experiments. Although she preferred more personal means when killing was required, she realized that in some situations, a quiet approach mimicking natural causes was more desirable.

The supervising military surgeon, Major Dallas Price, was a surprisingly competent doctor. Duval wondered for the hundredth time why he was not in private practice becoming rich. Price was overworked, and once he had seen the skill and competency of Duval in ministering to the sick and wounded, he had given her unrestricted access to the stores of medicines. Carefully, using only those cases that Price and his staff considered hopeless, Duval had tried out various combinations of drugs to see which made the most undetectable poisons. Laudanum she quickly ruled out. An overdose seemed always detectible by taste to the subject, and although death was quiet, the corpse left damning signs to anyone interested in an autopsy. Several other medicines had revealed similar drawbacks. Those signs were not noticed, even by the competent Price, whose full attention was devoted to those who stood a chance of recovery. Still, in Duval's . . . civilian life, she feared most of these poisons simply would not do.

Unfortunately, or fortunately, depending on the viewpoint, the youth who had just expired had received an overdose of digitalis, mixed with his evening dose of painkiller. The correct dose of digitalis could steady the heartbeat of those with certain kinds of heart disorders, a moderate overdose, undetectable to taste, could cause the heart to cease beating, and leave no sign, which even the most advanced chemical laboratories could detect. To all appearances, the dying youth's strained heart had simply given way. And people's hearts *were* giving way all the time, for all kinds of reasons. Teresa Duval smiled sweetly and laid her hand on the youth's head. She believed herself to have performed an act of mercy, as she had seen what peritonitis looked like in its last stages; and she was grateful for the unknowing service the youth had rendered by allowing her to explore what constituted a lethal dose.

"Miss Duval?" came a familiar voice from behind her. She was not startled, as she had heard the army physician's heavy tread coming up behind her. Summoning up one of her many useful arts, she commanded tears to well up in her eyes.

"Oh, Major Price, Lieutenant Willis has just gone to his reward," she replied, putting a catch in her voice. Price leaned forward, peering at the corpse with bloodshot hazel eyes.

"Well, we knew it was just a matter of time," he said, straightening up. "At least he seems to have passed peacefully, which is more than most of the gut-shot can expect. Heart must have failed. Not surprising, given what was going on in his innards. At least you were here for him so he would not die alone." The shambling, untidy doctor turned suddenly toward Duval. "Miss Duval, I might as well say to your face right now what I have been thinking for some time: that I was wrong to oppose your assignment to my hospital. I did not think that a woman could endure the horrors that we must see every day, that she would faint in the middle of an amputation. Lord knows enough men do. I was resentful, believing that I was being forced to accommodate a woman because Washington wanted to appease Clara Barton and the other do-gooders of the Sanitary Commission. I want to say now, humbly and to your face, that I was utterly wrong. I wish my male orderlies had half your gumption. You've assisted at a dozen amputations where you were steady as a rock. I have watched you tend to soldiers whose wounds will give me nightmares for the rest of my days. And this is not the first time I have found you standing vigil over the last moments of a wounded hero. Please accept my deepest apologies for my initial reservations."

"It is an honor to minister to these soldiers of the Lord; no apology is needed," she replied with feigned humility. In fact, she found, to her surprise, that she was taking pride in her work. She had performed genuine miracles for a number of soldiers whose lives hung in the balance; only the hopeless were material for her . . . experiments. She reflected that it was a novel experience for her to save rather than take a life and that she genuinely wished that she could save all of them so they could fight the damned aristocrats of the South and send the English-loving Confederacy straight to Hell . . . She shook her head slightly, to clear it of emotions before memories best left unexplored came to the fore of her mind. She had a job to do for Jay Gould.

"Beg your pardon, ma'am, doctor," came a weak voice from the next cot over. "Has Lieutenant Willis passed on?" Both Duval and Price turned to look at the wiry, sunburned man who had asked the question. A large, stained dressing was on his right shoulder.

"You should not be awake, Captain Larson," responded Price gruffly. "You have an excellent chance of completely recovering, but only if you lay quiet and let nature heal the damage done by man."

"I am afraid that Lieutenant Willis has indeed gone to his reward," replied Duval, allowing tears to once again fill her eyes. "The inner organs were perforated; there was never really a chance that he would get better."

The wounded captain digested the information, then began to speak softly. "It were my fault, I guess. Knew Willis' family back in Iowa; his mother's a widow, an' he's her only son. When they made me a captain in that colored regiment, thought I was doing him a favor when I asked him to apply for a commission in my company. Thought there was less a chance of a second lieutenant being shot than the corporal he was. Guess I was wrong."

"You must not trouble yourself with these feelings, Captain," Price responded. "This was not your fault, and there is no blame that can be laid at your door. Blame that devil Forrest. War is terrible enough, but what his men did to your regiment at Fort Pillow was murder, pure and simple. Your Negro friend, over in the next cot, is quiet now, but when the fever was on him, he raved about how your colonel raised the white flag, and the soldiers offered surrender, only to be slaughtered without mercy."

"Colonel shouldn't have tried to surrender to Forrest, not when he was commanding darkies," murmured Larson stonily. "Could've told him a slave-trader bastard like Forrest would go crazy at the sight of niggers with guns. Better to have died fighting than be slaughtered like sheep." Larson looked directly at Doctor Price, stony eyes softened by pain. "Now that Willis is passed, only survivor I know of is Corporal Samson there, and he's like not to make it, ain't he Doctor?"

Price found it difficult to meet Larson's gaze. "I have occasionally seen a soldier survive such internal wounds, so it's not impossible. And besides, there is word that a few others from your regiment did escape into the woods around Fort Pillow during the massacre."

"Darn few, Doctor, darn few," said Larson flatly.

There was an area in a corner of the barn where a tent-like structure had been erected. Suddenly, a flap was thrust aside, and Sergeant Lot emerged, looking around. Spotting Price, he carefully wended his way through the rows of cots, most filled with quietly suffering soldiers, until he stood before the doctor and Duval. Saluting, he said quietly, "Sir, have Captain Clay and Lieutenant Bierce arrived yet? They will be bringing a body . . ."

"Is that Sergeant Jeremiah Lot?" asked Larson softly.

The interrupted noncom started and peered through the dim light cast by scattered lamps at the captain's cot. "Sergeant Larson!" he exclaimed. "Lord, I didn't expect to see you here. You're hurt. May I ask how serious it is?"

"It's captain now," the wounded man responded with a thin smile. "Took a commission in a colored regiment; got tired of ranging out in front of the army killing fellers. Thought it would be better to order others to do the killing. Anyway, Doctor Price and Miss Duval here think that I'm out of the darkest part of the woods."

Lot turned to Price and Duval. "When I first met . . . Captain

Larson, he was acting as an independent sniper for Grant's army, before Vicksburg. He performed several important services for Captain Clay during that time."

"Let's talk no more on that," responded Larson, remembering the solemn oath he had sworn to Grant himself to preserve forever a secret that might finish the destruction of the Union. "Anyway, I got this here wound when that devil Forrest overran Fort Pillow. If it waren't for Sampson there, we wouldn't be having this little talk."

Lot glanced at the massive black soldier in the next cot who was drifting in and out of a feverish sleep, occasional uttering incomprehensible words. Lot recognized the man and remembered that night in Louisiana when they briefly met—that night of blood, of flame, and of a round horror sailing through the air. The night that Sampson had knocked Clay unconscious before he could enter a burning house with an innocent child inside in a suicidal attempt to save its life. A house burning from a fire Clay had deliberately set.

"I've heard rumors about what happened at Fort Pillow, but I can't believe they're all true," said Lot. "Yes, the Rebels are traitors and slavers, but they're still Christians, and I can't believe that any Christian could behave in such a barbaric manner."

"Believe it," Larson said flatly. "We were outnumbered and surprised; no time to organize a proper defense. Colonel raised the white flag as soon as he could. All the boys not cut down in the first assault stacked their arms and held up their hands. Then Forrest trotted up on a magnificent roan. No mistaking him. Felt a chill just looking at him. Never seen the Devil, but I imagine he would look like Forrest: skinny as a rail, small pointy beard, hair black as a crow's wing flowing straight back from his high forehead, and cold, dead eyes. He trotted on that fine horse of his up and down the line, lookin' at the white officers and the black soldiers, then the white officers again, his eyes getting colder and deader all the time.

"Then this big handsome major rides up to him. Could tell the major was from real quality from the way he held himself, just like you could tell Forrest had started out a scrub, no matter how rich and high and mighty he is now. That major said something with a laugh while he gestured to us prisoners. Then Forrest nods his head and trots away, and the major laughs again, takes out a cigar, and makes a show of lighting it. The major takes a few long puffs, all the while looking at us and smiling. Then without turning his head to face the Reb cavalrymen behind him, he says 'Boys, these here niggers are in rebellion against the Confederacy, and these white officers have been encouraging them in that rebellion. In peacetime, there would be only one penalty for them. The courts being disturbed by the current emergency, we will just save them the time and trouble. Kill them all.' Then the killing starts.

"Many of them Rebel fellers seem to hold back; from what I could see, nearly half of them did nothing. Must be those with a scrap of decency. Still, the other half were more than enough. A few of our fellers legged it into the woods, with the Johnnies whooping after them on horseback. Hope some of the poor souls made it. Most of us stood around like we couldn't believe what was happening; hell, I were there and can hardly believe it. Didn't even waste bullets, for the most part; the Reb cavalrymen just slashed away with them heavy sabers of theirs. I remember about a dozen darkies were on their knees pleading for mercy and getting none, when I sees Willis come up with a sword he picked up from where some officer had dropped it. He was screaming like a red Indian, slashing it back and forth, trying to stand between his men and the Rebs, who fell back a bit and laughed at him. Then that big major rode up close-like, drew a big LeMat revolver, and shot Willis in the belly, laughing while he did it.

"That seemed to shake me loose. I picked up one of the Springfields our boys had dropped and drew a bead on that major, but just as I fired, some Johnnie galloped his horse into my way and took the bullet in his head. The Johnnies waren't laughing then, but I waren't neither. While they drew their Colt Navies, I was standing there like a fool with an empty rifle. Course, they were fools, too. They started shooting at me from far aways on horseback, and the only fellers who ever hit what they were aiming at from that kind of distance, did so by accident. Still, accidents do happen, I guess.

"Before I could make a move to run, a pistol ball took me in the shoulder, spinning me around like a top. I staggered, dropped the rifle, looked up to see three of the Johnnies riding toward me, and prepared to meet my Maker. Then I'm bowled over from behind by Corporal Sampson there. I don't have much time to see him, going tip over arse like I was, but I saw enough. He was bleeding like a stuck pig from a belly wound, where you could see his guts like little sausages poking out. How a man could be alive with such a wound, much less walk, was a mystery to me. Before I could say anything, he smears a hand across my face, wet and sticky with his own blood. He hisses in my ear, 'Play possum, captain. Got to live to tell of this. Got to be a white officer; ain't no one going to believe a nigger about somethin' like this.' Then he flops onto me, clutching his guts, and I close my eyes and hold my breath.

"Over Sampson's groaning, I hear horses galloping up. Took a powerful lot of concentration, but I kept from moving or opening my eyes. I hear some Reb drawl, 'Major Ward, looks like that Yankee captain caught bullets in the shoulder and head; he's done for. Want that I finish off the darkie?' I heard a deep voice chuckle, then say, 'No, private. Let the ape feel the price of raising arms against his betters. His path to death should be long and hard.' I then hear all the horses gallop away, and pretty soon, the only thing a I hear is the wind in the trees and the cawing of some crows, along with soft moaning from Sampson.

"I figure it's safe to open my eyes and get up, but somehow, it don't seem I can do that. I keep trying, but my eyes just won't open. Then I guess I went to sleep or something. Next thing I know, I'm awake in the bed of a wagon, jouncing along a bad road with Samson on one side of me and Willis on the other. I cry out with each bounce the wagon takes; feels like someone has shoved a hot poker clean through my shoulder. Driver shouts out to hold on, best as I could; orders had come to concentrate all forces in east Tennessee, around Knoxville, and that there would be decent doctors when we got there. Meant to ask him how long it would be, but just then, the wagon hit some deep hole, and the whole world seemed to turn to flame. Next thing I know, this kind lady here is leaning over me, like an angel." He nods slightly to Duval, who felt herself blush and was angry at the feeling; she despised feeling pleasure at his complement, for some obscure reason.

There was a commotion at the entrance to the barn. Clay and Bierce stagger in, holding between them an army cot on which lay the lifeless body of von Lindau; Bierce was winded and red-faced, while the smaller Clay seemed completely relaxed, despite the burden of the portly major's remains.

Clay glanced around and saw the group around Larson's bed. Nodding to Bierce, they changed direction and approached. Placing their burden down temporarily, Clay saluted Price and said, "Sir, as I am sure that Sergeant Lot has informed you, it is quite important that a post-mortem be performed on a dead officer as soon as possible."

"Well, if it ain't Captain Clay," said Larson. "Looks like I catched up to you in rank, though not in seniority. Lieutenant Bierce, good to see you again too."

Clay turned his placid blue eyes on the wounded officer. "Larson. I am grieved to see you thus. How came you here?"

Larson repeated quickly the story he had already told. When he was done, Clay walked over to the cot where Corporal Samson lay drenched in sweat, feverishly muttering incomprehensible words, eyes occasionally opening, staring at nothing that the others could see. Clay stared at the black soldier for a long moment, then murmured, "Bottom rail is back on bottom, Samson. I should be in your place. I swear to you I will do whatever I can to let the rails rise as high in the fence as merit warrants."

Not understanding the strange statement, the puzzled Dr. Price asked, "Did you know this man, Captain?"

"I know him. He did a terrible wrong to me once, while meaning to be of service."

"Really," said the curious Duval. "And what was that?"

"He saved my life," replied Clay shortly. He focused his placid blue eyes on the woman. "My apologies, Madame; I have forgotten my manners. I am Alphonso Clay; this is my associate Ambrose Bierce. Together with Sergeant Lot, we are seconded to General Burnside from General Grant. May we have the honor of knowing your name?"

Duval looked at the slight blond captain for a moment, unaccountably feeling a flush in her belly. Hiding her confusion, smoothly she said, "Certainly. I am Teresa Duval. The Sanitary Commission has sent me to minister to the needs of these wounded heroes in a Christian manner."

"I see," Clay responded. He looked steadily at her for some moments, the faintest of smiles pulling at the corners of his mouth.

He suspects something thought Duval with a panic that she did not allow to show. How? *He has just met me for a moment. None of these fools question the Christian claptrap I spout. This man is a danger to me!*

Clay had turned to Doctor Price. "Sir, this officer has been found dead. It appears to have been suicide, but I have my doubts.

Recovering the bullet might be of some help in confirming that a particular pistol fired the fatal shot, which in turn might lead us to the killer. I have already confirmed that there is no exit wound, so I would be obliged if you could recover the ball from his remains."

Price looked at the cot and did a double take. "I'll be damned. Von Lindau."

"You knew the major?" asked Clay.

"Yep, saw him in a professional capacity back in Knoxville. Well, bring him to the table in the rear, and we will get this over with."

Bierce and Clay carried the cot to where the doctor had indicated, while the curious Lot and Duval followed behind. The body was transferred to a large metal table with drains in the corners. Taking a scalpel, with brutal efficiency, Price sliced away the dead major's upper clothes, revealing a pale torso with an ugly wound in its exact center. Taking some evil-looking instruments, the doctor began without preamble to probe for the bullet. Lot found himself looking away, while Bierce stared with a strange avidity. Clay looked utterly expressionless, while Duval struggled to conceal her . . . unhealthy interest in the butchering, very aware that Clay was occasionally turning his expressionless gaze upon her.

As the doctor worked, Clay suddenly broke the silence. "Sir, please do not take offense. However, I must comment that you show rather unusual detachment in doing this work upon someone you knew personally."

Price responded without looking up from the body. "Well, any doctor in this God-damned war would go plumb mad if he allowed himself to think of the patients as more than specimens. Besides, in a backhanded way, this was a mercy to poor von Lindau."

"How is that?" asked Clay unable to keep a note of surprise from his normally controlled voice.

"Oh, I doubt he would have lived more than another six months, and it probably would have been a hard six months. Came to me complaining about shortness of breath. Put my scope to his chest, and I swear to God it sounded like a steam engine about to explode. The heart is not my specialty, but I could tell he was in real trouble, and I doubt that the best specialists in Paris or Berlin could have done a thing for him. Put it to him straight, and he took it like a man, just saying he had some matters to put in order. Gave him some digitalis—what they've started calling extract of foxglove, but I told him it was unlikely to make much difference, given how bad he sounded. Ah, there's the bugger!" With a pincer-like instrument, the doctor drew out a misshapen piece of lead. "Here it is, captain. Hope you think it's worth it."

"Forty-four caliber," commented Clay, looking at the bullet. "I expected as much, but it is always wise to be sure. I will be indebted if you could wrap that in a small piece of cloth and give it to Sergeant Lot for safekeeping."

"What will we do with the major's remains?" asked the doctor.

"We'll arrange for a local burial," replied Clay. "Von Lindau appears to have had no family, at least in this country. Before we take care of that, I need to perform a more pressing duty. Sergeant, were you able to find the photographic equipment?"

"Yes, sir. Major Price was very helpful. I have established a small developing studio near the rear of the barn, shielded from the smallest light; I even have the developing chemicals ready."

"Very well. Bring the camera over while Lieutenant Bierce and I begin the process." As Lot hurried to comply, Clay turned to Price and said, "I will need an inkwell and several sheets of foolscap paper."

Puzzled, the army doctor replied "Well, I can get them from my work-table yonder." Quickly, the doctor snatched the items and handed them to Clay. Duval looked on with rapt attention, while Lot returned with the bulky camera and its tripod stand, which he carefully set up out of the way of the spectators. "Very well," began Clay. "Judging by his holster, von Lindau was right-handed. Let us lightly coat the pads of the fingers on that hand with ink and touch them to a piece of paper, taking care not to smear the marks."

While the others watched silently, Clay did as he had described, touching the inky digits one at a time to the blank sheet. He brought the paper near one of the oil lamps, and peered intently at the five marks.

"Nature is truly marvelous," he murmured to himself. Then addressing the others, he said more loudly, "Look at the incredible intricacy of the marks left by the ridges of skin. No two of his fingers leave patterns even remotely similar."

Clay passed the paper first to Lot, who studied it for a moment, nodding silently, before giving it to Bierce, who in turn passed it to Price.

Duval was the last to examine the piece of foolscap and worked hard to look interested rather than appalled. '*How many times have I left part of myself at the scene of a crime and not known*', she thought uneasily; she decided that she would in the future have to be cautious about touching things.

"Well, the patterns are pretty damn intricate," said Price dubiously. "But how can you be sure that everyone's fingers aren't complicated in the same way, if you see what I mean?"

"Nothing simpler, major," responded Clay. "Some experts believe the shape of the ear is equally unique; but for what I propose, I believe the fingers will be more practical. If you do not mind a little ink, we will place your marks on the paper, each finger's print alongside its counterpart from the late von Lindau's hand."

Swiftly, the process was repeated. After cleaning the stains from his fingers as best he could with a piece of cloth, Price took the paper from Clay and closely examined the pairs of marks. After a moment, he looked up and spoke with wonder.

"I'll be God-damned to hell. They're nothing alike. A blind man could tell the differences." Wordlessly, he passed the paper to Duval, who carefully worked at keeping her expression neutral. However, the unease within her grew. This could mean she had left clues of her presence where she thought no living person could prove she had been.

"Now, Lieutenant, this will be where we are entering uncharted territory," said Clay to Bierce. "Being very careful not to touch the grip, remove von Lindau's pistol and place it on this unoccupied table here." Bierce nodded. He was intelligent and could divine where all of this was leading.

After Clay handed him the bag, Bierce carefully unwrapped the gun; holding the big Colt clumsily by the end of the barrel, he placed it on the table.

"Now, Lieutenant, the package of talcum." From another pocket, Bierce produced the package of light fluffy powder. "Doctor, do you have a small, fine brush? The smaller the better."

Major Price looked thoughtful. "I think I got something in that cabinet over there." Quickly he went to the instrument cabinet along one wall of the barn and came back with a device looking like a shaving-brush, only much smaller. Handing it to Clay, he asked, "Will this do?"

"It will have to. Now, this is where theory will be tested by experiment. Even without ink, it is obvious that the oils in the skin leave subtle marks on whatever they touch; we have all seen such marks on glasses and spectacles. Talcum has absorbent qualities; I believe it may stick to such marks, if lightly applied. As the oils should be heaviest where the ridges pressed most heavily on the object, the talcum should adhere most to where the ridges were, in effect creating a photograph of the pattern of those ridges. Bierce, I want you to ink von Lindau's right fingers again and take their imprints on a fresh piece of paper, labeling which print was from which finger. Our first example is cluttered with Dr. Price's prints." As the lieutenant nodded and went to comply, Clay said "Doctor, Sergeant, I want you to be careful witnesses to what I am about to do."

Lightly dipping the small brush into the fluffy powder, Clay began delicately dabbing the handle of the weapon, treating first one side, then the other. As if by magic, a number of fingerprints began to appear. Clay grabbed one of the oil lanterns and carefully moved it about until he found a position where it cast its rays slantingly across the marks, making them more visible to the eye.

"Excellent. Please examine these marks and compare them to the paper where we recorded impressions of Major von Lindau's fingers." Bierce and Price peered intently, shifting positions several times to obtain a better view, periodically referring to the ink marks on the piece of paper. Duval hung back, an uneasy feeling in the pit of her stomach.

A smiling Bierce finally straightened up and looked at Clay. "An interesting experiment, Captain. However, as a hanging may result from this evidence, and as you are my superior officer, perhaps I should defer to Major Price's opinion."

The untidy doctor stood up straight, a pensive look on his face. "I will be God-damned to hell," he said quietly, staring at the revolver.

"Could you be more specific, Doctor?" asked Clay. "Please take your time and be accurate as to your impressions. It is possible that you may be called upon to repeat them under oath in the future."

Price responded without taking his eyes from the Colt. "A number of marks are badly smeared. At least one seems to be a combination of marks from two different fingers. However, two marks are clearly identical to the marks we have determined would come from the thumb and forefinger of von Lindau's right hand. There are two other clear marks; neither even remotely resembles any of the samples taken from von Lindau." He suddenly looked at Clay. "It was murder then, not suicide."

"I suspected as much from the lack of powder burns on the major's tunic, but this is proof beyond doubt. The murderer shot von Lindau with his own weapon, probably snatched from the table beside the major's bed, and then thrust it into his dying owner's hand. Now, we need to preserve this evidence, if possible; it is too much to expect that we can preserve these talcum smudges indefinitely. Sergeant, let us see just how much skill you acquired in exercising your photographic interests."

"As the Captain indicates, I made something of a hobby of photography before the war," said the black sergeant. "However, I never tried to photograph anything so close, or under such light. Still, the oil lamp burns steady enough, and length of exposure is not a problem with a stationary object. Let me see if I can get a good focus."

Lot removed the cap from the lens and then placed his head under the black cloth that trailed from the back of the boxy instrument; fingers flew expertly about the adjusting screws of the tripod until the lens was pointing directly at the handle of the revolver.

Then he fiddled incessantly with the lens, until he finally announced, "That is the best I can do. The marks are completely clear to my eye; the only question is whether the plate will record them with equal clarity." He removed his head from under the black cloth, gingerly replaced the lens cap, and said, "I will go get the plates. Please do not touch the camera in any way."

He hurried to the closed-off alcove at the back of the barn and returned immediately with a heavy wooden box that was hinged at the top, while the others waited silently.

Without uttering a word, Lot placed the box on the table beside the pistol. Opening the top, he removed a delicate-looking glass plate from one of several compartments and slid it deftly into the camera's slot. Checking the focus one last time, Lot uncapped the lens. Checking a pocket watch, he muttered, "Two minutes should be sufficient, given the light."

The time passed in silence, broken only by the moans of some of the patients scattered about the barn. Suddenly, Lot snapped his watch shut, deftly transferred the plate to the wooden box, shut it, and dashed to the curtained-off alcove.

A few minutes passed before Lot suddenly emerged from the curtains, again lugging the heavy metal box. Swiftly he approached the table, commenting, "I applied the wash to fix the image; the plate is now drying. While it does so, I will photograph the other side."

Lot carefully turned the weapon over, readjusted the focus, and repeated the time-consuming process. He again dashed to the curtained-off alcove. This time about five minutes passed before the sergeant emerged, gingerly carrying the first of the delicate glass plates, a wide smile on his face.

"Better than I had reason to hope," he announced as he rejoined the others. "The patterns are quite distinct. Of course, this is a negative, so the dark markings of the fingerprints appear as white lines against a dark background."

Holding the plate by its edges, one-by-one they all examined the marks.

"Well, I'm convinced," said Major Price, "but there are two things to think on, Clay. One, this is sort of like the recipe for rabbit stew: first, catch your rabbit. You have the murderer's finger-marks recorded, but until you actually catch the killer, that will do you no damn good. I mean, it's not like there is some kind of national library on the fingers of criminals that you can consult. Second, how in hell will you convince a court that the marks are truly unique, and could not possibly belong to someone else?"

"Valid observations, Major," replied the blond captain. "However, prior experience has shown me that evidence can have a cumulative impact. It is well that we retain this kind of permanent record.

"With your permission, sir, I will store this safely and complete the development of the other plate," said Lot to Clay, who nodded at his sergeant.

As Lot disappeared again into the alcove, Clay turned to the wounded Larson, who had been quietly following all that transpired while lying on his cot. "Well . . . Captain, what do you think?"

"I think you'd have made a fine sniper. To kill fellers at a distance and to keep from having them kill you, you need to take great cares, a step at a time. I think you'd get the hang of that right quick."

"Thank you, I think. However, I was more interested in what you thought . . ."

Clay was interrupted by a commotion at the front of the barn. He turned to see three cavalrymen and an officer make their way in from the darkness outside.

"Who is in charge here!" announced the officer in a loud voice that disturbed some of the fitfully resting patients. The large man, dressed in a lieutenant's uniform that seemed too tight for him, had a cheerful, breezy manner seldom found in the early hours of the morning. Behind him, two of the cavalrymen supported the third between them; the man in the middle seemed unconscious, his head lolling back and forth.

"I am, Lieutenant," answered Price, advancing toward the new arrivals with a frown. "These men need their rest. I would appreciate it if you would keep your voice down."

"My apologies," said the new arrival, without noticeably lowering his voice. "We were bushwhacked by some of Forrest's boys, and one of my men here was wounded. He needs help right badly."

"Well, bring him over here toward the back," replied Price. "I've got some empty cots. We'll take a look and see how bad he is." The army surgeon led the new arrivals over to an empty cot near where the quietly observant Larson and the semi-conscious Samson lay.

The large lieutenant looked at the feverishly muttering black and commented "Well, there's a sight. A nigger soldier. Is he from that fuss I hear that they had over at Fort Pillow?"

"Yes, he is," responded the gruff Price.

"Any others here from that place?"

"Yes, Captain Larson here. These are the only survivors that I know for sure."

At the sound of the big lieutenant's voice, Larson had risen up on his elbow, staring intently at the new arrival. Meanwhile, Samson had stopped his feverish muttering and opened his eyes wide, a small noise not unlike a growl issuing from his mouth.

At the same time, Clay was studying the four new arrivals intently, a slight frown of puzzlement marking his normally placid face. He sensed something was wrong about the new arrivals and tried to analyze the source of this feeling. He noted that the lieutenant's holster bulged oddly, indicating a pistol even larger than the massive Colt .44. He glanced over the holsters of the three cavalrymen and noted that their side arms seemed to be the somewhat less massive Colt .36. Standard issue for regular Federal cavalry was the Colt or Remington .44, although the Confederacy was fond of copies of the lighter .36. Of course, states sometimes purchased Colt .36s for their volunteer units, but Clay quickly observed that the buckles of the soldiers had the "US" of the regular army, rather than the "USV" of a volunteer unit. He then studied the lieutenant for an instant and noted that the left breast of his tunic had a faded area, indicating repeated scrubbing and cleaning efforts, centered roughly on a small rent in the fabric.

Smoothly, Clay began to draw his Smith & Wesson. However, the large lieutenant had been paying more attention to Clay than was obvious and swiftly grabbed the astonished Duval, holding her in front of him, while with one hand producing a large LeMat revolver, which he proceeded to level at the hesitating Clay with mocking slowness.

Then a number of things happened within the space of a few moments.

The laying of threatening male hands upon her triggered memories of fifteen years before, setting off an automatic reaction in the normally self-controlled Duval. Screaming *"Erin Go Bragh!"* she viciously kicked the lieutenant's ankle and twisted out of his grip, raking his face with her nails, narrowly missing his left eye. The man howled and fired his pistol wildly, waking all of the patients who still slept. They began to shout with confusion and fear. Clay took careful aim on the officer, when suddenly a screaming black mass crossed his line of fire. The dying Samson had been roused from his delirium by the sound of a familiar, hated voice.

With shouts of inarticulate rage, he cannon-balled into the lieutenant, knocking him to the ground, fixing his powerful hands around the man's throat.

The three newly arrived "cavalrymen" began to draw their Colts; that included the man in the middle, no longer faking a debilitating wound. Lot had emerged from the closed-off alcove, saw what was happening, and despite being unarmed, ran full tilt into the melee.

While Dallas Price stood frozen in shock at the eruption of violence, Ambrose Bierce drew his Colt .44 and pulled the trigger. However, he had been negligent in maintaining the grease that prevented the ignition of loose powder in one chamber of the revolver from igniting the others. An instant after the one bullet was fired, the other five chambers fired, causing the pistol to explode in his hand in a "chain fire."

Screaming obscenities and clutching his wounded hand, Bierce stumbled backward into the table where they had photographed von Lindau's gun.

One of the enemy soldiers, seeing Bierce's helplessness slowly drew a bead on him, but before he could fire, Lot slammed into him, grabbing the man's gun hand, and tried to wrestle the weapon away.

The other two intruders aimed their weapons at Clay. Clay knew that he was unlikely to shoot them both before he himself was killed, but nonetheless, he calmly fired at the man on the right, the bullet striking him square in the chest. The man fell screaming to the ground. Clay did not have enough time to switch his aim. However, the second enemy had no chance to fire at Clay. Duval had produced a four-shot Sharpe's pepperbox gun from a concealed pocket and fired three times, striking the man twice in the side. While the astonished Clay watched, the wounded man staggered into the table where two oil lamps had been placed, knocking one to the straw-covered ground where the dripping oil quickly ignited the tinder-dry straw. Small pistol in hand, Duval moved to where Samson was trying to choke the life out of the false lieutenant. Before she could intervene there was a loud roar, and Samson seemed to fly off the officer, a huge bloody wound in his side, glassy eyes showing he had died instantly. With shocking quickness, the lieutenant surged to his feet, striking Duval's wrist with a vicious upward swipe of the heavy LeMat. The central barrel of the unique handgun, in essence a small shotgun, was smoking, showing that Samson had been killed by a point-blank discharge of buckshot.

Lot's opponent had managed to twist the revolver around to where the barrel pointed into the sergeant's face. With a yell of triumph, he started to pull the trigger. However, the shot that rang out did not come from his gun. A small hole appeared above his left ear. He staggered away from Lot, a look of surprise on his face, and collapsed to the ground. Duval spun around to see the wounded Larson, breathing heavily, holding her small pistol, a look of satisfaction on his face. Despite his wound, he had rolled off the table and joined the battle.

The sight of the fire had released Price from his paralysis. Furiously, he stomped at the growing flames as they spread slowly along the straw-covered ground, while soldiers too wounded to move by themselves cried out in terror. At that moment, the big lieutenant ran for the door. Clay tried to aim at him, but those soldiers able to get on their feet were already trying to gain the exit as well, and Clay did not want to risk wounding someone who had already suffered for the Union. He set out in pursuit of the intruder, who had just slipped out the door, but before he could get to the exit, he heard Dr. Price scream, "God damn you, Clay! Get back here and help me put out the fire! We'll never get the badly-wounded out in time if it spreads!"

For a moment, Clay considered ignoring the doctor and pursuing the murderous spy, believing that to be more important in the grand scale of things than the death of some wounded soldiers. However, he suddenly remembered an evening in Louisiana and a death by fire—a horrible death by fire. Casting a regretful glance at the door, he holstered his pistol and turned to rejoin Price and his growing band of amateur firefighters.

By the narrowest of margins, the fire was put out before it could spread to the entire structure. Clay admired the competence with which Price organized the sounder patients into an impromptu bucket brigade while Clay, Lot, Duval, and even the wounded Bierce used blankets to smother the hot spots as best they could. The exhausted group was taking their first rest just after dawn when Generals Parke and Sanders arrived.

"What the hell happened here?" demanded the short, intense Parke without preamble. Clay summarized the events of the evening, but with curious omissions.

Price, Bierce, Lot, and Duval looked at him strangely when he told the generals of the autopsy of von Lindau but not of the elaborate experiment in fingerprints. They all had the sense not to volunteer more than Clay was willing to tell.

After he had described the battle with the intruders, the melancholy General Sanders asked, "Just who were they, and what did they want?"

It was Captain Larson who volunteered the answer. "Can't say for them enlisted men, but the lieutenant was that Major Ward, him that was with Forrest at Fort Pillow. Never saw him close up, but I'd recognize that oily, laughin' voice anywhere."

"Why did he come here? What in God's name was he trying to do?" asked the solemn Sanders.

"I believe he was trying to eliminate witnesses at the order of General Forrest," responded Clay. "Even for Forrest, what happened at Fort Pillow was a criminal atrocity. He must fear retribution at some point. Somehow he learned of Captain Larson and the late Corporal Samson, and decided to tidy things up. The few other survivors are all former slaves, I imagine, and he knows they are unlikely to be believed by a public reared on legends of Southern chivalry."

"How in the hell did they get into the camp?" asked Price who was sitting on a table while Duval efficiently bandaged his right shin where it had been seared by the flames as he had stomped on them.

"They murdered no less than four of my men who were on picket duty," responded Sanders grimly. "Those uniforms, which they must have scavenged off dead Union cavalry, let them get close to the pickets. All four had their throats cut, no time to give an alarm. Ward must have found it easy enough to get out again."

"Well, lucky things weren't worse," commented Parke. "Major Price, I know that on top of what you've just been through, this is hard, but you need to start loading up those who are too bad off to move on their own. Longstreet is across the river. General Potter's boys are skirmishing to slow him down, but you will need to be ready to hit the road at 10:00 a.m. That's only four hours from now."

"Some of these boys can't be moved without killing them," growled the doctor.

"Leave them in the care of the locals," replied Parke abruptly. "They'll be safe enough. I know Pete Longstreet. He's no Forrest and will see our wounded are treated as well as his own."

"If you will excuse me, I must make arrangements for my wife, Marjorie. She, of course, will be coming with us," said Sanders.

Clay could not keep a note of surprise in his voice. "I understood officers were not permitted to bring their families on campaign."

"General Burnside was kind enough to make an exception for me," replied Sanders somberly. "She is from Mississippi, and well, there is nothing for her there now—and no one she knows in the North."

"Very well, gentlemen," said Parke impatiently. "We all have much to do. Let's get to it!" Burnside's chief of staff strode purposefully from the barn, followed by Sanders.

"Doctor, I know that you are going to be exceedingly busy in the next few hours. However, with your permission, I'd like to borrow a couple of your healthier patients to help me bury Major von Lindau and Corporal Sampson. It is the very least that they deserve."

"I can help too," announced the Bierce cheerily, holding up his bandaged right hand. "The cuts and bruising were not as bad as I feared, and the charming Miss Duval was exceedingly efficient in patching me up."

The army surgeon looked as if he was about to say no, but then shrugged. "I'll get you a couple fit for shovel duty, but don't keep them long. We owe as much to the living as to the dead."

As Lot and Bierce organized the burial party, Clay approached Duval, who was busy packing up the medicines and instruments. He bowed, and said, "My apologies, Miss Duval, but I wish to compliment you on your quick wits during the emergency that just happened. I was especially impressed with your proficiency with the Sharpe's pepperbox. It is very unusual for an Eastern woman to have such a weapon, or to be skilled in its use."

Duval faced Clay, successfully burying a feeling of alarm. "Why, Captain Clay, I had to learn a little of firearms during my ministries on the frontier. A clear conscience is no protection against evil men, be they red or white."

Clay shook his head slightly, the faintest of smiles returning to his lips. "It is strange. I would have thought that a woman on the frontier would have a larger, more accurate Colt. The Sharpe's something I would expect to see used by a city criminal or gambler—not accurate at a distance, but deadly at close range and easy to conceal in the clothing."

Panic burbled within Teresa Duval. "I do not understand what you are driving at, Captain," she responded, still hiding her inner fears under a prim exterior.

"I suppose I did not take into account cultural differences," continued Clay. "A recent arrival from Ireland might be more comfortable with the weaponry of the slums of, say, New York. Frankly, I was surprised to discover that you must be from Ireland."

"I am no Papist bogtrotter!" she exclaimed angrily, masking her panic with rage.

"During the fight with Ward's men, I distinctly heard you say '*Erin Go Bragh*.' In my European travels, I heard that phrase and had it explained to me. It means 'Ireland forever,' does it not?"

"I recall saying no such thing," she replied stonily. "Of course, I might have picked up that phrase from the poor immigrants to whom I was ministering at one time. In any event, does this hectoring have a purpose?"

Clay looked at her appraisingly. "Just this, Miss . . . Duval. I would really have liked to question one of Ward's men. When we collected the bodies, after the fire was put out, I discovered a curious thing: the one whom you shot did not seem to have died of his initial wounds. There was a big pool of blood under him, but it did not come from the bullet holes in his side, which do not appear to have inflicted injuries that would be immediately fatal. Instead, it would appear that the femoral artery in his left leg had been neatly severed with an extremely sharp instrument. With your knowledge of nursing, you would of course know that would cause a man to bleed to death in less than half a minute. I could find no sign of the instrument that had inflicted the wound."

"I still do not see the point of what you are saying. What does this have to do with me?"

Clay lowered his voice so that he was certain no one could overhear. "I have certain tasks to undertake, certain goals to achieve. I am not certain whether you knew you were interfering with me in the past. However, you are on notice. Do not hinder me again—else I might be forced to make . . . inquiries." Clay bowed, turned, and strode over to where the bodies of von Lindau and Samson were being placed on stretchers.

Duval watched his back, thinking furiously as to how best to go about dealing with this threat to her. Unconsciously, she inserted her right hand into the cleverly concealed pocket in her frock and fingered the closed straight razor it contained, sticky with the blood of the dead Confederate.

CHAPTER 4

THE ROAD TO ZION

Clay, Lot, Bierce, and Larson stood bareheaded before five fresh mounds of earth in the scraggly woods behind the hospital barn, two of which being marked by crosses. Lot had just finished a simple, dignified prayer over the graves. Bierce idly massaged his bandaged hand, showing the look of sneering contempt that even the most sincere expression of faith seemed to bring to his face, while Larson looked hard and grim. As usual, Clay's face gave no hint as to what was going on in his mind.

Finishing his prayer with a firm "Amen," Lot restored his forage cap to his head.

"Well, thank the problematic God that is over," said Bierce in a jaunty tone of voice. "I understand the hygienic necessity to place the decaying remains underground, but spending time invoking the mercy of a hypothetical deity is pure waste, especially as to those Rebel spies."

"I reckon that's enough of that, Lieutenant" said Larson, now dressed in his rumpled captain's tunic, still stained with the blood from his wound at Fort Pillow. "Don't mind saying I don't under-stand all the words you use, but I get their drift. You be a free thinker; that's fine with me. Only don't mess with those who ain't. As for the Rebs in the ground, it's our job to kill them in this world, but the Lord's to judge them in the next."

The handsome young lieutenant threw back his head and emitted one of his unlovely, barking laughs. Then he touched the kepi he had never removed during Lot's prayer and said, "Yes, sir."

Lot cast a troubled look at Bierce, then turned to Clay. "Sir, what shall we do next? Ask all the officers who were on the third floor of the hotel to ink their fingers and give us samples of their marks? That will be tricky. The innocent will be enraged and insulted, and the traitor will hide his guilt in their rage."

"The matter will probably have to wait until Knoxville," replied Clay. "All of the suspects will be in the saddle constantly until then. Even in Knoxville, it will be difficult to obtain the samples required."

"You could get General Burnside to order cooperation," interjected Bierce.

"Ah, but what if Burnside himself is the traitor?" responded Clay.

The small group was shocked into silence, broken only when Larson said slowly, "I figured you was here over some kind of treason, Captain. After what happened in Vicksburg, won't nothing you be doin' surprise me. Still, I figure you're barkin' up the wrong tree with Burnside. Ain't the smartest feller to ever wear stars, but he seems a straight shooter."

"You're probably correct, Captain Larson. However, it's always a capital mistake to make assumptions in matters of this importance. For reasons I will tell you later, the traitor must be one of only six, and General Burnside is one of those six."

The group all turned at the sound of approaching hoof beats. Captain Orlando Poe reined his galloping steed up sharply, quickly returned the salute offered by the standing soldiers, and said, "General Parke sends his compliments and tells you to make the utmost haste. General Potter's boys are just outside of town and will only be passing through. Longstreet is pressing hard and will undoubtedly be at this spot before noon."

The arrogant young engineer suddenly looked over at the door to the hospital barn, where Teresa Duval had just emerged. The sleeves of her dress had been rolled up to the elbows; her forearms were streaked with red stains, which she was absently rubbing off with a scrap of damp cloth.

"Miss Duval, my compliments. We must accelerate our move to Knoxville. General Burnside feels that the coming days may present risks that ladies should not endure, so he has offered a squad of cavalry to escort Mrs. Sanders and yourself to Louisville on a little-used northern trail. Mrs. Sanders has refused, insisting on remaining with her husband—made quite a scene about it when he tried to order her north. In any event, the offer still stands as to you."

Duval hesitated before replying. "My thanks to the general. However, my place is here, more than ever. All I ask is that I be allowed to telegraph my family in the North."

"Best make haste, then. Go to the telegraph room at headquarters as soon as may be. After Burnside finishes sending messages up to Louisville, he has ordered the equipment dismantled and the wires cut."

"Thank you, Captain," replied Duval briskly, striding toward the headquarters in a swirl of skirts.

Poe watched her retreating figure for a moment, then addressed himself to the burial party. "I feared she would make that decision. Well, I have set aside a wagon to transport her and Mrs. Sanders. As they will be moving with the army, there is no need for the cavalry squad, which, in truth, is sorely needed elsewhere. Still, I would be more comfortable if you four accompanied their wagon and made sure that nothing untoward happens to the ladies."

"Of course," responded Clay, answering for them all.

"Thank you. It will be a load off my mind. Now if you will excuse me, there is much to do and precious little time in which to do it." He jerked his horse's head around and viciously applied the spurs, galloping off without a backward glance.

"That's no way to treat a horse," commented Lot to no one in particular.

"I have an impression that Captain Poe gives little thought to the feelings of others, animal or human," responded Clay absently. Then he turned to Larson and said, "Captain, we need to retrieve our horses; as I believe you have no mount, you should be in the wagon with the ladies. If you please, go help them make their arrangements; we will meet you outside Burnside's headquarters presently."

Clay, Lot and Bierce carefully urged their horses through the controlled chaos in front of the hotel that served as Burnside's headquarters. Screaming officers urged ragged regiments onto the road leading to Knoxville, while supply wagons jolted over the deepening ruts. The only thing that did not appear to be in motion was an open wagon directly in front of the hotel. On the front bench sat Captain Larson, restraining the pair of skittish horses with gentle pressure from the reins. In the back, seated on bags of feed that served as cushions, was a startlingly attractive blond woman. Sitting on a horse beside the wagon was the solemn-looking General Sanders, who was speaking to her urgently. As the three horsemen rode up, they could hear the tail end of the conversation.

"You know I would never order you to do anything," said the solemn Sanders. "However, please reconsider. General Burnside's gracious offer still stands. It is not too late to send you safely to Louisville. God alone knows what can happen in Knoxville."

The blond woman tilted her dainty features upwards and gazed at her husband with adoration. "I will tell you again, and for the last time, my love. I will not wait fretting among strangers while you are at risk. Our fates are entwined."

At this statement, the impassive general seemed about to break into tears. However, spotting the new arrivals, he quickly recovered and said somewhat brusquely if formally, "Gentlemen, may I introduce my wife, Mrs. Marjorie Sanders."

Clay swept off his kepi and bowed from horseback. "My pleasure, madam. I am Captain Alphonso Clay. These are Lieutenant Bierce and Sergeant Lot. If I may be so bold, may I recommend that you follow your husband's advice, which is motivated from the deepest concerns for your welfare. The dangers in Knoxville could be considerable."

The woman nodded regally, saying, "The pleasure is mine, Captain. However, you must appreciate that if my husband is unable to dissuade me, a recent acquaintance can do no better. Please respect my desire to remain with General Sanders."

Clay restored his cap with a flourish. "I respect your devotion, madam. No more will be said." Turning to the general, Clay asked, "Where is Miss Duval? We should be on our way as soon as possible."

Sanders nodded toward the entrance to the hotel. "In there, Captain. She entered the telegraphy room just as the operators were about to take apart the equipment and load it into a wagon." He smiled briefly. "Our nurse has a firm way about her. She made them wait until she had finished a telegram to her people."

"I will see what is causing the delay," replied Clay. He smoothly dismounted, wrapped his reins about the hitching post, and strode into the hotel while Sanders rode off to direct his men. Once inside, Clay heard tell-tale tapping coming from a small side parlor. Stepping gingerly over a tangle of copper wire, he entered the room to find Teresa Duval staring grimly at a frantic operator who was transmitting her message.

Suddenly, the balding young man finished. "Done! I hope that you appreciate the favor I've done you. Yours is the only message gone out today that wasn't to either Stanton or Grant."

"Indeed I do, sir. Now you may go about packing your machinery for the move to Knoxville." She turned and saw Clay. "A pleasure to see you again, Captain," she said, giving only a moment's hesitation to the slightest hint of unease she felt. Clay bowed to her slightly, a faint smile upon his lips.

"My compliments, Miss Duval. I must urge you to make haste. Mrs. Sanders is already in the wagon, and we should depart immediately."

"Thank you, Captain," Duval responded curtly. She swept out of the parlor toward the hotel door without a backward glance, snagging a carpetbag by the entrance without a pause.

Clay stared after her briefly, then turned his attention to the young operator who was frantically packing heavy batteries into straw-filled crates. On the table where his key still lay, was a pile of telegram copies. While the telegrapher's back was turned, Clay casually palmed the message on the top of the pile and strolled out of the room. At the door to the hotel, he paused to scan the brief message, addressed to Janice Duval, care of a hotel in New York City. It said simply, "LOVING MOTHER STOP LEAVING FOR SOUTH STOP MAY NOT BE HOME FOR CHRISTMAS STOP TELL PAPA NOT TO WORRY STOP." Clay frowned as he pocketed the message. Knoxville was due east of where they were, not south. He strode out of the hotel and swung into his saddle just as Duval finished settling herself in the bed of the wagon beside the aloof Marjorie Sanders.

Somewhere far to the west there were a series a booms. The soldiers trudging in irregular groups eastward along the road cast uneasy looks over their shoulders.

"Ladies and gentlemen, let us proceed," announced Clay. Larson snapped his reins, and without further ado, the wagon and three horsemen slid into the stream of retreating soldiers.

Teresa Duval was a woman who hated not being in control, and she was not in control of the wagon and its escort. Out of boredom, she attempted to strike up a conversation with the aristocratic Marjorie Sanders, but the delicate-looking blonde disdained carrying on a lengthy conversation with a middle-class New Englander like Duval was pretending to be, and she soon abandoned her efforts.

After an hour, Lieutenant Bierce brought his horse alongside and initiated a conversation, overtly proper but subtly sugges-tive, trying to see if the nurse was open to a liaison. For some minutes, Duval amused herself by pretending to be too innocent to understand Bierce's hints, until the grim Larson told him in no uncertain terms that he should ride forward of the party and join Clay and Lot in their post about twenty yards in advance of the wagon. With an insolent salute, Bierce spurred his mount on ahead, pretending to be oblivious to the level, hostile stare he was receiving from Larson. As soon as the lieutenant was out of earshot, Larson spoke to Duval as the wagon jounced along the uneven dirt road.

"My apologies for that, ma'am. That feller Bierce is a good enough soldier, but he ain't been brought up right. Needs a good horse-whippin' to learn him how to behave to a lady. He give you any trouble, let me know. Might just give him that horse-whippin' myself."

"Why, whatever do you mean, Captain? Lieutenant Bierce's conversation had nothing improper in it."

Larson glanced over his shoulder and looked for a moment with keen penetration at Duval before returning his attention to the road. "I reckon you found it easier to pretend not to know what he was aimin' at, but I can tell you're a heap smarter than that. Sometimes things are easier for a smart man—or woman—when they try not to seem so smart."

Duval found herself instantly re-evaluating Larson. He looked like a stupid strawfoot scrub from the north fork of the creek, but no one knew better than she that appearances could be deceiving. While Marjorie Sanders continued to aloofly study the slowly passing scenery, Duval decided to open up a conversation with the lean officer.

"Captain, you seem to know Lieutenant Bierce and Captain Clay well. How did you come by their acquaintance?"

"During the siege of Vicksburg, ma'am. Didn't see it myself but heard Bierce an' that darky sergeant rode out and rescued General Sherman from in full view of the Rebs, when Uncle Billy got his horse shot out from under him. Was near onto suicide—would have been, but dang if Captain Clay didn't gallop his own horse right along the front of the Reb line, daring the Johnnies to take a shot at him. Distracted enough of 'em so that Bierce and Lot could get Sherman back to our own lines. Don't rightly know how any of 'em lived to see sunset that day."

"I do not mean to take away from their bravery, but isn't it possible the danger was exaggerated?"

"Well, ma'am, Lord knows soldiers tend to make stories bigger than they were, but I reckon that it pretty much happened that way. Heard General Sherman himself talk on it once."

"I am surprised to hear of Captain Clay's bravery. Pardon me for saying so, but he appears to be one of those soft, upper-class youths who imagine it would be fun to play soldier and faint at the first hint of danger."

Larson paused and considered at length before answering. "Well, ma'am, I guess I can see how one could think so. From a distance, he does have the look of one them nancy-boys you see from time to time, if you'll pardon me for mentioning such things. Hair long and soft as a woman's, pale complexion, lightly-built. But get to know him, and you'll get some different notions right quick. There's something different about him; I'll give you that, but it ain't that he don't like women. And he might look like a short drink of water, but he's stronger than nature should allow."

"How do you know that?"

"Well, it came from the time he saved *my* life. We was talking in a trench outside Vicksburg, when a 3-inch shell with a sputtering fuse came over the edge and plopped into the dirt at our feet. Some Johnnie had lit it and rolled it downhill into our line. Quicker than a snake, Clay grabbed that shell and threw it near thirty feet uphill right back into the Reb trench, where it blew a couple of Johnnies to glory."

"Quick-witted, I grant you, but hardly extraordinary."

Larson stared forward at the road for a long time before finally replying, "Ma'am, ain't no disrespect to you to say you don't know much about artillery. That three-inch shell must have weighed over twenty pounds, and Captain Clay threw it more than thirty feet up a hill. The strangeness of that didn't strike me until later, but the more I thought on it, the more I realized no feller could do that, least of all a skinny little one like Clay."

Duval had no education that she had not obtained on her own, but she was highly intelligent, and the more she considered it, the more she realized it was impossible for Clay to have thrown such a heavy object such a distance. "Perhaps under the stress of the moment he drew on reserves of strength. It's well known that people perform amazing feats under the spur of rage or fear."

"True enough, ma'am. Still, there are limits. Not long ago, I offered this bear of an artilleryman ten dollars if he could throw such a shell thirty feet. He had a powerful thirst, that one, and really wanted that money, but he couldn't even make it a third that distance."

"So, what are you trying to say, Captain?"

There was another of Larson's long pauses. "Don't rightly know, ma'am, except I sure am glad Captain Clay's on our side."

"So where does the Captain hail from?"

"Kentucky blue grass, they say. I hear tell if he ain't the richest man in those parts, he knows the richest. Pappy was a cousin of Henry Clay. Hear tell he died on him the year the war started and left him more than six thousand acres of prime land."

This gave Duval pause. She had always thought that when she "retired" from the service of Jay Gould, she would ensnare one of his rich acquaintances into marriage. Nothing would be easier, she had decided, as all men were such fools in the hands of a beautiful woman. She had always thought that after a decent interval, her husband would sicken and die, leaving her free and even richer than before. However, chance may have placed an excellent opportunity before her, right here, right now.

"What does his family think of his bravery?"

"Don't know that he has any kin closer than cousins. No wife, though I get the feeling there was a woman who has passed away— hard to say why, just something about him gives me that feeling."

Duval decided to probe Larson further on a matter that had been bothering her. "Some people seem nervous about being around Clay. I've noticed that several times."

"You really do not recall that horrible incident last December at the Devereaux plantation in Louisiana?" interrupted Marjorie Sanders, anger in her voice.

"No, Mrs. Sanders, I do not believe so," replied Duval, surprised at her haughty companion's sudden intervention.

"It is a disgrace to our glorious cause that he still wears a uniform! Sabered to death Mr. and Mrs. Devereaux right in front of their children, along with an overseer. Then he set fire to the house, with an infant still inside. Horrible!" She shuddered delicately.

Duval was surprised to hear of such savagery on the part of the mild, slight Clay, so apparently in perfect control of himself. Surprised—and more than a little . . . interested.

"Really! I find it difficult to believe that such a gentleman as Captain Clay could do such a thing. Are you certain the news-papers didn't get things mixed up?"

Larson answered for Mrs. Sanders. "Well, I always say, 'Let sleeping dogs lie, unless something big is at stake. Then you should get a newspaper to do it.' Still, I reckon that they got it pretty much right. Hear tell, he won't even deny what the papers say to those fellows with guts enough to ask him about it."

Duval was intrigued. "Well, if it's true, why has he not been court-martialed and hanged, or at the very least dismissed?"

Larson paused for a long moment as the wagon jounced along the road. "Well, ma'am, I have a fair idea that General Grant figures he owes the captain, though you'll pardon me for not going into the details." There was something about Larson's attitude that showed he would say no more.

Mrs. Sanders spoke again. "I declare Miss Duval, you should not feel safe around a man so . . . ungentlemanly. Be careful that you do not allow yourself to be alone with Captain Clay."

Duval feared being alone with no man and found herself looking forward to a private meeting with Alphonso Clay, for several possible reasons.

The jolting of the wagon as it left the road awakened Teresa Duval. She experienced a moment of confusion, seeing only dim outlines in the ghostly light of a quarter-moon, then realized she had managed to sleep the remainder of the day away. She had the trick of sleeping whenever she was unoccupied, and had slept in far worse places than the back of a wagon in motion. Far, far worse. The wagon came to a halt, and three shadowy horsemen came alongside. With the voice of Alphonso Clay, one of the shapes spoke. "Ladies, we must tend to the horses and give them some rest. My apologies for the crudity of the conditions. Larson, Bierce, Lot and I will take turns guarding you against any impertinence. Discipline is always lamentably loose in a retreating army."

"Where are we, Captain?" asked Mrs. Sanders disdainfully.

"Campbell's Station, madam. As nearly as I can tell in the dark, it contains scarcely a dozen buildings. However, two roads branch out from it in the direction of Knoxville. I understand that upon the advice of General Parke, General Burnside has determined to leave a portion of Potter's corps, aided by your husband's cavalry, to fight a delaying action, while the remainder of the army makes haste to Knoxville."

"Is there any risk, Captain Clay?" asked Duval.

After a pause, Clay replied, "There is always a risk. However, we will be in the column of wagons on the road to Knoxville while Potter's corps detains the main Confederate body."

With surprising ease, given the darkness, the horses were detached from the wagon to be fed and watered, and a small fire started. Clay caused a skillet to materialize and began frying up pieces of unappetizing-looking salt pork. The others settled uncomfortably around the fire and watched with some amusement the aristocratic Alphonso Clay perform the menial duties of cook. Lot brought out a number of cheap tin plates and eating utensils, laying the plates in a neat row beside his friend. Clay deftly divided the cooked meat between the plates and added to each a single army cracker. Taking one plate in each hand, he walked to where Marjorie Sanders and Teresa Duval sat uneasily side-by-side. Bowing slightly to the general's wife, he said, "My apologies for the crudity of the sustenance, Mrs. Sanders. I realize this may not be appropriate for a woman of your station, but it's all that we have, and I urge you to maintain your strength for the days ahead."

She took the plate reluctantly and prodded the unappetizing contents gingerly with her fork.

Clay turned to Duval and with a faint smile added, "And as for you madam, I am sure you have made do with worse in your life." Smile still on his lips, he turned to distribute the remaining plates.

Duval felt her heart pounding. '*He suspects something*', she thought. 'What does he suspect? *What does he know? Has he told anyone else? No, that kind of southern "gentleman" would never utter a word against a lady unless he had proof. Has he proof? No, he would have denounced me by now. If I am careful, he'll probably never get it; but probably is not good enough. I must really do something about that little captain. Such a shame, too; he is so very . . . interesting. There may be an opportunity in the confusion of battle . . .*'

"What is so interesting about Captain Clay?" With a start, Duval broke her reverie to see that a grinning Lieutenant Bierce had strolled over to where the ladies sat and was looking at her intently while he stabbed at a piece of meat on his tin plate. He had noticed her concentration on the blonde captain. The sardonic lieutenant speared a stringy piece of pork, carried it to his mouth, and swallowed with a minimum of chewing.

"I wouldn't waste much time on him," continued Bierce in a low voice. "For the time being at least, he is impervious to feminine charms. He has suffered a loss, and his romanticism leads him to believe that what he lost was unique, and never to be replaced. You should turn your attentions to someone with fewer illusions, someone who knows how to truly enjoy life."

Although she was not being addressed, Marjorie Sanders angrily answered Bierce. "Lieutenant, you forget yourself. You may be accustomed to speaking in that manner to a certain kind of woman, and that is your affair. However, Miss Duval and I are ladies, and your conversation should take that into account."

Unexpectedly, Bierce threw his head back and emitted one of his barking laughs. The others around the fire all turned their attention to him, various degrees of concern on their faces. "Ah, yes, ladies. Ladies . . . we all know what fragile, angelic creatures ladies be. No possibility of crudity—no possibility of hidden secrets . . ."

Suddenly Clay appeared, grabbing Bierce's arm and spinning him around. In a calm voice charged with terrible menace, Clay said, "Lieutenant, I suspect you are in liquor." In fact, that was the case, as Clay's nose immediately told him. He had not realized that Bierce must have been furtively tippling during the day's ride from his battered hip-flask. Clay hesitated in saying what he had intended to say. Instead of drunken anger or misplaced humor, what he saw in Bierce's face was a flash of pain and despair, a pain and despair so intense that in an instant, Clay's anger over his ill manners had turned to concern.

Sergeant Lot appeared at his side. "Captain, I believe the lieutenant is unwell. He had complained much of dizziness on the ride today. Let me take him for a walk through the woods. I am sure that and few hours of sleep, will restore him."

Clay silently nodded, and the black sergeant gently took Bierce's arm. As Bierce turned away unresistingly to take the walk that would "clear his head," Clay noticed that tears were welling in the lieutenant's eyes. That sight disturbed him more than he would have thought possible.

Larson walked up to Clay. "You should put that feller on report. Drunk on duty, for a start."

Clay did not respond for some moments. Then he replied, "I believe I will accept Sergeant Lot's verdict. Lieutenant Bierce was . . . ill. I believe that he is in the process of advising him to be more circumspect in the medication he uses. We'll leave it at that. Unless, that is, one of the ladies wishes to complain."

Marjorie Sanders began to open her mouth. However, before she could say anything, Duval smoothly said, "Of course, he was not himself, Captain. I have seen those with a touch of malarial fever behave in a similar way. It would be un-Christian for us to discipline poor Lieutenant Bierce for a sickness."

Sanders looked put out, but apparently decided not to contradict the nurse; she closed her mouth without uttering a syllable.

"Well, you're senior captain here, Clay," said Larson. "I just hope you're right about the sergeant knocking some sense into that funny head of Bierce's."

"For some reason, Sergeant Lot has some influence with Lieutenant Bierce. Let us hope that it is sufficient." Clay stared into the darkness, a slight frown on his face, and said nothing else.

At 2:00 a.m., Clay was keeping watch over the party. All were asleep, including Lot and Bierce, who had returned after an hour in the darkness. Refusing to meet Clay's eyes, Bierce had crawled under the wagon and fallen into an uneasy sleep without so much as a blanket. Lot had wrapped himself in a horse-blanket and slept beside Larson under the stars. Sanders and Duval had been given the one small pup-tent the party possessed to share. Despite the occasional sound of horse-hooves and tramping feet from the nearby road, the campsite was surprisingly still, the crackling of the small fire more noticeable than the sounds of an army in motion. Clay sat motionless on a feedbag, staring unseeing into the fire, his mind alternating between memories of a dark beauty and a round horror sailing through the air.

Gradually Clay became aware that Bierce was sleeping uneasily. Hearing the sound of limbs shifting position ceaselessly, Clay looked over to the wagon; the small fire cast enough light under it so that Clay could see Bierce's head thrash back and forth, while his booted feet dug furrows in the forest floor. Bierce began muttering in his sleep, blurred, confusing words.

"Stop . . . don't . . . it hurts . . . mama . . . where . . . help . . . ma . . . God . . ."

Although Bierce's voice was low, it had awakened Lot, who was a light sleeper. Clay looked at his friend, who had sat up, a look of concern and pity visible in the blue eyes that glittered behind the spectacles in the flickering light from the fire. Lot looked back at Clay; their eyes met, and a silent understanding passed between them.

"It is not his turn, but perhaps we should ask Lieutenant Bierce to take the next watch," suggested Clay.

Lot nodded, got up, and approached the thrashing Bierce. Reaching under the edge of the wagon, the sergeant gently shook his shoulder, saying "Lieutenant, time to take your watch."

Bierce's eyes flew open; even in the flickering light, Lot could see the look of wild, lost despair they contained. Then blinking, the lieutenant's eyes focused on Lot, and the handsome face settled into its accustomed look of cheerful cynicism. "Ah, Sergeant, what time is it?"

"Nearly two in the morning, Lieutenant."

"I thought my turn would not come until four. Well, no matter. I wasn't sleeping well, anyway. Bad dreams, although I can't remember exactly what they were."

"I am restless myself. With your permission, I will stand watch with you. Besides, you can tell me that idea for a work of fiction you mentioned you wished to write up for the magazines."

Bierce clambered out from under the wagon, brushed the worst of the dirt and leaves from his tunic, and said jauntily, "That is kind of you, Sergeant. I find it useful to put my ideas to an interested party before immortalizing them with pen and ink." Bierce and Lot settled themselves on cracker boxes next to the fire. Bierce threw a cynical salute at Clay, saying, "Sleep tight, Captain. Tomorrow may be filled with excitement, so get your rest."

Wordlessly, Clay picked up a horse-blanket and walked to a nearby tree. Wrapping himself in the coarse woolen object, he settled into a sitting position, back and head firmly braced against the trunk.

Near the fire, Bierce began to spin an ominous tale for Lot in a low voice, designed not to disturb Clay or the sleeping members of the party. They obviously thought that even if he remained awake, Clay would not be able to hear, but Clay's hearing was astonishingly acute. Lot did not have to fake interest as Bierce unfolded a grim tale of Union sentry who shoots a Confederate cavalryman in order to prevent disclosure to the enemy of the Union position. Only at the end was it revealed that the Rebel was the sentry's father.

While the two men at the fire discussed how to vary the story for maximum effect, Clay turned his head away, staring into the unlit blackness of the nighttime forest. As he reflected on his own youth and what must have been the youth Bierce had experienced, Clay thought of how there were so many undisclosed horrors of different types in this world.

The party joined the stream of military traffic on the road at first light. As the sun was poking above the horizon, they slipped through the small hamlet of Campbell's Station and were greeted by an incredible sight.

Just east of the village, the road forked into two, their paths running parallel eastward for fifteen miles until they rejoined just outside Knoxville itself. Off to the sides of the road just before it forked were scores of army wagons; some were already burning, while soldiers scurried about setting fire to the others. A stream of soldiers and horse-drawn artillery continued eastward, the blue-clad figures looking uneasily at the growing fires before their units took one or the other of the highways leading from the fork. Meanwhile, thousands of blue-clad soldiers were frantically digging trenches and throwing up breastworks on either side of the fork, stretching to where the walls of the narrow valley began to rise.

Off the road, Clay spotted a group of officers on horseback, arguing furiously. Long before the others could recognize them, Clay could discern that the group consisted of Captain Poe and Generals Parke, Potter, and Sanders.

"Reckon this is a good place to pass on by," said Larson over his shoulder to the ladies. "When the bulls fight, it's the grass that gets stomped." Then he muttered a curse under his breath.

Ahead of him, Captain Clay had veered off the road and ridden right up to the quarreling officers, Bierce and Lot trailing reluctantly behind. Having little choice, Larson directed the wagon off the road and jounced the short distance toward where Clay had led them.

"Let me repeat, I am speaking for General Burnside," Parke was saying. "The Rebels are not encumbered with many wagons or heavy equipment. We will not have the slightest chance of making it to Knoxville burdened with the wagons and their contents. The men must march with only their weapons and ammunition."

"God damn it!" exploded Captain Poe insubordinately. "Without the equipment in those wagons, I will not be able to entrench around Knoxville properly. Without the food they contain, many of the men will be too weak to properly man the fortifications I will be able to build!"

"Captain, restrain yourself," said General Sanders. "General Parke does raise a valid issue. However, perhaps we should ask

General Potter to hold off the enemy a bit longer and try to save the wagons."

Potter removed his hat and wiped his balding forehead, glistening with sweat despite the early-morning chill. "I, ah, must agree with General Parke. My boys will only be able to hold this line long enough to force Longstreet to deploy his forces into line—two hours at most. Then we must pack up and go fast as we can for Knoxville. If we wait long enough for the Rebs to fully engage, any men left here will be lost. Even if we skedaddle in time, the rest of the army must get to Knoxville as soon as may be, to start organizing the defenses. Every minute lost is precious. The wagons must be sacrificed."

"General Potter, sir, you will tie my hands in Knoxville if I don't have those wagons and what they contain!" grated Poe furiously. "You and General Parke are proposing actions so detrimental to this army that they might as well have been proposed by Richmond!"

There was a shocked moment of silence, then General Parke said quietly, "Captain Poe, you may consider yourself under arrest."

Unexpectedly, Clay injected himself into the high-level dispute. "General Parke sir, you are fully within your rights in relieving Captain Poe for insubordination. However, I believe that he is the only trained military engineer currently with the Army of the Ohio. His presence is vital in the coming days; I am certain that his sense of patriotism and yours would show him the wisdom of apologizing right now for his intemperate speech, and you the wisdom of accepting his apology."

General Sanders said morosely, "In this case, apology is insufficient, Captain Clay. The maintenance of discipline and respect for command requires Captain Poe's arrest and court martial as soon as we attain Knoxville."

In a petulant voice, Potter complained, "Can't this wait? We must make a decision, one way or the other, I almost care not which."

Poe looked furiously at Clay and back at Parke. Then taking a deep breath, he said, "General, my concern for the safety of this army led me to be intemperate in my language. I apologize for my statement and . . . beg . . . your forgiveness."

A stunned Parke, who obviously had not expected the haughty young engineer to so humble himself, came to a decision and replied, "Very well, Captain, I will consider it an outburst caused by the extremity of our current situation. General Burnside and I determine how this army will be protected. You will continue to burn the wagons and double-harness their horses to the artillery pieces so that they move that much faster to Knoxville."

As if summoned by the mention of his name, General Burnside came galloping up on his wild-eyed gelding, Bob, a horse supposedly so fierce that only a superb horseman could safely ride him. Behind Burnside trailed a number of aides and cavalry guards. Burnside viewed the flaming wagons with a frown, then turned to Parke and said, "General, I don't understand. Why are we setting fire to our own wagons?"

There was a moment's silence, broken only by Clay replying, "Sir, General Parke said this was being done at your order."

Handsome face looking thoroughly confused, Burnside turned to Parke. "My order? General, I gave no such order."

In a smooth voice, Parke replied, "General, they misunderstood. I said that I was speaking on your behalf. You have honored me with your confidence and permission to make decisions on your behalf. I made the decision that if we retain these wagons, Longstreet's less-encumbered men will overtake us on the road to Knoxville while we are strung out and unable to organize a proper defense. It is a shame that so much of value must be left behind, but unavoidable."

Burnside looked dubious but then slowly said to the party in general, "Gentlemen, since I have had the pleasure of having

General Parke as my chief of staff, his advice has always been good. On only one important matter did I fail to follow that advice: that was when I commanded the Army of the Potomac, and he begged me not to order the assault at Fredericksburg. That assault, and the death of all of those brave men to no purpose, was . . . my fault entirely and would not have occurred if I had listened to General Parke. I will trust his judgment on this. Please consider any orders from General Parke as if they came directly from me."

"I thank you for your confidence," said Parke, eyes shining with what seemed to be admiration. "Now, with your permission may I suggest that you proceed directly to Knoxville and begin organizing the defense. I will be able to shepard the rearguard and the stragglers."

Burnside nodded saying, "Very good, General Parke. Generals, Captain Clay. Lieutenant. Ah, Lieutenant, we will meet again in Knoxville." Burnside turned his mount's head sharply, and Bob reared, but the general retained his seat and galloped toward the East, trailing his escort behind him.

Parke turned toward the remaining party, a slight smirk on his face. "Gentlemen, you have your orders. Now execute them. Captain Clay, please be so good as to escort the women to Knoxville with no delay."

With that, Parke viciously spurred his horse toward a tangle of artillery pieces whose crews were having trouble harnessing the double teams of horses.

With no attempt at concealment, General Potter removed a flask from an inner pocket of his tunic and took a long pull. Then wiping his moist forehead yet again, he turned nervous eyes toward Sanders and said, "General, you have three regiments of cavalry. Be so good as to deploy one on each of my flanks, and one in front to establish contact and force the Rebs to waste time moving up slowly."

The somber cavalryman nodded and made as if to gallop off but hesitated, checked his horse, and cast an agonized glance toward his wife in the wagon. Then he said, "Captain Clay, I charge you to guard . . . your passengers well. There may be more danger on the road to Knoxville than any of us suppose." Having uttered that enigmatic remark, he clamped his mouth shut and galloped toward the west to rejoin his horse soldiers.

From his seat on the wagon, Larson commented, "Captain Clay, the General's advice is good. Let's make some tracks."

Clay nodded and led his party back into the eastbound stream that was taking the southernmost of the two roads that led to Knoxville. Lot and Bierce took their places to the left and right of Clay. Almost at the same moment, both glanced at Clay and noticed a look of abstraction on his face, as if he were thinking hard on what had just transpired rather than the road ahead of them. Both were made uneasy by Clay's expression.

Rain had begun to fall—a cold, unpleasant rain, accompanied by stiff winds, completing the misery of the retreating soldiers. Clay's party grimly slogged on, aware that their only hope against death or capture was a speedy arrival in Knoxville. The men's woolen uniforms were heavy with frigid water; the women huddled under a horse-blanket that provided indifferent protection from the rain.

The road twisted like a snake through second-growth timber growing on low hills on either side. Although the better part of a division was using this road, only a couple of platoons of weary infantry were currently visible in the short portion of the road that Clay's party could observe.

Suddenly, a series of distant booms were heard far off on the west. Clay's head jerked up, and he said softly, "I hear continuous volleys of musket fire. I believe Potter is putting up a stout defense; let us hope he is able to disengage and save the rearguard."

Lot frowned. "Are you sure? I hear cannon fire, I think, but nothing like the sound of muskets."

Clay smiled thinly. "Trust me, Sergeant. They are being fired, and the fire sounds organized, rather than the ragged discharge of panicky regiments. The men are giving good service; I suspect better than many of their officers."

Bierce suddenly spoke up. "I don't pretend to understand high strategy, but tell me, how in the Hell can Potter now disengage without Longstreet tearing him to bits?"

With a knowing air about him, Clay responded. "I believe that General Parke is counting on the fact that although Longstreet is one of the South's most reliable generals, he is cautious and somewhat slow, somewhat more prone to see dangers rather than opportunities. His disappointing performance at Gettysburg proved that, to the benefit of the Union. If Potter's soldiers disengage carefully, as the fire slackens, Longstreet will fear ambush and a Union counterattack. He will not rush his men in until he has reconnoitered the position. Of course, much will depend on the speed and skill with which Potter and Sanders guide the men along the roads while retreating—and protect the flanks against infiltration by cavalry."

Suddenly the rain-drenched air was split by the inhuman Rebel yell. Seemingly out of nowhere, about 80 cavalrymen came charging out of the timber to the left of the party. At the head of the charge was the large, handsome officer that Clay had last seen in the confusion of a burning hospital. Platoons peeled off to the left and the right, attacking the isolated squads of Union soldiers in front and in back of Clay's party. The main body charged at the wagon, led by the smiling officer who shouted, "Kill the escort, but don't harm the ladies!" Curiously, only a few held revolvers; most of the attackers charged with only swords in hand.

Larson looked frantically in front and behind the wagon and

saw that his only paths of escape were blocked by swirling masses of Confederate cavalry on the road, busily slaughtering the few Union soldiers, who had not even had time to place percussion caps on their muskets' nipples. Larson dropped his reins, leaving the horse to its own devices. With the speed of weasel, he slid into the bed of the wagon and roughly knocked the women flat with a muttered, "Pardon me." Then he smoothly drew his Colt and began firing. He let off six shots in as many seconds, and an attacker fell for each shot, but he now faced the enemy with an empty weapon. Calmly he reached into his cartridge pouch and began to reload; he knew he had no chance of doing so before he was killed, but had no intention of dying meekly.

Bierce drew the new revolver he had been issued to replace the one that had exploded during the fight in the hospital. He was an indifferent shot at best, and in addition was firing from atop a skittish horse, so even at close range, only two attackers dropped for his five hasty shots. As a Confederate pistol-ball ripped through the side of his tunic, grazing flesh, he pointed his revolver at a bearded opponent coming at him with a raised saber and pulled the trigger for the sixth time. However, the percussion cap flashed weakly without igniting the gunpowder in the chamber; the young lieutenant had not been careful in keeping water from his holster. "Goddamn it!" screamed Bierce.

Suddenly the sharp crack of Clay's .32 caliber Smith & Wesson rang out in Bierce's right ear, and a black third eye appeared in the bearded man's forehead. With a look of surprise, the man dropped his sword and slid off the horse to lie still on the ground. Calmly and with precision, ignoring one bullet that took his kepi from his head and another that grazed his thigh above the knee, Clay continued firing, a Rebel dropping for every shot.

Meanwhile, one cavalryman had rounded the wagon and took careful aim with his Colt navy at the furiously reloading Larson.

Suddenly, Duval popped up from the bed of the wagon like a jack-in-the-box, aimed her Sharpe's pistol at the Confederate's chest, and discharged all four barrels in lightening succession. The man dropped his pistol, clawed at his chest, and with a long howl of agony, slid slowly out of his saddle. Beside Duval, Mrs. Sanders sat up, a look of aristocratic indignation rather than fear on her face.

Lot had emptied his own pistol, bringing down three of the enemy, having only suffered a wound to his left forearm. However, he was now effectively disarmed and stared with horror as the big Confederate officer pointed at Clay with his sword shouting, "Kill that Yankee bastard first, then the other blue-bellies!"

Lot saw that the situation was hopeless. His party had nothing left but the officers' swords, and they were still facing over twenty unwounded Rebels, not counting the ones blocking either end of their stretch of the road. With mingled despair and pride, Lot saw Clay smoothly holster his empty revolver and draw his saber, waiting calmly for the end. It was more than Lot could stand. It was possible that a lone horseman could escape into the woods during the melee, but Lot did not even consider it. Screaming "Alphonso," Lot spurred his mount forward to be with his friend at the end.

At almost the same moment, surprising himself, Bierce drew his own sword, put his horse in front of Clay's, and shouted "Redeploy to the rear, Clay!"

The large officer shouted, "Cease fire!" in a voice that cut through the confusion of the fight like a cannon-ball. It was a tribute to the discipline of his unit that all were suddenly stock-still. "Alphonso Clay," the officer muttered in the silence. "This does alter . . ."

The sound of scores of muskets firing came from the road behind them. A dozen Confederates were knocked from their mounts to join the Union soldiers they had just killed. The survivors spurred their horses toward their leader, one screaming, "Major Ward, a whole Goddamn regiment on the quick march!"

"Retreat! Back the way we came!" shouted Major Ward. As his men began to gallop back into the woods, he drew a large LeMat revolver and began to point it at Larson, who had continued the cumbersome reloading of his Colt as if he had not a care in the world. Still clutching his saber, Clay spurred his mount directly into the line of fire, and stared at the Confederate.

Around the bend in the road came a trotting company of about sixty infantry, bayonets affixed to their muskets, behind an overweight, puffing captain with lengthy side-whiskers. Ward looked at the reinforcements, snarled a curse, turned his horse toward the woods, and fled after his retreating men. By the time the red-faced captain had reached the wagon, the only sign of the Confederates were their dead and wounded on the ground, and the horses they had ridden.

The wheezing captain saluted Clay and managed to choke out, "My God, what happened here? We were told Forrest's men might stage raids, but I never dreamed . . . I mean look at . . . and a wagon with ladies, too."

"Captain, we are indebted to your timely arrival. I am Alphonso Clay, on detached duty from the Army of the Tennessee."

"Captain Burton of the 27th Ohio," choked out the ill-conditioned officer. He glanced about at the mingled blue and grey bodies scattered along the road, a few moving or groaning piteously. "The rest of the regiment is right behind us," he said, gesturing toward more blue-clad soldiers coming around the bend in the road. "We have an excellent regimental surgeon; I guess I better get him up here." With a hurried salute, the portly officer began trotting back down the road.

Clay turned his attention to the wagon. "Mrs. Sanders, are you hurt?"

"I am not, Captain. However, it would seem there was some

neglect in patrolling by the cavalry. It is hard to understand how such a large body of men could get this close to us undetected."

"Indeed it does, Mrs. Sanders. It troubles me." Clay shifted his attention to Teresa Duval, and a small smile graced his lips as he looked at the pistol she held in her hand. "Miss Duval, may I say that I am not surprised at how well you conducted yourself. I expect nothing less from someone of your . . . antecedents."

"Thank you for your concern, Captain," she replied as she slipped the small gun back into a pocket of her frock, an edge to her voice. She glanced at Larson, who had finished reloading his Colt and now was busy attempting to calm the skittish horse attached to the wagon. "Tell me, Captain Clay, do you not find it strange how almost the last act of that . . . Confederate was an attempt to kill Captain Larson in particular?"

"Not strange at all. It is merely an attempt to finish what he started back in the hospital."

"Reckon he's scared there might be an accounting someday about the Fort Pillow business," added Larson. "Far as I know, I'm the only white man who actually saw the order for the massacre given."

"In any event, Miss Duval, it would appear that your nursing services are needed for our wounded."

"For *all* of the wounded," added Lot with emphasis. "The battle is over, and now all we have are Christian souls in need."

Bierce, who had been leaning over a wounded Rebel, straightened up and snorted his contempt. "Christians be damned! These are Forrest's boys. This Johnnie has just confirmed it to me. If Forrest's men are Christians, then I'm proud to be a free thinker. You're a good man, Sergeant, but you waste your concern on offal such as these."

Duval looked about twenty yards behind them, where an officer who was obviously the regimental surgeon was starting to organize the relief of the wounded. "Gentlemen, if you'll pardon me, I think my duty calls me to the care of these poor souls." Without a further word, she strode off toward the informal dressing station that was being set up. Clay stared after her, his face absolutely devoid of expression.

An hour later, Clay, the recently returned Duval, and Larson had finished dressing Lot's wounded arm. Mrs. Sanders sat regally in the wagon at the side of the road, daintily holding an umbrella over her head, disdaining to look either towards the party under a tree, which provided some protection from the intermittent rain, or at the thickening stream of Federal troops trudging eastward on the road. The bullet had passed through the outer layers of Lot's forearm, barely missing the bone, leaving an injury that was more of a gash than a hole. Lot had born the process stoically, uttering no groans as Duval deftly probed the injury with a curious instrument from a small box she carried for the scraps of cloth that might fester in the wound, only hissing when Bierce doused the site liberally with cheap whiskey borrowed from Bierce's flask. As the lieutenant watched Duval bandage the wound she had skillfully stitched with gut from the same small box, Bierce commented, "Damn if your skills never cease to amaze me, Miss Duval."

She did not bother to respond to Bierce. Instead, it was the on-looking Larson who broke the silence. "Pardon me for asking, but can anyone tell me why we're still alive?"

Bierce barked out one of his unlovely laughs. "Well, we put up a damn good fight, Larson. Damn good. That, and the sudden arrival of the 27th Ohio, saved our hides."

"That was part, but only part, Lieutenant," responded Lot as he gingerly started to put on his jacket. "Only a few of those attacking the wagon used the revolvers that every one of them seemed to have had. I think what the captain means is that if they had all used guns instead of swords, we would have been dead before the 27th came on the scene."

"Heard that murderin' officer shout to be sure not to kill the women," said Larson. "Figure they held back on their fire to have . . . well to take . . ." The deadly former sniper had suddenly turned beet red. Turning his eyes toward the ground, he spotted an officer's kepi and pretended to busy himself picking it up.

A faint smile upon his face, Clay replied, "Captain Larson, no one has a lower opinion of Rebel forces than I, especially those of Forrest. However, in all of his atrocities, save for what we observed at that farm, there has never been a known case of such an outrage by his men. No, for some reason, they wanted to be sure to take the ladies alive—at least one of them alive."

Still blushing, the prudish Larson thrust the kepi at Clay. "Reckon this is yours. Has a hole at the very top; couldn't have missed your skull by a quarter inch."

"Thank you, Captain." Clay took the piece of damaged headgear and placed it carefully on top of his dripping head; it was too late for protection from the drizzle, but Clay was at all times a stickler for correct attire.

"That does not make sense, Clay," commented Bierce. "Why the hell would that major want either Miss Duval or Mrs. Sanders?"

"Why indeed?" murmured Clay, who then strolled over to the waiting wagon. When he got there, he bowed slightly to Mrs. Sanders. "Madam, the Confederate major known as Ward gave an order to take the women alive. By any chance is the major known to you?"

"Certainly not," she sniffed. "It is far more likely that Miss Duval would know him. I would not be surprised if a woman of . . . that background might have acquaintances of a low nature. Why do not you make inquiry of her?"

Clay glanced back down the row of trudging soldiers on the

road and saw approaching the surgeon of the 27th Ohio. "Perhaps I shall, at a more opportune time."

The small, compact surgeon came up to Clay, saluted, and said, "Captain, I wish to thank you for the services of Miss Duval and to tell you in her presence that she is a wonder. Most of the poor souls were beyond help, but those who could be helped, she worked miracles with. There is at least one corporal who will end up alive and whole because of her; he had an arterial leg-wound that I feared could only be treated by an amputation that would like to have kill him in any event. But without a word she shoved me aside, went in and tied off the artery, cleaned and dressed the wound, and stitched him up as quick as you please—almost quicker than it takes to tell of it. In fact, all of our wounded can be moved, at least as far as Knoxville, which is due primarily to Miss Duval."

"Oh, tush sir," responded Duval with simulated New England briskness. "You and your bandsman did most of the work. The Lord only allowed me to help."

"Miss Duval is a woman of many rare talents, sir," said Clay with the slightest trace of a smile. "What about the Confederate wounded?"

"Only five survived," said the surgeon morosely. "The two fit enough to move, I've turned over to the Provost as prisoners. I'll stay with the other three until the Confederate army arrives, and their doctors can assume their care."

Clay looked intently at the surgeon, then said, "Sir, when Longstreet's forces arrive, you will be taken prisoner, and probably sent to Andersonville. You have heard what that place is like?"

The surgeon paled at the mention of the infamous prison camp but responded resolutely. "That cannot be helped, sir. I cannot abandon men in such need until I am certain they are in capable hands."

Clay looked at the man for a long moment, then slowly and formally saluted his inferior in rank. "Sir, you have my respect. Would that your devotion be bestowed on more worthy objects than Forrest's men."

"Thank you, sir. Is there anything that I may do for your party before I return to my charges?"

"Nothing, thank you."

"Let me again thank you and Miss Duval." The surgeon turned toward where she had stood, but she was nowhere to be seen. Puzzled, he muttered "I fear that I may have embarrassed that excellent Christian lady with my praise. Please, give her my apologies." He saluted, turned, and began shambling along the side of the road, a lone figure heading west against a stream of eastward-bound men and horses.

Clay turned to the rest of the party. "Come, we must be under way. It is still a good six miles to Knoxville, and we do not want any further surprises from Confederate cavalry. Let us load up our equipment."

As the few items in question were hurriedly stowed in the bed of the wagon by Lot, Bierce, and Larson, Clay checked to assure himself that a large wooden box was carefully braced between bags of feed. Mrs. Sanders noticed the care he was taking, and broke her long silence.

"Captain, I have been wondering about that box this whole trip. You have treated it like it contains a great and delicate treasure."

"In a way it does, madam. They are glass photographic plates, very subject to breakage and disfigurement. A trip such as this raises risks of both."

"And what is so precious about these particular plates?"

Clay finished cushioning the box, looked directly at Sanders, and replied, "They may hold the key to acts of murder and treason."

Sanders shuddered delicately. "Whose murder? What treason?"

"With my deepest apologies, I beg that you wait for me to answer those questions. At this time, I have only suspicions, not proof, and if I tell you of my suspicions, it may wrong an innocent party." Smoothly changing the subject, Clay turned to Lot and asked, "Have you seen Miss Duval? We must be under way."

"I believe that she may have been, ah, seeking a moment of privacy." Suddenly, Duval emerged from behind a tree, smoothing her frock. "Are we ready to depart?" she asked as she approached the wagon.

"Indeed we are, Miss Duval," responded Clay with a deep bow. "Allow me to hand you up into the wagon." With subtly exaggerated gentility, Clay assisted her into the bed of the wagon while Larson seated himself up front.

Then Clay, Lot and Bierce untied their own horses from nearby saplings and mounted. With a soft play of the reins, Larson urged the wagon into motion, the mounted soldiers taking the lead. The party slid with a minimum of fuss into the eastward-bound stream of blue-clad soldiers.

They had only been proceeding for a few moments when Lot spoke aloud. "You may all think me fanciful, even silly. However, when I look at this mighty army moving as one, even moving in retreat, it seems like an army of the Lord. I cannot believe this road is the road to defeat. It must be the road to Zion."

Bierce laughed until he coughed. Then he said, "On the road to Zion? Sergeant, you are brave man, and I owe you my life, but sometimes you're the damnedest fool that could be found in a month of Sundays. Look at our own little party, never mind the whole army. Look at me! Do you think that the road to Zion would have such travelers upon it?"

Lot answered with simple dignity. "Yes, I do believe it. I believe those on the road to Zion will have many strange companions;

it will matter little exactly what they are like, so long as they are bound for the same destination."

Bierce cast a glance at Lot and suddenly turned somber. "Yes, Jeremiah," he responded quietly. "You may find some very odd companions indeed on the road to Zion."

Surrounded by the Army of the Ohio, the party rode on in silence.

The 27th Ohio's surgeon trudged wearily up to the tent where the wounded Rebels were kept. He dreaded the thought of Andersonville and felt little love for Forrest's troopers. Still, he knew his duty before God and would do that duty. He squared his shoulders and threw back the flap of the tent. His eyes adjusted to the murkiness inside, and he suddenly cried out. Even in his horror and shock, he felt a small kernel of guilt over the joy he had from knowing that Andersonville would not be in his immediate future.

The throat of each Rebel had been cut to the bone.

CHAPTER 5

". . . WE WILL WELCOME TO OUR NUMBERS THE LOYAL TRUE AND BRAVE . . ."

It was nearing noon as the party caught sight of Knoxville. The road had crested a low ridge, and Clay and his companions beheld the city of Knoxville. The town was compact, scarcely a mile square of frame and brick buildings on a small plateau bordering the north bank of the Tennessee River.

"Sure is disappointing," muttered Larson to no one in particular as he casually flicked the reins of the wagon's horse. "Kinda expected a regular city, not some jumped-up village."

"It is certainly not that impressive in appearance," replied Clay over his shoulder, from his position on horseback in front of the wagon. "However, it is the political and economic center of eastern Tennessee. All the highways and railroads of this part of the state pass through here, such as they are. Furthermore, I believe it has the only regular telegraph terminus for fifty miles in any direction. Of course, Forrest's raids have destroyed so many bridges and miles of track that the railroads are worthless, and I would not be surprised if the telegraph is down. If it's not, it certainly will be shortly."

"Sounds like we're heading straight into a God-damned trap," muttered Bierce darkly.

"Not entirely," replied Clay. "If worse comes to worse, the army can retreat over the eastbound trails into West Virginia and safety, providing it starts that retreat before Longstreet has the opportunity to properly encircle Knoxville."

The party had begun to approach the outskirts around the town. To their left and right, they saw blue-clad figures furiously digging rifle-pits and trenches. In front of them, they noticed that the outskirts of the town were crowded with the crude shanties and tents of haggard-looking civilians, some of whom were black.

"What are all those white trash and Negroes doing hanging about?" asked Mrs. Sanders with a sniff.

"Refugees, ma'am," replied Lot quietly. "The Union loyalists that have so concerned Mr. Lincoln, along with some slaves that have fled to what they thought would be freedom. The very reason the Army of the Ohio was sent here was to protect people like them. General Burnside must stay here. He must. If the army flees, these people will be in no shape to flee with it. The men will be slaughtered, the women will lose what property they have, and they and their children will starve."

"Come, Sergeant," replied Bierce. "I hear Longstreet is a hard man, but not a bad one. He would not order a massacre."

Lot glanced at the lieutenant with unaccustomed fierceness. "He may be a Godly man, but I doubt that he has complete control over Forrest and his men. Have you already forgotten what we found on that farm?"

Bierce's eyes became unfocused. For a moment, he was remembering the slaughtered boy, blinded farmer, and obscenely violated girl.

"This army must stay here," continued Lot. "The people of eastern Tennessee have already suffered far too much for their loyalty to the Union. God will grant us success here, if we have the belly to stand, for we are in the right."

Bierce barked out one of his unlovely laughs, devoid of genuine amusement. "I believe with the little emperor Napoleon, Sergeant. He said that God is always on the side of right, but before He decides what's right, He counts the cannon. Better send up your best prayer that the accounting is in our favor."

By now the stream of blue-clad soldiers in which the party was embedded had begun to enter the town proper. The disheveled civilians were waving enthusiastically, a few giving ragged and uncoordinated cheers. Here and there were knots of blacks, even less well-clothed than their white brethren; when their eyes lit on Jeremiah Lot, the joy in their faces was almost painful to see. They had undoubtedly heard rumors that Lincoln was beginning to arm slaves, but this was the first they had seen of it for themselves, and freedom was now and forever a tangible reality to them.

Duval watched the crowd, unaware that a hard, bitter expression was creeping over her features. The refugees reminded her of the early stages of the Famine, before the people actually began to die of starvation. In her mind, she heard snatches of remembered speech, the words from different men, but in her mind always, always in a drawling English accent: '. . . *She's dead, lassie.. your old man shouldn't have hit that soldier . . . well, there is still a way to get a spud, Colleen . . .*' She shook her head, cramming those memories back into the dark corner of her soul where raging madness lay. Then she looked to the left where Clay trotted alongside the wagon. He was staring at her, that faint enigmatic smile on his face, and Duval had for a moment the irrational feeling that he knew her thoughts. *Ridiculous*, she thought, shaking her head again. *Ridiculous.*

To their left on the main street was a stately three-story brick hotel. The presence of sentries and pennants announced that army headquarters was already established inside.

Clay nodded toward the building, saying, "We had better establish ourselves there before every square inch is taken," as Larson deftly maneuvered the wagon toward the one unused hitching post for blocks in either direction.

Larson dismounted and began to secure the horse. Duval noticed the small telegraph office next to the hotel, soldiers continuously scurrying in and out.

"The lines must still be up. I must let Mother know how I fare." Without waiting to be handed down by one of the men, she vaulted easily out of the wagon and strode into the telegraph office.

Lot stared after the nurse for a moment then said, "She must be very fond of her mother."

"I am certain that she is," replied Clay, dismounting from his own steed, tying it to the back of the wagon. Only Lot was familiar enough with Clay to detect the faintest trace of mockery in his friend's voice and stared strangely at him for a moment.

While Clay, Lot, and Bierce secured their mounts, Larson helped Mrs. Sanders down, and the party entered into the lobby of the hotel. Immediately, they were witness to a remarkable scene. Captain Poe was standing in front of Generals Burnside and Parke and addressing them. Actually, it was more like berating them. Every member of the party felt varying degrees of shock as they listened to the arrogant young engineer make his demands of his superiors. "Sirs, I must insist. Expel the crackers immediately— every man, woman, and child. Niggers too, but keep the young bucks; I'll need strong backs for the fortifications. They will work, or out they will go as well. Anyone who cannot work is a useless mouth, and must go."

Burnside looked appalled. "Captain Poe, you cannot mean that.

The countryside hereabouts has been picked clean. Even if they are not swept up by the Rebels, they will starve. The women and children will starve, sir! And I don't even want to think what will happen to the darkies! They all came here for the protection of the Army of the Ohio!"

"I am as troubled as you are by the necessity," replied Poe, not looking troubled at all. "However, the Union must be preserved. To preserve the Union, this army must survive until Grant can drive off General Bragg and come to our relief. We only have the food we brought with us and undoubtedly will have to go on half-rations in any event. I cannot erect the defenses of this town with starving men. Useless eaters must go. It is the greater good, sir, the greater good."

"So we will survive, and the people we came to protect will perish?" asked Parke, actually quivering with suppressed fury.

"With the greatest respect, sir," replied Poe, respect noticeably absent from his voice, "this army is far more important than a couple of thousand crackers and contrabands. This must be looked at rationally."

Parke's face was turning scarlet with rage, but before he could issue an explosive response, Burnside placed a restraining hand on his shoulder. "This discussion has gone on long enough," he announced quietly. "The decision—and the responsibility—will be mine. No civilian, white or black, will be expelled against their will from our lines. You will have the word passed among them that rations will be scarce. Civilians will receive quarter rations, based on the standard allotment while on march. Soldiers and civilians working on fortifications will receive half-rations. Quarter rations will sustain people not doing physical labor until—well, until help comes. Once they understand how little quarter rations are, they may wish to leave, but it will be their choice."

"Sir!" exclaimed Poe. "If we do not receive supplies from the outside, that will exhaust all our foodstuffs in less than ten days—perhaps less than a week!"

"Captain Poe, you are an excellent engineer and do the best you can by your lights," responded Burnside. "My decision is made; I expect you to do nothing less than your best under the conditions I have laid out."

Apparently not trusting himself to speak, the red-faced Poe silently saluted, spun on his heel, and strode out into the street, where a moment later he could be heard barking furious orders. Parke was the first to break the silence.

"General, how can you tolerate his blatant disrespect?" asked Parke. "He should be placed under arrest and court-martialed for insubordination."

"Perhaps so, John," replied Burnside. "But where would I find as good a military engineer? His manners are deplorable, his heart of stone, but you must admit he knows his business." The commanding general shifted his attention to Clay and his party. "Captain . . . ah . . . Clay. Is there something I can do for you quickly? You can imagine how many demands there are on me at this moment."

"Yes, there is sir," replied the slight blond captain. "Despite the pressing needs of the army, I must ask for an hour of your time this evening. That also of Generals Parke, Potter, and Sanders, and of Captain Poe.

"What in the hell are you about, Clay," responded Parke angrily. "In case you haven't noticed, we are about to become besieged in an isolated town by a superior Rebel force. The people you have named are the most essential officers in the Army of the Ohio. What possible reason could you have that would justify taking them away from their duties at such a time?"

"Possibly the very survival of this army, General," responded Clay quietly. "Nothing else would prompt my request."

Parke snorted in disbelief. "I don't care if you do have General

Grant's ear, Clay. Everyone knows that you can go off the reservation from time to time; just look at what happened in New Orleans."

The lobby was suddenly filled with a shocked silence, a silence that seemed to emanate from the young captain. In that interval of silence, Teresa Duval slipped quietly into the room, her mission in the telegraph office accomplished.

"The incident to which you allude is not relevant to the current conversation," replied Clay in a voice that was terrifyingly devoid of emotion. "It related to a . . . personal matter. No one has ever doubted my devotion to the Union and its forces. When I say that the meeting I require is vital to the survival of this army, I am stating the literal and exact truth."

Burnside's face had acquired the petulant expression it usually held when he attempted to look fierce and decisive. "Well, Captain Clay, I imagine we can spare you a few minutes around midnight; I don't expect any of us will be getting much sleep. In the meantime, Parke will see to it that the ladies have a room to themselves, and that you and Lieutenant, ah, Bierce have a room to share next to theirs. Your man will have to . . ."

"Sergeant Lot will squeeze in with us, General," interrupted Clay. "I thank you for your consideration."

"I imagine this is the first time colored have stayed as guests in a Knoxville hotel," commented Burnside. "Well, I expect the innovation will do no harm. Until tonight, then."

Having already helped the ladies settle into their own room, Clay, Bierce and Lot arranged their meager possessions in a space intended for at most two guests. In the corner furthest from the door, Clay was gently positioning the heavy wooden case containing the photographic plates. Finally satisfied that it was positioned where it could not be accidentally jostled, he turned to the others.

"Sergeant, I would appreciate it if you would obtain a quantity of ink and clean foolscap paper. If anyone asks, say it is for writing dispatches. The traitor undoubtedly suspects we will attempt to unmask him tonight, but we do not need to forewarn him of exactly how. In the meantime, I have an errand."

"Can't say I'm not looking forward to tonight, Clay," responded Bierce cheerfully. "I remember the last time you had one of your pow-wows. Wouldn't miss this one for all the tea in China. Just give me a chance to go check that our wagon and horses are secured; Larson will be staying with them all night at the headquarters' corral, to make sure no light-fingered quartermaster 'requisitions' them. I'll find out if I can get him anything before he settles in."

"I'll see if I can find us something to eat while you are both out," added Lot. "If there is any choice, what should I get you to drink? Coffee?"

"Thank you no," replied Clay with a grimace. "Never liked coffee—especially Army coffee. Tea, if it is available; otherwise water."

"Coffee for me. Lieutenant Bierce, you wish coffee as well?"

"So long as I can lace it with whiskey, it'll do."

Unknown to the three soldiers, Duval was already in the next room and could hear their conversation clearly through the deplorably thin wall. A plan quickly unfolded within her mind.

Nodding a farewell to his friends, Clay swiftly left the room. He descended the stairs rapidly, exited the hotel, and in moments was in the cramped telegraph office next door, where pandemonium reigned. The telegraphers and several soldiers were whooping for joy, some pounding others on the back. Raising his voice to cut through the noise, Clay asked, "What has happened?"

A civilian telegrapher brandished a scrap of paper like a weapon. "A God damn miracle, Captain! A God damn miracle! Grant and Thomas have the Rebs on the run!"

Clay was a hard man to surprise; however, he knew the desperate plight of the Army of the Cumberland, and could not keep his surprise from showing on his face. "How is that possible? General Bragg held an impregnable position on the ridges over-looking Chattanooga."

"Well, I guess Bragg's gonna have a baby in nine months," chortled another telegrapher. "Seems Grant ordered Pap Thomas to drive back the pickets from the lower slopes of the mountains. Thomas gave the job to that little mick division commander of his, Phil Sheridan. Sheridan led his men right smart-like and drove the Rebs up the side of the mountain. Looks like he notices Bragg had thinned out his lines at the top more'n than he should'a. I bet old Braxton's sorry now he didn't hold onto Longstreet's boys. Anyway, Sheridan didn't wait for any orders or spend any time thinkin' on it. Message says he just waived his sword from atop that big black horse of his and yelled, '*Follow me, you bastards!*', if you'll pardon me, Captain. He took off up the mountain on a trail, with five thousand whooping heroes behind him. Must'a really spooked the Rebs; they hardly fired a shot before taking to their heels. Word is Bragg's army don't look like it'll stop running this side of the Georgia line. Anyway, Army of the Cumberland is now sittin' pretty damn pretty."

The clicking telegraph key suddenly fell silent. One of the telegraphers swore eloquently, then said, "Well, we knew that was goin' to happen sooner rather than later. Someone better go tell Burnside and Parke the lines are down until this is over. At least we know Grant will be on the way, so it's just a matter of holdin' on."

While most of the crowd in the room headed for the door, Clay leaned over the counter, appearing to inspect the now-silent telegraph key. However, his fingers rapidly riffled through the flimsy copies of outgoing messages while he scanned them with surprisingly acute peripheral vision. When he found the one he wanted, he deftly slipped it into his tunic pocket and calmly walked out of the office.

Once in the street, he extracted the message and examined it in detail. It was from Teresa Duval to a New York hotel and only said, "HEADING NORTH NO MATTER WHAT YOU FEAR MOTHER STOP HOME BY CHRISTMAS."

Clay frowned slightly in puzzlement before pocketing the message. No one was going north from Knoxville anytime soon. Clay reflected that Teresa Duval did not seem to be the kind of person to make a promise that would not be fulfilled. Or a threat.

Clay found Sergeant Lot standing outside the entrance to the hotel in the gathering twilight, a worried expression on his face. The occasional pop of a musket far to the west could be heard. The black sergeant addressed Clay without looking at him.

"Reb scouts are running into our pickets. Longstreet's feeling us out."

"Longstreet is a cautious man," replied Clay. "He will not order a full assault until he has inspected our defenses in detail, and the more time he takes, the more rifle pits and cannon emplacements Poe will have waiting for him."

"I just heard something that worried me," replied Lot, still looking off toward the west as if he could unravel the future if he just stared hard enough. "Word got back to Burnside and Parke that Poe's taken a good portion of the skilled construction troops off the trenches and artillery emplacement projects and put them to work building a single earthen fort. Construction of all other defenses has been slowed in favor of that one little fort. I was in the lobby when a messenger brought the news and heard what was near an argument between the two generals. Parke was demanding that Poe be relieved for incompetence, while Burnside mulishly insisted that Poe must know his business."

Clay was shocked into silence for almost a minute. Finally, he said, "I am not a strategist and do not pretend to be one. However, it seems to me that Longstreet would simply bypass such a fort, no matter how strong it was, and storm into Knoxville."

Lot finally looked at Clay. "If Poe is one of the people you suspect of being the secret traitor, this could constitute a brilliantly subtle act of sabotage."

"Poe could hardly be arrested on a charge of treason based only on professional incompetence," mused Clay. "Tonight's demonstration should, with luck, give us the proof we need for an arrest."

"Before it is time for us to set the stage for our little drama, we should get something in our stomachs," commented Lot. "I scrounged up some fried pork and hardtack—even some of your tea. I left it in our room; Bierce has already gone up. We better go up ourselves and enjoy dinner before it before it gets cold."

'Everything is falling into place,' thought Teresa Duval, as she heard Lot leave the room next door. *'The Sanders bitch is off with her husband, and the darky left their dinner in their room before going out in search of Clay and Bierce. Couldn't have planned things better. Nonetheless, I may have only seconds.'*

She opened the door to her room and confirmed no one was in the hall. Moving with the stealth of a cat, she glided up to Clay's room. She found it locked, but the flimsy lock succumbed in moments to one of her hair pins. She glided over to the room's one table where three cooling drinks resided along with a disgusting mess made from Army contract meat. It took only a moment to see that two of the drinks were coffee, the third tea. Swiftly she produced a small brown bottle from one of her frock's pockets and uncorked it. She went to pour half the contents into Clay's tea but was surprised to find herself hesitating. Silently she cursed herself; yes he was attractive, but the risk he posed to her far outweighed any pleasure that could come from a dalliance. She forced herself to pour the overdose of digitalis into the tea, corked the bottle, and restored it to her pocket. She glided out of the room (not forgetting to relock the door), and attained her own with no one having seen her.

She lay down on her comfortable cot, and to entertain herself, she visualized Clay's death. The digitalis was tasteless, and he would suspect nothing. Then the tremors would start, followed by increasingly severe convulsions; finally, heart palpitations of increasing intensity would hit him, until the heart gave up the ghost altogether. A frown came to her face. For some reason, and unlike all prior times, she was getting no pleasure from imagining her victim's death.

Duval heard the click of the lock to Clay's door; strangely, no voices could be heard. She frowned at the sudden sound of fragile glass being broken, especially since the absence of any voices continued. The crunching sound of breakage ceased, and the silence became absolute. Uneasiness building up inside her, she got up and pressed her ear directly to the wall; still, she could hear nothing. She was debating with herself whether to risk going out in the hall to check the condition of Clay's room, when suddenly she heard all hell break loose.

Clay and Lot entered the hotel and rapidly ascended the two flights of stairs to the floor where their cramped room was located. As they entered the third-floor corridor, they became aware of shouting voices. One belonged to Ambrose Bierce, his cultivated phrasing gone, to be replaced by a string of sulfurous curses. The other belonged to John Parke, shouting responses in a high-pitched voice where anger warred with fear. Clay and Lot saw that the door to their hotel room was open and rushed in to find an astonishing sight: Lieutenant Bierce had twisted General Parke's right arm behind his back and had him jammed up against the wall. On the floor, at their feet, was the precious wooden container for the glass photographic plates. The top was open, and in front of the box were the remnants of the plates themselves, ground into small fragments as if repeatedly crushed under heavy boots. The red-faced Bierce caught sight of the new arrivals.

"Here's the bastard we want! Traitorous son-of-a-bitch!"

"Captain, get your crazy lieutenant off me!" shouted Parke.

"Bierce, release the general," commanded Clay in his soft yet penetrating voice.

With a muttered obscenity, Bierce released Parke's hand; the chief of staff turned away from the wall and, breathing heavily, began to massage his injured wrist before saying, "Captain Clay, place this madman under arrest! We'll sort out the exact charges later, but I will see to it that he's breaking rocks for a decade after this war ends!"

In a silky voice, Clay responded. "Sir, before we address the actions of Lieutenant Bierce, I think I would like to know how you came into our room."

"That's of no importance, Clay."

"Please, sir. Humor me."

Hesitantly, Parke began to speak. "Well, I was in my room, catching a few winks. Haven't had much chance to sleep. Must have been lightly dozing because a voice no louder than a whisper woke me—seemed to be calling my name several times from outside the door. I shouted for whoever was there to come in; reckoned it was a courier with some message from Potter or Sanders, but the whispering suddenly stopped. Pretty damn cross, I got up and threw the door open, but no one was there. All I could see was the door to this room standing ajar. Went in, saw that open box and a Goddamn mess of broken glass. Was trying to figure out what it meant when suddenly this madman Bierce grabs me from behind and starts calling me several kinds of . . ."

"Horse shit!" exclaimed Bierce. "I come into this room and find him standing over the smashed plates. Doesn't take a Harvard man to figure out what happened."

"I seem to recall that not too many months ago, I found you alone with a freshly murdered officer," replied Clay thoughtfully. "Many would have thought no further inquiry was necessary. It is fortunate for you that I was not among them."

"Damn it Clay, that's not the same, and you know it!"

"True enough; every situation is unique. Let us see if we can find out what's unique about this one." Turning to the red-faced general, Clay asked "Sir, did you see anyone when you came out of your room? Anything unusual at all?"

"No, nothing. Just this open door. I spotted the mess and was trying to figure out what it was when this jackass . . ."

"Lieutenant Bierce is to be commended for his attention to duty—and his fearlessness. He has already demonstrated his physical bravery a number of times. However, many are the brave lieutenants who would catch a general in a compromising position and decide to see nothing. Bierce has responded appropriately under the circumstances. That will be in the report I will make, to go as far in the chain of command as need be. To Grant himself, if it comes to that."

"Still don't see what set him off," muttered Parke. "Seems to be all that was damaged was some photographic plates. Box may have fallen off the bed and flown open, the damn things smashing to bits. A shame for whoever took them, but hardly a cause . . ."

"They were more significant than you may suppose," interrupted Clay smoothly. "With respect, I will not reveal why at this instant. Who else is on this floor?"

"Don't know. As I said, I just woke up," replied Parke with heavy irony.

"Then I beg your indulgence. Let us find out."

The four Union soldiers emerged into the hallway and quickly began knocking on doors. Most rooms proved to be empty, their occupants involved in various ways preparing for the siege. However, one room disgorged General Potter, who stared with bleary-eyed befuddlement, turning a crumpled kepi over and over in his hands. A faint odor of whiskey drifted into the hall.

"What? What?" blurted the division commander in confusion.

"General Potter, did you recently enter my room, perhaps by mistake?" asked Clay.

With perceptible difficulty, Potter focused his bloodshot eyes on Clay. "No, no. No reason to. Was taking, ah, a little nap. Taking a rest. A rest."

"Sir, did you see anyone going into or coming out of that room?" asked Bierce.

Potter looked crossly at the lieutenant. He wiped a thin film of sweat from his balding forehead, jammed on his kepi crookedly, and muttered "How could I? Was resting. Excuse me, have to get to the division. Have to lead the boys." With steps that were ever so slightly unsteady, he passed by the soldiers and began to heavily descend the stairs. Parke looked after him with naked disapproval.

"The lives of good men are going to be in the hands of that sot," the chief of staff muttered.

"I suspect General Potter conquers his fear with alcohol," said Clay.

"You mean he's a coward," growled Parke with contempt.

"Not quite. I mean he conquers his fear with alcohol. If he were a coward, he would have run away long ago. It is hard to know who is more worthy of admiration: a man who knows no fear or a man who knows fear yet still risks his life. In any event, let us check the remaining rooms."

They knocked on the door to Duval's room. After a moment,

the nurse opened the door and peered at her visitors bleary-eyed, apparently having just awakened.

"Miss Duval, did you hear anything unusual taking place in our room next door?" asked Bierce.

"Why no. I was sleeping."

"But your room is next to ours, and the walls are quite thin," commented Clay.

"I am sorry, Captain, but I was very tired and was sleeping soundly."

Clay stared at her for a long moment, then said, "Our apologies for disturbing your sleep." He then spun on his heel and led the group in search of the remaining occupants of the floor. Duval left her door slightly ajar and lay back down on her cot, patiently awaiting developments.

It was in the room assigned to the absent Orlando Poe that they found the remaining occupants of the floor. Their knocking was answered by General Sanders, the tall, solemn cavalryman, a look of anguish on his face. Behind him, seated on the edge of the bed, was his wife, dabbing daintily at the corners of her eyes with a silk handkerchief. Sanders looked at the new arrivals with puzzlement and then looked particularly hard at Parke, a strange expression flitting across his face; Clay could have sworn it was akin to revulsion.

"Sir, what is the meaning of this visit?"

Clay answered for the chief of staff. "General Sanders, did you or Mrs. Sanders enter my room for any reason recently?"

"Certainly not," snapped the southerner in an offended voice. "I have been here with my wife, who is disturbed by the situation that the army finds itself in. Captain Poe was kind enough to lend me his quarters so that we could have some . . . privacy."

"Did either of you hear anything amiss in the hall?" asked Bierce.

Mrs. Sanders answered for both of them. "Not until a few

moments ago, when we started to hear a lot of going to and fro outside the door." This was obviously in reference to the search party itself. "Just what is wrong?"

"Ma'am, General Sanders, if you will be so kind as to accompany me to my room, I will be better able to answer your question," responded Clay.

Along with the rest of the party, the cavalryman and his wife crowded into Clay's small chamber. Pointing to the box and shattered plates, Clay said, "Those plates may have contained incontrovertible evidence concerning the guilt of a traitor and a murderer."

"What kind of evidence?" a voice from the doorway inquired.

Frowning at the interruption, Clay glanced at the room's entrance to see Teresa Duval, a look of innocent curiosity on her face. "Miss Duval, if you will be kind enough to join us and stand by Mrs. Sanders, I will use you in a demonstration."

Showing no sign of the sudden wariness she felt, Duval entered the room and did as she had been asked.

"Now gentlemen, please look closely at one of the ears of Miss Duval, then at the corresponding ear of Mrs. Sanders." Frowning, the various officers did as they had been asked. After they had finished, Clay continued. "Do any of you notice something interesting?"

Among general grumbling, Parke said, "Two ladies' ears. So what?"

"Please look again carefully, paying attention to the ridges of cartilage. You will note that the patterns they make are quite different."

The officers did as they were asked; the grumbling was replaced by puzzled silence.

"Now, I assure you that I could produce as many women as you would like for you to compare, and you would find no two with exactly the same patterns of cartilage. Many European scientists, the Frenchman Bertillon among them, have found that when examined closely, there are some physical aspects of every human being that are absolutely unique."

"I am afraid you have me at a disadvantage," said General Sanders in a slow, deep drawl. "It's interesting, but how does this relate to treason?"

"It would seem that the ridges of skin on the tips of our fingers are similarly unique. Furthermore, it would seem that the fingertips contain oils, which leave imprints on objects that an individual has touched. Under some conditions, those marks can be photographed and preserved. A sample can be taken from a criminal suspect and compared to the impression left at the scene of a crime. Those plates contained photographs of the marks left by a murderer and a traitor. Somehow this person found out about the plates and smashed them to remove evidence, hoping I would believe it to be an unfortunate accident." Clay noted that General Park looked at the tip of his fingers then glanced furtively at Sanders but decided not to comment. "However, the traitor was both too thorough and not thorough enough. Fragile as they are, photographic plates tend to break into large fragments, not small ones such as these; this was no accident. Yet the murderous criminal was not thorough enough; although the pieces are small, I have no doubt that with some effort, I can reconstruct enough of the fragments to obtain prints sufficient for comparison. I will then be requesting everyone here, along with Generals Burnside and Potter, to submit samples of their finger-markings. What I had planned for tonight will only need be delayed for a day or so."

"I don't think General Burnside will hold with such nonsense," said Parke. "Anyway, I'm sure he agrees the idea of a traitor among the officers of the Army of the Ohio is ludicrous."

"General Parke, it is well known that you have been very loyal to General Burnside during his troubles, and you are to be commended for that loyalty," replied Clay. "He has many enemies among the general officers of the United States Army, but so far, Grant is not among them. I remind you that I report to General Grant; it is really in the best interests of your superior that you persuade him to cooperate with my investigation."

Parke cast a murderous glance at Clay but seemed to see the force of the captain's argument. In a surly voice he responded, "Very well, tell me when you are ready, and I will see to it that General Burnside will order all concerned to participate in your damned . . . experiment."

"Thank you, General. Now ladies, gentlemen, if you will excuse us, Lieutenant Bierce, Sergeant Lot, and I must begin the daunting task of gluing together these fragments. General Parke, please be so good as to inform General Burnside that we must delay for one day the meeting I requested for tonight."

With expressions ranging from impatience to puzzlement, the others filed out of the room. Clay carefully secured the door, and turned to the other remaining occupants.

"I've said it before and I'll say it again, Clay; you're a corker," said the grinning Bierce. "Standing up to Parke like that, threatening to go over his head; it looked as if he would explode." The smile faded from Bierce's face, and he continued. "You said some highly complementary things about me, Clay. Why? I was under the distinct impression you did not care for me all that much."

Clay looked blandly at Bierce for a long moment before responding. "How I feel about you personally is irrelevant, Lieutenant. I gave you your due, nothing more or less."

Bierce looked at Clay for a moment and then turned his head away, gruffly saying, "Well, should we start piecing together the plates?"

Clay waived dismissively at the shards on the floor. "That? Oh, let us just sweep up the mess; there is no chance of getting anything useful from those fragments."

"Then why . . ." began Bierce.

"I believe Captain Clay wants to keep the traitor under pressure," interrupted Lot. "The more insecure he feels, the more likely he will be to make a mistake."

"Then what will we do while the others think that we are working?" asked Larson.

"Get a good night's sleep," replied Clay. "There is nothing useful to do until tomorrow, a day on which I expect we will need our wits fully rested and at the ready. However, first dinner."

"I'm afraid the coffee and tea may be getting cold," said Lot apologetically.

The three friends sat down to their informal repast; although it had indeed begun to cool, they forced themselves to enjoy what was probably the finest meal to be found in rations-short Knoxville. With his usual lack of manners, Bierce gobbled with unseemly haste, while Lot cast disapproving looks at him, which were studiously ignored. Clay merely picked at his salt pork, seeming more interested in his tea than the food.

When Bierce began to lick his tin plate, Lot could take it no more. "Ambrose, I know you know better than to eat like an animal. I know it pleases you to irritate others by defying convention, but in the Lord's name can you not . . ." Lot's voice trailed off as he saw that Bierce was looking fixedly past him, a dawning look of horror coming to his face. Lot twisted in his chair and saw what the young lieutenant saw.

Alphonso Clay was trembling all over; he seemed to be trying to say something, but no words were passing his lips. The tin plate dropped from his left hand, scattering its contents on the floor; it was quickly followed by the fork Clay had held in his left. Both hands scrabbled at Clay's tightly buttoned tunic, trying to loosen its collar, but the shaking allowed no purchase. Clay began to slip to the floor, but between them, Lot and Bierce caught him under the arms and leveraged him onto one of the room's narrow cots.

"What is it? What's wrong with him?" shouted a panicky Bierce.

"I don't know," replied an equally-panicked Lot. "Aside from occasional indigestion, his health has always been perfect. Quick! Get Miss Duval from next door!"

As Bierce tore out into the hallway, Clay locked eyes with Lot and gasped out, "Poisoned . . ."

"Are you sure, Alphonso?" asked the frantic Lot.

Clay mutely nodded his head affirmatively. An idea came to Lot. He grabbed Clay's saddle bag and frantically rummaged till he came up with a tin of charcoal biscuits, with which Clay treated his occasional indigestion. Lot tore open the tin and began breaking one of the soft cookies into pieces, virtually ramming them down Clay's throat. Then Duval rushed into the room, followed by the pasty-faced Bierce.

"What is wrong with Captain Clay, and what are you putting in his throat?" demanded Duval in a stern voice. '*Damnation! The dose I gave him should have killed him in seconds. Did I miscalculate?*'

"Clay has been poisoned, I don't know how," blurted the harried Lot as he continued to feed bits of biscuit to Clay. "The charcoal biscuits he takes for indigestion should absorb the poison before it all enters his blood stream. I pray we have acted in time. Is there anything else that we can do, in your experience?"

It was all Duval could do to maintain her poise. *Hell! Not only did Clay not die as quickly as he should, they are applying exactly the correct antidote. The charcoal will indeed absorb what poison is still in the stomach. I don't dare give them bad advice; their knowledge is too much for me to risk giving advice.*' "No, Sergeant, you are doing all that can be done in a case of poisoning. If it is indeed poisoning, it must have been in some of the army food; it is a scandal how careless some of the meatpackers are. Bad food kills more soldiers than Reb bullets. Lieutenant Bierce, please go and get a bucket of fresh water from a well far from any privies; we will lavage his stomach as soon as the charcoal has had a chance to take effect. Sergeant, please stand back so I can examine the captain for myself."

As Bierce scurried out of the room and Lot retreated to a far corner, Duval knelt beside Clay's bed, taking his pulse. She found it thin and erratic but not obviously failing; she was certain he would recover. '*Damnation and Hell! I gave him enough to kill half a dozen men, and he just ends up with a bellyache. Just what is Clay?*'

Suddenly Clay's right hand clamped down on her wrist with a grip of iron. The surprised Duval looked into Clay's pale blue eyes and saw them fixed on her with a weird combination of hatred and amusement. In a whisper too soft for Lot to hear, he hissed, "We will settle this another time." He then released her wrist.

As Duval stood up, she announced to Lot, "I believe the danger is past." She found herself amazed that a part of her was glad that it was so, despite the even greater risk Clay now posed to her.

After a hasty breakfast in which a still unsteady Clay refused to participate, Clay, Lot, Larson, and Bierce emerged from the hotel shortly after dawn. Although his friends begged him to rest, Clay's iron will was not to be denied; he was determined to see the perimeter before the discussion with Burnside and his officers, and that was that.

Low, thick fog covered the ground to about three feet, above which the chill air was absolutely clear. The blue-clad figures scurrying up and down the street on army business seemed to be disembodied torsos, legs largely invisible. The effect was eerie; Larson, the phlegmatic former sniper, shuddered superstitiously at the sight.

"The guard in the lobby says that Poe is already at his precious fort," commented Clay. "I think it is time for us to interview him and see with our own eyes what he is up to with this army's fortifications." Walking west through the ghostly mist, they had just left the town proper when Clay jerked his head up, just like a dog having heard an interesting sound. "Something unusual is happening off to our left," he said. "I think it may be worth a short detour to investigate." Without waiting for a response from his companions, he set off at a right angle to their path.

"Didn't hear nothin'," grumbled Larson to Bierce. "Clay must have one powerful set of ears." Bierce, who remembered the last time Clay had heard something others could not hear, frowned but did not respond.

In less than a minute the entire party could hear the murmur of flowing water, the mutterings of a number of voices, and an occasional splash. The mist parted, and they saw a stretch of the river before them. A lieutenant was directing about twenty shivering soldiers, most in frigid water up to their waists, as with pruning hooks and similar instruments they wrestled a large, crude raft to the shore. The raft contained no people; instead, it was covered with bags and barrels, each one carefully lashed to the raft.

"That's right, boys, tie it up to the shore. Don't wait to unload. Go get dry and warm in the shacks first. The cargo'll wait."

"Lieutenant, what is going on here?" inquired Clay of the officer.

The lieutenant, a short, thin youth who seemed scarcely old enough to shave, turned to respond. "Captain, a wonder for sure. Word got through the lines that the loyalists upriver heard we were about to be besieged, and that they would be floating what supplies they could find down the river on unmanned rafts, right under the noses of Reb pickets." He gestured at the contents of the raft, now safely tethered to the shore. "Just look at that. A dozen barrels of salted pork and twenty sacks of feed for the animals. Been a raft like that every three to four hours since late yesterday.

Course, it doesn't do all that much for an army of our size, but every bit helps."

Bierce frowned. "But the country hereabouts has already been stripped pretty much clean. How is it the loyalists have anything to spare?"

"They don't, sir," responded the young lieutenant. "They're starving themselves to help keep us in business. It's one thing for rich businessmen up north to claim how patriotic they are; it's another thing for a hungry man to get even hungrier for his country."

"It is indeed," responded Clay somberly. He saluted the young officer and led his party back to their original path.

As they walked on, Lot spoke suddenly. "You see why we can't abandon these people to Richmond. Their loyalty must not be rewarded by the rule of the slavocracy."

"Abandonment is no longer an option," responded Bierce with a harsh laugh. "I heard one of the officers in the lobby of the hotel say that pickets are running into Reb patrols in all directions. We're well and truly surrounded now."

With surprising suddenness, their destination loomed out of the mist. They were faced with a crude-looking, rectangular earthen structure a hundred yards on a side, where swarms of men were busily wielding picks and shovels, adding to the walls already twice as tall as a man, mainly with dirt excavated from a ditch surrounding the structure that was already deeper than a man. They could see that at the top of the steep walls soldiers were grimly sandbagging positions intended for a number of cannon. "Impressive", murmured Clay. "Am I to understand that there was literally nothing here twenty-four hours ago?"

"That's what some fellers in the lobby said," replied Larson.

The attention of Clay's party was suddenly drawn by a string of curses ringing out in Captain Poe's voice. Looking through the thinning mist, they recognized him in a group just to the west of the incomplete fort by his rigidly-erect posture. He was swearing at a group of soldiers who appeared hunched over, looking for the entire world like they were trying to tie their shoes while walking. The new arrivals approached the engineer and were able to hear with perfect clarity his next furious statement.

"Idiots! God damn you! I don't want the wire up where they can see it. Down, down in the grass and weeds. If it's more than six inches high, it's too damn high!"

Casting surly glances at their tormentor, the soldiers continued at their job, a job that seemed most peculiar. They all seemed to be tying lengths of telegraph wire to tree stumps where they existed, or to stakes driven in the ground where they did not, then anchoring them tautly to another stump or post, leaving a wire suspended between them some inches from the ground.

"Captain Poe, I must ask for a few minutes of your time," said Clay.

Poe turned his hard, disdainful eyes on Clay. "I do not have time for nonsense, sir. I have a duty to this army, and I do not care if you know Grant or Abe himself. Go meddle somewhere else, sir." He turned as if to recommence directing the strange task of the soldiers, but Clay would not let it go at that.

"Sir, I must really insist. If you care as much for the army as you say, you will spare me a few minutes."

"A few minutes! Do you have any idea how little time we have before the Rebels come charging out of the west? Every minute counts, sir. Only a few moments ago the three batteries of cannon I had pleaded for arrived. Under the best of conditions, it will take them several hours to be emplaced up on those parapets, and they must be there before Longstreet's boys attack."

"Captain Poe, what makes you think they will be coming from the west at this section? Why not go around?"

"Don't be a fool Clay! I know Longstreet will not be one. The river guards the south of the town, the east and the north have numerous hills and gullies that will break up any attack by a large body, and which give us defensive positions so strong that a handful of regiments could hold the Rebs off until Doomsday. No, a major attack will come from the west, up that slight slope; this fort is right in the middle of the only feasible avenue of attack."

"Will not Longstreet's men stream past the fort and into the town, taking just a few casualties?"

Poe looked with arrogant disdain at Clay. "You are not a West Pointer, are you?"

"I did not have that privilege."

"Then take the word of a West Pointer, a trained military engineer. I am assembling a killing ground here. The trenches and rifle pits stretching from the fort to the river on one side and to the hills on the other may not look like much. However, when manned, they will be enough to cause the Rebs to pause. You will note that I am preparing six cannon positions on opposite sides of the fort, in addition to the six facing forward. Those cannon will be double-shotted with grape, firing scores of half-inch balls with each blast. I will be able to kill as many Johnnies as Longstreet cares to send, so long as my ammunition holds out. He will have to take the fort before he can move on, and I am preparing some unpleasant surprises for Pete Longstreet. But I need time! If the cannon are not in place by the time the assault comes, then it is all for naught. So you see, I have no time for your nonsense, Captain Clay!"

Clay's attention seemed to have wandered; he was looking at the line of entrenchments stretching away from the fort, then at the fort itself. Nodding slightly to himself, he said, "Captain Poe, I believe that the risk to the army may be as great within it as without. That inner risk may indeed render your efforts for naught. If you would spare me an hour, I might guarantee that the only risks you need face are from the west."

Poe looked sharply at Clay, as if he could read some hidden meaning in his face. Clay's countenance was as bland as it usually was, but the intelligent engineer seemed to see something that gave him pause. Slowly he responded, "I suppose I can trust Lieutenant Benjamin to continue in my absence. He is less foolish than most of the subordinates with which I must deal. Let me have a word with him, and you may have your hour."

As Poe strode off toward the fort, Clay turned to the rest of his party and began to speak in a low but urgent voice. "I believe I have begun to see my way clear. However, I am still not certain. Larson, locate Potter and do whatever it takes to get him to Burnside's headquarters, but tell him that the situation will be formal, his best uniform and boots. Lieutenant, Sergeant, do the same as to General Sanders. Make sure that they clean themselves before coming to Burnside. I will handle Burnside and Parke. Now Sergeant Lot, I must ask an unpleasant task of you, one that is demeaning yet vital . . ."

Sergeant Lot finished giving a last swipe to General Potter's boots. "Very good, Sergeant, very good," said Potter in his distinctive New York accent. "Haven't seen a gloss on those in a month. Of course, you didn't really need to do it. General Burnside's seen muddy boots before." He carefully buttoned his tunic, the better of the two he had, and started for the open door of his hotel room.

"My pleasure, sir," said Lot as he straightened from his uncomfortable squatting position. "This meeting is at Captain Clay's request, and as you might have noticed, he is fussy about matters of attire. I have already performed a similar service for General Sanders."

"Well, I saw him going past the door toward the stairs a few minutes ago. I best hurry, or I'll be the last one there. Always hated being late." Potter started to reach for his hip, then caught himself. Lot realized Potter had automatically reached for his flask to "fortify" himself, and felt a pang of pity for the general.

"I will escort you, sir. Captain Clay has requested my presence as well." Potter cast a puzzled glance at the black sergeant but said nothing. The pair entered the corridor and swiftly clattered down the stairs to the first floor. To the left of the front desk was a large room that in better times had probably served as a dining room; on either side of its open door stood an expressionless sentry. Lot followed Potter into the room and firmly closed the door behind them.

Clay stood in front of the room's large, single window, his back to the occupants of the room; he stared out as if he could see the activity outside, although the thick curtains were tightly drawn. Lot approached and whispered briefly in his ear. Clay nodded curtly but did not turn. Lot joined Bierce and Larson, who leaned casually against the wall to the right of Clay.

The five other occupants of the room were seated in plush armchairs that had been arranged in a semicircle facing Clay. Ambrose Burnside was obviously trying to look fierce but only managed to appear angrily befuddled. John Parke glared at Clay, as if his stare could make him disappear in a puff of blue smoke. Orlando Poe sat ram-rod straight, his back not touching the chair; his hard eyes were unfocused, as if his thoughts were far away. Robert Potter fidgeted, licked his lips, and once furtively wiped his glistening forehead. William Sanders sat quietly wreathed in melancholy, several times casting strange glances at Parke.

Clay finally turned to face his audience. He removed his kepi and placed it on a small table to his right. He smoothed back his long, straight hair; then he produced from an inner pocket of his tunic a small photograph case, which he opened and placed alongside his cap. The crude picture in the case was obviously from the first days of photography; it showed a young, handsome man bearing a noticeable resemblance to Clay, a triumphant smile on his face, while next to him posed a woman of disturbing beauty, whose large eyes and high forehead made all who saw them uneasy for no reason they could easily say.

Clay turned to the waiting officers and clasped his hands behind his back. "Gentlemen, the time has come for me to resolve a matter of extreme unpleasantness. You are of course all aware of the death of Major von Lindau, a bullet from his own pistol through his chest. There are however, two matters of which all but one of you are ignorant. One, that he had communicated to General Grant his belief that there was a high-ranking traitor in the Army of the Ohio. Grant sent me specifically to confirm the truth of that accusation. Two, that he did not die a suicide. More accurately, he died as a sacrifice, offering up a life he knew was drawing toward its end in order to compel the traitor to incriminate himself."

A series of angry exclamations erupted.

"Lunatic."

"Deranged,"

"Impossible," and less pleasant words were traded.

"Silence!" came a bellowed command. All occupants turned to stare in surprise at Captain Orlando Poe, who had spoken to a roomful of his superiors as if they were squabbling children. Into the silence, the engineer spoke. "I wish to hear what Captain Clay has to say. If he indeed has evidence of a traitor, this must be known before Longstreet attacks. If he is a lunatic spreading defeatism, he should be arrested and court-martialed. If he intends to levy such an accusation on my honor, I will kill him."

The room was stunned. Burnside literally gasped, staring slack-jawed at his chief engineer. Then recalling himself, the commanding general said, "Well, it can't hurt anything to hear Clay out. Let us follow Captain Poe's suggestion."

Clay nodded slightly to Poe, a slight, grim smile on his face. There was no returning smile on Poe's face, only the piercing glare of the engineer's intelligent, cold eyes. Clay resumed speaking.

"There is also a matter of which all but two of you are ignorant: the destruction last night in my room of photographic plates that might have identified the traitor. One of the two people is that traitor. I do not know how von Lindau learned of the traitor, and for the moment that's not important. What is important is that he apparently had suspicions, but not proof. However, von Lindau knew himself to be dying. The surgeon Dallas Price has confirmed that he informed von Lindau of the state of his health. It must have occurred to von Lindau that the best way to give meaning to his impending death was to bait a trap for the traitor with himself. I believe that he privately did or said something that communicated his suspicions to the traitor, making it appear to be inadvertent. The evening of his death he went alone to his room in the hotel, knowing that the traitor had heard of my planned meeting with him and would suspect that von Lindau would communicate his suspicions to me. Von Lindau thought that the panicked traitor would be caught in the act. However, his murderer behaved with swiftness and lack of panic, regaining his room before any of the other occupants of the floor had opened their doors."

"This is a theory built on sand," interjected Burnside. "Without exception, everyone on that floor of the hotel was unquestionably loyal to the Union. It had to be some outsider."

Clay shook his head. "With respect, General, it was simply impossible. No one could have safely clambered out the third-story windows, at least in the brief time available; even if they had, the sentries around the hotel would have certainly noticed. There was no conceivable hiding place on the floor that we did not search, and Lieutenant Bierce was coming up the only stairway at the time, and saw nothing. No, von Lindau's death proved the truth of his belief that there was a high-ranking traitor in the Army of the Ohio."

"But why would any of us betray the country we love," blurted Burnside, anguish in his voice.

"There are many possible motives, sir. For instance, let us consider you."

"What in the hell do you . . ."

Clay waived a hand. "Hear me out. Is it not true that your best friend since your days at West Point is Harry Heath, a division commander under Lee? That you in fact have mining investments out west with him? Is it not true that you invented an admirable breech-loading carbine and founded a company for its manufacture? Is it not true that the Army refused to purchase any until after you lost control of the company in the panic of '57, and then provided contracts for tens of thousands of the weapons to the new owners? Also, during your tenure as Commander of the Army of the Potomac it is known that many of your subordinates, especially General Hooker, worked very hard to make you look worse to the country at large than your actual performance warranted. It might seem to you that the only real friends that you have were Southerners like Heath; certainly the Army of the United States has not acted as your friend."

Burnside shot to his feet. "Sir, I demand you retract that foul accusation!"

"Please be seated, General. I was only illustrating possible motives for treason. In fact, anyone who has studied your career would have found that an uncomplicated sense of honor pervades all of your actions. When your firm went bankrupt in '57, you labored for several years to pay debts that you were not legally obligated to pay, out of a sense of moral obligation. After the unfortunate attack at Fredericksburg, you could have justifiably diverted blame on subordinates such as Generals Hooker and Sumner. Even if the attack was ill-conceived, they could have served you ever so much better than they did. I concluded that you could be dismissed as a suspect."

Grumpily, Burnside resumed his seat.

"Of course, my attention then turned to General Parke," said Clay. The chief of staff turned red in the face but said nothing. "However, a seemingly irrelevant fact convinced me he could be dismissed as a suspect. General Burnside himself proclaimed that General Parke begged him not to order the frontal assault at Fredericksburg, the assault that led to General Burnside's removal from command of the Army of the Potomac. I regret saying so, General Burnside, but my study of the circumstances surrounding that unfortunate battle leaves me with the conclusion that a Confederate agent would have been urging you *to* the attack, not arguing against it." Burnside cast his eyes downward. Parke reached out and touched his commander's arm while glaring at Clay. "Also, General Parke is a highly intelligent man; it is extremely unlikely that he would have allowed himself to be caught smashing the plates. It is much more likely that the real traitor lured him into a trap, to divert suspicion."

"Of course, I considered Captain Poe." The saturnine engineer leaned forward, looking, for all the world, like a tiger preparing to leap as Clay continued speaking. "It is obvious that Captain Poe has a reluctance to submit to authority—and an unusually high opinion of himself. I have noticed these are common traits in Southerners—and those who sympathize with them." Clay favored the room with a tight, humorless smile. "In fact, it has been alleged that I myself possess these traits. Furthermore, he seemed to take several actions that would weaken the army in its coming conflict. To name two, he supported General Parke's burning of the supply wagons during the retreat and has slowed the fortification efforts to concentrate on one particular fort. However, I have concluded the things I have mentioned have no bearing on Captain Poe's loyalty. A touchy sense of pride and honor do not make a traitor, as I hope I myself prove. Next, what appeared to be actions harming the army on closer examination seem to be harsh but necessary steps taken for its preservation. Longstreet's army barely failed to catch us during the retreat. If we had been further slowed by a cumbersome wagon train, he would have undoubtedly succeeded. And the single fort upon which he is focusing all of his effort does indeed seem to be a vital link in blocking the only feasible route by which we can be assaulted with any chance of success. Although not a trained military engineer, I could see for myself that the fort is cleverly situated to devastate enemy forces to its left and right as they inevitably pause to assault the rifle pits.

"So, two are left. I considered Generals Potter and Sanders." Potter took out a handkerchief and wiped his damp forehead. Sanders looked impassively at Clay as the small blond officer continued to speak. "General Potter had no obvious motive, save certain . . . weaknesses . . . which might have left him open to blackmail by Confederate agents—and perhaps a desire for a rapid Confederate victory ending the war. Frankly, it did not seem enough of a motive, but since only he and General Sanders were on the floor when the photographic plates were broken, I had to continue to give him consideration."

"Wait a moment," interjected Parke. "How could anyone have known of the plates and their importance? You only told us of this fingermarks nonsense after they were broken."

"I am afraid that was due to an error on my part. Mrs. Sanders inquired innocently concerning the contents of the case, and I was unwilling to be rude to a lady of her station. She must have repeated what I said, not truly appreciating its importance. In any event, the traitor must have believed himself safe after he had stamped the plates into small slivers. Nevertheless, he neglected one thing. Small pieces of glass have extremely sharp edges, edges that can easily force their way into boot leather; walking further drives them in. It occurred to me that the soles and heels of the traitor's boots must have at least a few small slivers of glass. Once that occurred to me, the question became how best to obtain a careful examination of the bottoms of the boots of two generals. A demand by a captain might be met with all kinds of obstruction and unpleasantness, even outright refusal. However, if one were getting ready for an important meeting, an examination by a black man, even one in the uniform of a sergeant, might seem the most natural thing in the world to someone used to the colored boot-blacks one sees on every street corner."

Both Potter and Sanders started and looked reflexively at Jeremiah Lot, who returned the stare of one of them with implacable hatred.

Clay walked over to the chair where one of them sat and looked down expressionlessly at the general. "Yes, General Sanders, Sergeant Lot identified not less than four slivers of glass in your boots—and not a single one in those of General Potter."

The solemn cavalryman looked up at Clay, a strangely melancholic expression on his face. "That is proof of nothing, sir. Broken glass is to be found in many places. Besides, what possible motive could I have to betray my country?"

Clay's features took an expression that was not short of sorrow. "One of the best, I fear. In von Lindau's notebook, he wrote 'It was always thus with 'Sampson' and 'Delilah.' Cryptic references to a strong and honorable man undone by his love for a woman. I draw your attention to the assault by a party of Forrest's men led by Major Solomon Ward on the group I led during our retreat to Knoxville. It was obvious that the focus of the attack was on the wagon containing Mrs. Sanders. It was also obvious that the attackers were under orders not to harm the women. That is why there was little use of firearms in the assault. Major Ward and his men had already shown a distressing ability to come and go through Federal lines at will—witness their attack on the hospital before the retreat began. I do not know how Ward established contact with you, nor do I know how von Lindau discovered it. However, I believe Ward established that contact, possibly during one of your personal patrols. He must have informed you that your wife's continued safety relied on your cooperation with the goals of Forrest and Longstreet. The attack on the wagon established that you could not protect your beloved from capture or death."

"Wait a moment," interjected Parke. "Assuming that you are right, why didn't Sanders send her away when he could?"

"He tried to do so," responded Clay. "In fact, I personally witnessed one such attempt. However, Mrs. Sanders refused, out of misplaced devotion, and he could not reveal to her the urgency of her leaving without betraying his own disgrace to her. In any event, Major Ward must have established regular rendezvous locations at which to meet Sanders, at which time Ward could receive information on General Burnside's dispositions and, in turn give, instructions on how to impede the army. For instance, I remember that it was Sanders who advised against abandoning the burdensome wagons. In any event, such meetings were relatively easy, as he had legitimate reason to be riding out ahead of the army, ostensibly to confer with cavalry scouts but really to meet his new master. It was also Sanders who denounced Captain Poe's fort as a wasteful folly, when even a non-expert, such as myself, could see that that it was cunningly located and laid out."

Burnside looked at General Sanders and shook his head disbelievingly. "Captain Clay, this is unconvincing. I know William Sanders, and he would never . . ."

A frantic knocking exploded at the door. It was flung open to reveal an agitated lieutenant, eyes wild with fear. Burnside surged out of his chair and angrily said, "I told the guard no disturbances! What do you mean . . ."

"Sir, I beg your pardon," interrupted the lieutenant breathlessly. "This cannot wait. The Rebs are coming up the road. They'll be at Captain Poe's fort in half an hour; it's a major assault, and we are not ready to receive it!"

Poe stood up. "I must have three hours, at the least. Three hours! There must be a counterattack to hold Longstreet off for at least that long."

Potter also stood up. "I, ah, don't know if I can get the boys on line in that time. It will be all they can do to hold . . ."

With no warning, Sanders launched himself from the chair to the window, knocking the surprised Clay aside as he broke through the glass, the heavy drapes saving him from serious injury. Clay quickly bounced to his feet and looked out the broken window in time to see Sanders vault into the saddle of a horse and spur it smoothly into a gallop. Swiftly, Clay swept up his hat and picture case from the table and sprinted past the astonished Burnside out the door, through the lobby, and out to where the horses were hitched, followed closely by Poe, Larson, Bierce, and Lot. As each swiftly mounted a steed, Poe screamed "To the fort! To Hell with Sanders! We can deal with him later!"

In his turn, Clay screamed, "Bierce, Lot, locate Mrs. Sanders and keep her safe! Larson, come with me; we'll follow Poe."

As Clay savagely spurred his mount and stared at the rapidly dwindling figure that was Sanders he shouted, "It would appear that our errant cavalryman is making in that direction in any event." Despite the wild pace of the pursuit, Sanders was soon lost from view. He was, after all, a superb horseman. Now their attention was focused on Poe's unfinished fort. Clay risked a glance at Poe and found, to his astonishment, that the arrogant engineer was crying tears of anger.

Poe led the party galloping through the sally port, skittering to a halt in the central parade ground. Vaulting off his horse before it was fully stopped, he screamed, "Lieutenant Benjamin!"

"Sir!" came an answering shout from the western parapet. Poe scrambled up the wooden steps two at a time, followed by Clay and Larson. They achieved the parapet and glanced toward the west; less than a mile away, they saw thousands of butternut-clad soldiers, marching in grim unison. On a small hill just behind the front ranks, a group of horsemen could be spied. Despite his spectacles, Clay's vision was better than many would have believed, but at that distance, even he could not be sure that the heavily-bearded, stolid horseman in the middle of the group was General Longstreet—or that the whipcord-thin rider next to him was General Forrest.

The lieutenant snapped a salute at his superior. "Sir, the cannon will be in place in two hours, which will be about sunset. They wouldn't dare have a full-scale attack in the dark, so we would be good and ready in the morning, but I don't see how we'll get that two hours . . ." The lieutenant trailed off, looking over Poe's shoulder, and saying with wonderment, "I will be damned," he pointed to the south.

The officers looked and beheld a magnificent sight. Coming from the direction of the cavalry bivouac near the river, galloped a thousand screaming Union cavalry. In their lead, Sanders could be distinctly seen, saber pointed straight at the advancing ranks of the enemy. Although they were heavily outnumbered, they were a terrifying sight to the Confederate advance, which stopped their steady marching and prepared to receive the charge.

"He is leading his men to massacre!" exclaimed Poe. "A final act of treason."

"I suspect not, Captain," replied Clay thoughtfully. "I believe he is seeking expiation, once he is no longer able to protect his wife by doing Ward's bidding. I believe you will have your three hours. Put them to the best possible use."

Poe looked at the distant charge. The cavalry struck the Confederate front lines. Then, amidst clouds of dust and the sounds of gunfire and men screaming, most of Union horsemen dismounted; in every group of four, one was given the reins of all four horses while the other three began to fire rapidly with the Spencer carbines. Through the dust, Sanders could occasionally be spotted, directing men at weak spots, slashing at enemy officers, exposing himself suicidally at every instant. Poe finally said, "I believe you might be right. Benjamin! Come with me!"

The two engineers left Clay and Larson on the parapet to watch the progress of the battle.

Sanders was brought into the fort after dark by two burly troupers who were unashamedly crying their eyes out, carrying him in a crude stretcher. As Poe and Benjamin were busy with the final touches to the fortification, the cavalrymen were met by Clay and Larson. One, a corporal whose bright red hair screamed his Celtic origins, saluted and through his sniffles said, "Beggin' yer pardon, sir. General Sanders is dyin'. Gut-shot twice. He'd never make it to the hospitals in Knoxville; but didn't seem right to leave him out on the field. Man as brave as that shouldn't die alone in the dark."

"How did you boys do?" asked Larson.

"Shot to hell, an' that's a fact," replied the corporal. "Casualties near twenty percent. Cavalry division won't be good for nothin' for months to come. Still, General Sanders said a day was needed to make Knoxville ready, an' we gave you that day. Now, if you'll excuse us, there's still a lot of boys out on that field, and come dawn, the

Johnnies will be marchin' across it." Saluting hurriedly, the corporal and his companion scurried out of the fort into the darkness.

Clay stared down at the stretcher containing William Sanders. The dying general was conscious, but in deep shock; his jaw was set grimly, as if determined not to let a single moan escape. With difficulty, he focused his eyes on Clay and recognized him despite the dim, flickering light provided by the few oil lanterns around the sally port.

"Captain Clay," came his voice in a weak murmur. "Don't hold a grudge. You did the right thing. Gave up my honor for my wife. Shouldn't have . . . couldn't help myself. Didn't know at first all that devil would want. Lot of my boys died because of me . . . forgiveness not possible. Did wrong to Parke."

"It was you that whispered at Parke's door after you smashed the photographs," said Clay. "You left the door to my room open, knowing he would be likely to look in there first and be caught in the apparent act of destroying evidence."

"Yes." Sanders closed his eyes for a moment, then opened them and focused his gaze with feverish intensity upon the blond captain. "Parke's a revolting beast, but he's no traitor. Thought . . . if I had to sacrifice someone to protect myself, who better than that animal." A shudder passed through his body, and nearly a minute passed before he spoke again. "No right to ask, but I have two requests."

"If I can grant them with honor, I will," replied Clay solemnly.

Gingerly, Sanders moved his hand inside his rumpled tunic and slowly produced an envelope spotted with bloodstains. "Give this to General Burnside. Wrote down, just in case . . . needs to know truth about a man he trusts. Good man, Burnside—too good for this killing business."

"And the other?" asked Clay.

"My wife . . . do what you can to keep her from harm . . . was all for her I lost my honor . . . pray that . . . this last . . . balances books . . ." A gurgle came from his throat; his chest heaved once, and his eyes glazed.

Clay looked down at the general's body, an unaccustomed look of pity on his face. "I also pray that your books are balanced, General."

The assault the following morning was almost anticlimactic. The Rebels came charging out of the morning mist, screaming their inhuman yell, only to trip by the scores over the hidden telegraph wires Poe had cunningly placed six inches above the ground. Formations destroyed, and wasting time in getting to their feet and reforming, the cannon and infantry support in Poe's fort began to extract a terrible toll. Many regiments tried to swerve past the forts, only to run into the rifle pits manned by General Potter's determined men. They recoiled from blue riflemen, at the same time coming under horrible fire from the cannon on the flanks of the fort.

Clay and Larson had stayed in the fort to lend a hand. Larson had commandeered a private's rifle, assumed a place on the parapet, and was calmly and methodically firing. The ex-sniper had not lost his skill; every time he shot, a Rebel fell. Clay watched as the cannon methodically chewed up the advancing Confederates with grapeshot; he noted with unpleasant fascination that after each blast he could see objects flying into the air, objects such as rifles, knapsacks, limbs, heads, less describable parts of the human body. Yet they kept coming—these brave warriors. Clay truly wished they were serving a better cause.

At one point, at the height of the battle, Clay's attention was drawn to the left flank. To his amazement, he saw General Potter walking slowly along his lines, fully erect, apparently indifferent to the death that was splitting the air all around him. His men cheered as he walked by; some waived their kepis. At Potter's nearest approach, Clay's acute hearing alerted him to what seemed, to his amazement, to be singing. It could not be; yet it was. In the midst of the battle, General Robert Potter was singing "*The Battle Cry of Freedom*" at the top of his lungs, with those nearest him joining in as they continued to fire at Longstreet's men. Clay heard three verses quite distinctly, with Potter's surprisingly clear tenor leading a ragged chorus of his men:

> "*Yes, we'll rally round the flag, boys, we'll rally once again*
> *Shouting the battle cry of freedom,*
> *We will rally from the hillside, we'll gather from the plain*
> *Shouting the battle cry of freedom!*
>
> *The Union forever!*
> *Hurrah, boys, hurrah!*
> *Down with the traitors, up with the stars*
> *While we rally round the flag, boys*
> *Rally once again*
> *Shouting the battle cry of freedom!*"

Potter paused for a moment, then with exaggerated gestures snapped his fingers several times in the direction of the enemy. The men near him cheered, and he continued singing.

"We will welcome to our numbers, the loyal, true and brave

> *Shouting the battle cry of freedom!*
> *And although they may be poor, not a man shall be a slave*
> *Shouting the battle cry of freedom!*
>
> *The Union forever!*
> *Hurrah, boys, hurrah!*
> *Down with the traitors*
> *Up with the stars*

While we rally round the flag, boys,
Rally once again
Shouting the battle cry of freedom!"

Potter now paused in his slow march, placed both hands on hips, and visibly laughed at the approaching enemy. To increasing cheers of his men, he sang a third verse.

"So we're springing to the call from the East and from the West
Shouting the battle cry of freedom!
And we'll hurl the rebel crew from the land we love the best
Shouting the battle cry of freedom!

The Union forever!
Hurrah, boys, hurrah!
Down with the traitors
Up with the stars;
While we rally round the flag, boys
Rally once again
Shouting the battle cry of freedom!"

As Potter began his slow return walk along his lines, and the sound of song faded away, the Confederates made their final push. Realizing there was no hope of success without taking Poe's fort, the Rebels made a last desperate assault, plunging by the thousands into the deep ditch surrounding the structure and clawing their way up the steep opposite sides. However, Poe was ready for them. He had assembled scores of artillery shells with short fuses. On his screamed command, soldiers lit the fuses and heaved them into the ditch, where a rapid series of explosions turned the moat into an abattoir.

And then suddenly it was over. The surviving attackers were

streaming back to the west as fast as their legs could take them. Clay and Larson found themselves beside Poe, hardly daring to believe that it was over. Clay turned to Poe, whose face was bearing a look of smug satisfaction, and said, "Captain Poe, my congratulations. You have served your country well." Clay saluted the engineer, who did not deign to respond, but simply continued to stare into the west with pride oozing from every pore.

As they road back into Knoxville proper, Larson said to Clay, "Reckon we better stop at the hospital. They'll need to send some doctors out to the fort; we got the best of it, but there's still a lot of our boys in a world of hurt out there. Also, best make arrangements for bringing Sanders' body in for burial. Can't say I'm looking forward to telling his wife, neither."

"Neither am I," responded Clay. "In any event, here we are."

The hospital was actually a series of large tents and miscellaneous buildings, already beginning to fill with wounded as bandsmen scurried in with stretchers bearing awful burdens. Suddenly from one tent rose a scream of "Murder! Murder!"

Without hesitation, Clay spurred his mount to the tent in question. Muttering, "Here we go again," Larson followed him. The two officers swiftly dismounted, to find at the entrance a familiar figure. The man doing the shouting was the surgeon of the 27th Ohio that they had met on the road to Knoxville.

"Sir, what is amiss," inquired Clay with surprising calm.

The surgeon's eyes were wild, and it seemed to take him a moment to recognize Clay. "Oh, Captain! They shot Major Price. They kidnapped the nurses! The women . . . we must rescue the women!"

Drawing his revolver, Clay shouldered his way past the shocked surgeon into the tent. In an instant, he took in an awesome scene.

A badly wounded man lay on a table. He had apparently been

prepared for an amputation of his leg. Beside the table, Major Price was on the ground, a bleeding wound in his midsection.

"Captain, they took Mrs. Sanders and Miss Duval. A posse is needed. Captain! Captain?"

Clay did not respond. His attention was focused on an inert form on the ground not far from Major Price. It was Jeremiah Lot.

CHAPTER 6

"... WE'LL HURL THE REBEL CREW FROM THE LAND WE LOVE THE BEST ..."

The revolver slipped from Clay's fingers and thudded softly on the dirt floor. Ignoring the moans of the injured man on the table, ignoring Major Price's corpse, Clay staggered three steps forward and dropped heavily to his knees next to Lot's silent form. Tenderly he gathered the black sergeant into his arms and began rocking slowly back and forth. After a moment, a low, keening sound began to issue from his throat, a sound unlike any that the witnesses to the scene had ever heard. Periodically, it would drop to impossible depths, reverberating like the lowest notes of a cathedral's organ and then ascending multiple octaves to a sound so high it almost faded away. The survivors in the tent hardly knew how to respond and were frozen in place until a flap was thrown back and Lieutenant Bierce entered cheerfully whistling a snatch of "*The Yellow Rose of Texas*," bringing a whiff of cheap whiskey with him. He took in the scene, froze for a moment, then blurting an obscenity, rushed to Clay's side.

"Clay! Clay! What has happened here?" He shook the captain's shoulder but received no response. Bierce examined Clay's face carefully but saw only a horrifying blank expression, from the mouth of which issued the inhuman sounds of grief. Bierce turned his attention to the motionless Lot. To his own surprise, he found his eyes filling with tears.

Working gently around Clay's cradling arms, he examined the bleeding wound at the back of Lot's head, then placed two fingers to the sergeant's neck. Bierce started, then began to speak to Clay like a small child. "Clay, Jeremiah is alive. His pulse is strong. Clay, do you hear me? Clay, we need you to let him go, so the surgeon here can examine his injuries. Clay. Listen to me, Clay."

Slowly Clay turned his head to Bierce and seemed to notice him for the first time. "Alive. Are you certain? Alive?"

"At least for the time being. Come on Clay, I need you to be strong. Help me move him to the unoccupied cot."

Clay slowly shook his head as if confused by something. Then, taking a deep breath, he said, "Of course. I'll take the legs, you the arms." With extreme gentleness, they moved Lot past the table holding the moaning soldier to the unoccupied table beyond, stepping gingerly over the body of Dallas Price. The surgeon of the 27th Ohio rushed over and began to efficiently examine the wound.

"Doctor, what happened here?" asked Clay quietly.

The surgeon's voice quavered, but his fingers were swift and assured. "It happened so quickly, I can hardly say, Captain. Just as we were preparing a poor soul for an amputation, a large lieutenant came in with two cavalrymen, saying he heard someone named Captain Larson was here and that he was needed at Burnside's headquarters."

"I'm Larson," said the former sniper. "A large, handsome feller with a cheerful way about him?"

"That's the one, sir. Seemed disappointed until he noticed the two ladies that were helping Major Price. Then he said something about having to settle for the ladies and ordered his men to take them. Mrs. Sanders screamed, and Price stepped forward and asked him just what this was about. Then the lieutenant drew this big, strange-looking revolver and just . . . shot him dead. Dead, sir! Cold-blooded murder. Then the sergeant here made a lunge for the bastard, but before the brave fool could be shot, Miss Duval smacked him in the back of the head with a bottle, and he went down like he was pole-axed. Then cool as you like, she tossed the bottle down and said, 'No sense in this getting out of hand. Shall we go?' The Lieutenant looked surprised but recovered real quick. Had his men grab the ladies and told me that if I gave the alarm he'd have their throats cut. I must've stood here five minutes or more; then I just couldn't take it anymore. Couldn't take it. Started yelling, and that's when you came in."

Bierce looked meaningfully at Clay. "Sounds like our friend Solomon Ward." Bierce then shifted his attention to Larson. "Looks like he's still determined to eliminate the witnesses to the Fort Pillow massacre."

"Seems like he's worried about some sort of trial," responded Larson. "If I catch him before the law does, he won't have to worry about no rope." Larson's eyes had acquired a flat, dead look.

The surgeon had finished. "Doesn't seem to be any fracture. No real dilation of the pupils. I expect the sergeant has a concussion. Tricky, but there is no obvious reason for him not to recover."

Clay giggled, startling everyone in the room. The sound he emitted was definitely a giggle, but was devoid of any trace of amusement. In fact, it made all who heard it uneasy for no reason they could say. A shudder passed through his narrow chest; then, as if nothing out of the ordinary had happened, he turned to the surgeon and said, "I am pleasantly surprised to see you, sir. You decided not to stay with the wounded Rebels after all? Not that I blame you. Forrest's offal is not worth a visit to Andersonville."

"No, sir, I intended to stay. However, there was a real tragedy. Some straggler snuck into their tent and killed all three before I returned. Slashed their throats. What kind of monster would do that to wounded prisoners? Anyway, no point in staying for bodies."

"Indeed. I am glad that you remain free and for the service you rendered my sergeant." Clay glanced at the inert form of Major Price. "There was no point in killing that man. He was unarmed, and a skilled physician. No point at all. His killer seems to be in love with death for death's sake." He turned to address Bierce. "Best notify the provost of what happened here."

"Should I alert the pickets to be on the lookout for three soldiers with two women?"

"There is no reason, Lieutenant. Ward undoubtedly has the passwords and countersigns from . . . well, he has them. He is long gone with his hostages."

Bierce nodded grimly, and strode out of the tent. Then with some hesitation in his manner, the surgeon of the 27th Ohio turned to the two captains. "Sirs, as gruesome as it may seem under these circumstances, the soldier on the first table has the beginnings of gangrene in his leg; if there is not an immediate amputation, he is a dead man. While we wait for the provost, could you assist me by holding him steady? There was only enough chloroform to make him woozy, and I fear he will thrash around. It will not take long."

The two officers nodded and approached the table while the moaning soldier began to scream.

Clay, Larson and Bierce stood with heads bowed before two fresh graves with crude wooden crosses. At Clay's insistence, the burial party had left them alone.

Larson suddenly broke the silence. "I hear Sanders held with the Episcopalians. Anyone know Major Price's church?"

Bierce emitted one of his barking, humorless laughs. "General Potter told me Price was a free thinker. I expect he stopped believing in a God of mercy about the time the cholera epidemic in '59 carried off his wife and all three of his children." Bierce paused and added almost reluctantly, "Maybe that was why he became so obsessed with treating the sick and wounded."

"Can't say I'm much of a church-goer, so I'm not one to talk down his beliefs," replied Larson. "Still, it ain't right to leave a good man in the ground without a few words." The lanky former sniper removed his kepi, bowed his head, and began to speak. "Lord, you know the sins of the two men here a sight better than me. Major Dallas Price may not have been able to believe in you because of the hurts inside him, but he did a powerful lot of healing, and died tryin' to protect a lady. General William Sanders believed in you, but he betrayed his country and his fellow soldiers, just about the most doggone awful crime there is. Still and all, he did it because he loved his wife, to protect her, and he died tryin' to set things right. Taken together, they were good men, tried beyond the trials of other men through no fault of theirs. Sinner that I am, I ask that you forgive them and give them eternal peace. Amen." He restored his kepi and saluted the graves.

Bierce looked sharply at Clay; he could have sworn he heard the captain whisper "amen" as well. Bierce shook his head as if to dismiss the thought; it simply was not possible.

The three officers began to walk towards the hospital tents nearby. "How is Sergeant Lot progressing?" asked Larson.

Looking straight ahead, Clay said, "Very well. The surgeon is perhaps being overcautious in still keeping him confined to bed. However, I agree with the doctor that concussions can be tricky, and no chances should be taken."

Throwing back the flap to the tent, they entered to find Jeremiah Lot groggy but awake, covered with a thick army blanket to ward off the autumn chill, another folded blanket acting as a crude pillow. The surgeon was elsewhere, undoubtedly tending to other survivors of Longstreet's failed assault. The only other occupant of the tent was the soldier whose leg was amputated, now sleeping the unnatural sleep that laudanum provided.

As the three officers approached him, Bierce, with artificial cheerfulness, said, "Well, good to see you awake, you goldbricker. It is about time you stopped lolling in the shade near the water barrel and got back to duty."

"You will do no such thing," interjected the humorless Clay. "It is sheer good fortune that you are alive, no thanks to your foolishness in attacking an armed man with your bare hands. You will stay here until the surgeon tells me you are completely recovered. In a backhanded way it was good that Duval struck you, although, even there, you were fortunate. Despite what the dime novels say, it is extremely hard to hit someone in the head hard enough to render them unconscious without killing them."

"I get the point, sir," responded Lot in a feeble voice, smiling wanly. "It was just that when I saw Dr. Price murdered in cold blood, for no reason at all, something snapped inside of me. At that moment, I wanted to kill Ward and would have done so if it had cost me my life."

"I still can't figure why that Duval woman struck you," commented Larson thoughtfully.

"I blame myself for that," replied Clay impatiently. "I knew that there was something wrong about her from the moment I first clapped eyes on her."

"How could you possibly have known that?" asked Bierce.

"There was no objective reason," replied Clay bitterly. "Call it an instinct or perhaps a hunch. I didn't trust my feelings and refused to move against her because, in my own mind, I couldn't point to an objective reason to do so. I tend to worship at 'the alter of reason,' but it would seem that, upon occasion, reason can be a false god."

"Unbelievable," added Lot from his cot. "A lady with such a Christian demeanor, acting as a spy for the barbarian murderer, Ward, from the beginning. She helped deliver Mrs. Sanders into his power. When Ward learns that General Sanders died frustrating the first assault on Knoxville, he will have no hesitation in adding one more murder to his total. I fear that there is nothing we can do to save Mrs. Sanders now, much less bring Ward and Duval to justice."

Clay placed a reassuring hand on Lot's shoulder. "Do not disturb yourself about what you cannot change. Save your strength for your recovery. Sherman's forces will be here any day, and matters might proceed rather quickly when they arrive."

"Sherman will be here?" asked the surprised Lot. "What about Longstreet?"

"While you have been lollygagging around, there have been some major events," responded Bierce. "Looks like Longstreet learned of the approach of Sherman's boys and felt that with all the losses he'd had, he could not stand up to them. Our scouts have confirmed that the Rebs are leaving. It appears they're circling around Knoxville and heading east into Virginia, undoubtedly to rejoin Lee. Aside from a few roving bands of Forrest's cavalry, the danger is over, Sergeant."

"Then we've saved the loyalists," responded Lot. "I knew that somehow God would grant us victory." A wan smile flitted over Lot's face, while the atheist Bierce, genuinely fond of the black sergeant, firmly held his tongue in place.

"We will leave you to rest," said Clay abruptly. "Gentlemen, come with me." With affectionate waves to the wounded Lot, the three officers exited the tent. Once outside, Clay said, "Be so good as to walk with me for a while, gentlemen."

The three officers left the grounds of the hospital area and began strolling down the main street of Knoxville. The atmosphere was very different than it had been just a few days before. Soldiers still bustled back and forth on innumerable errands, but there were smiles on their faces as they did so. The civilian refugees that they encountered, white and black, still looked ragged and hungry, but hope and optimism shined in their eyes. The siege of Knoxville was over, and it showed.

Suddenly Clay began to speak without looking at his companions, as if thinking aloud while they walked. "During the first assault on Poe's fort, I thought I saw in the distance Longstreet and Forrest on a hill. It was so far away that I could not be certain. Still, some instinct inside of me insisted that it was them. In that moment, I felt an urge to leap on a horse, charge right through the battle and up to Forrest so that I could kill him with my own hands. It was what I wanted to do more than anything on earth, and I could die content once it was done. Of course, I resisted the impulse. Logic told me I could not make half the distance to them before I was inevitably killed."

Bierce knew the story about how the slave-trader, Forrest, had taken Clay's lover Arabella, sister to Jeremiah Lot and his cousin by Clay's uncle, and sold her to a Louisiana family who maltreated her until she took her own life. The family paid a terrible price in an evening of blood and flame. Unlike Bierce, Larson did not know the story and looked uneasily at Clay.

"I can't help but see you've got a powerful hatred for Forrest and his boys," said the lanky sharp-shooter. "Don't mind that. After what I saw at Fort Pillow, I'd pay gold to see Forrest hang, but what have *you* got against him?"

"It is a personal matter. In any event, the fate of General

Sanders set me to thinking. I am certain that Generals Grant and Burnside will want Sanders' treason kept a secret, for a number of reasons. Therefore, Sanders' death, a genuinely brave one, will elevate him to the status of a national hero. That made me realize that even if I succeed in killing Nathan Bedford Forrest, I might only succeed in making him a hero to the Confederacy. It's not enough to kill Forrest. He must be utterly destroyed, now and after his death."

Larson looked away from Clay, taken aback at the calm, unemotional way such undying hatred was expressed. Even Bierce felt a chill go through him, a chill that had nothing to do with the crisp autumn air.

"Forrest must be brought to trial, for the Fort Pillow murders and . . . for other crimes," continued Clay. "His depraved bestiality, his barbaric, uncivilized nature must be demonstrated publicly to the world. There must not be the slightest trace of sympathy or admiration for him when he goes to the gallows, even in the Confederacy." He turned his calm blue eyes on Larson. "That's why it's so important to me that you survive to testify against him. You are the only one living who actually witnessed the command to slay. With your testimony, he will not be able to claim that his men went out of control without his knowledge. And that's why I must go and see if I can capture Solomon Ward alive. I am certain that I will be able to persuade him to testify to his commander's orders. Also, if possible, I will rescue Mrs. Sanders from his clutches, if she still lives. I promised Sanders I would try to protect his wife while he lay dying, and a Clay will not go back on such a promise."

"You aim to do that alone?" asked Larson. "It don't seem the smartest thing in the world. Should at least let me and Bierce tag along. Besides, how do you aim to find Ward, short of walkin' up to Longstreet's whole army and asking for him?"

"I believe if I move quickly, it is possible to snare him. When we were going through General Sanders' effects, I found a small scrap of paper. It contained, in his own hand, directions to a small farm that appears to be northeast of Knoxville. The paper has no indication of what the place is. It might possibly designate a meeting-place, directions to which were provided by Ward during their last meeting between the lines. There would almost have to be such a meeting place, in order that Ward could receive information from Sanders. Ward did not dare use his disguise of a Union officer too many times to penetrate our lines. As leader of our cavalry and responsible for scouting, Sanders could venture alone outside our lines without arousing too much suspicion. Right now, time is of the essence. As part of Forrest's cavalry, Ward is undoubtedly staying in the area to screen Longstreet from Sherman's advance, but as soon as Longstreet has a good head start, the cavalry will follow. That's why this must be done today."

"Sounds like another one of your corkers," added Bierce cheerfully. "I really wish you'd let Larson and me come along for fun."

"Gentlemen, it is not a question of your bravery; both of you have demonstrated that many times over. It is just that I am likely to fail, with or without your help, and I would prefer that neither of you suffered the consequences of my failure. Please be so good as to watch over Sergeant Lot. That is the greatest assistance you can render me." They had reached the hotel that served as the army headquarters. Clay turned and saluted his fellow officers saying, "Good-by gentlemen. We will meet again within one day, if we meet again at all." Without awaiting their response, he strode into the building.

Clay walked into the ground-floor parlor that served as Burnside's office. To his surprise, it was General Potter sitting behind the commander's desk. Potter himself was surprised. He had been staring moodily at a hip flask clutched in one hand

and glanced at Clay guiltily. As Clay saluted, Potter lay the silver container carefully aside and said "Yes, Captain, what is it?"

"My apologies, sir. I expected to find General Burnside here."

"He is gone for several hours with General Parke, out to the west. They're hoping to establish contact with General Sherman's vanguard this very day. General Burnside could easily have left that to subordinates, but he felt very restless and decided to go himself. In any event, he has left me in command in his absence. How may I be of service to you?"

In a few clipped sentences, Clay explained his madcap plan. Potter looked at him and occasionally nodded, but it was obvious that the general's thoughts were elsewhere.

"In any event sir, I need your permission to leave our lines—and a pass to assure no trouble from the pickets," said Clay in conclusion. "Ward's repeated penetration of our lines in the guise of a Union officer has left our people suspicious, if not positively jumpy."

"If this is what you want, then be it on your head," replied Potter with surprising fatalism. He took a pen and a small piece of paper, swiftly wrote a couple of lines on it, and scrawled his signature at the bottom. Handing it Clay, he said morosely, "I fear your chances of success are small, Captain, but you do have my best wishes for securing Ward and liberating Sanders' widow."

Clay took the pass and pocketed it but did not immediately turn to leave. Instead, he focused his pale blue eyes on Potter for some moments, and then spoke. "General, I was privileged to witness your bravery during the final Rebel attack on our lines. The way you slowly walked back and forth in full view of enemy marksman, showing not the slightest concern for danger—even singing a patriotic song. It must have greatly heartened your men in the moment of their greatest peril. They must have believed you the bravest officer they had ever seen."

"The greatest fraud they had ever seen," murmured Potter.

"You might as well know, Captain, I was terrified. Terrified out of my wits."

"That may be, sir, but you showed no sign of it. They all must have seen what I saw: a calm, collected leader who placed himself in great peril to provide an inspiring example."

"That may be what they saw, but that is not what I am. I am a fraud who fears dying with every waking moment and can hardly get through a day without alcohol."

"Were you in liquor during the attack?" asked Clay quietly.

"No. No, I wasn't. Strangest thing, Clay. At the height of the battle, I had no need of it at all. It's only before or after that I seem to need its help. Thank God for the men that I hadn't . . . well, I had held off . . ." Potter's voice trailed away, and he glanced at the flask on the desk with something akin to fear.

"General, I will now be presumptuous, and I would not blame you if you took offense," said Clay. "Nevertheless, this must be said, just between the two of us. You may be afraid, but you are not the coward you fear. A coward would have run away during the attack—or drank himself senseless. When your men needed your example to overcome their own fears, you did not fail them. Nonetheless, you must consider that if you continue to . . . overindulge, you will be of no use to them. Someday there might be a sudden call for your leadership, and you will fail that call. I do not believe that you need to rely on spirits, but you must be your own judge on this matter."

Before the astonished Potter could respond, Clay smartly saluted, turned, and left the room.

The bearded Confederate leaned lazily against a tree, slowly chewing tobacco while he considered his future. There was no doubt that being in Major Ward's "special squad" beat the hell out of being with the rest of the company, never mind with Forrest's other units. True, there was a good chance of being killed in Ward's service, but there was a much better chance of that with the rest of the army. No frontal assaults against entrenched infantry or into the maws of cannon for Ward's pets.

Aside from that one botched raid on Burnside's column just before the bluebellies made it to Knoxville, it seemed service with Ward was just about the safest place you could be in the Confederate army. Even that raid would have been a cakewalk if they could have all used their Colts, reflected the man. Still, Ward had ordered no chance be taken of killing the women by accident, and if the man had learned one thing, it was that you did not cross Major Solomon Ward. He remembered the punishment that had been meted out to a cavalryman who had not followed orders exactly, and he shuddered.

The man spat tobacco juice and continued to think on his future. Yes, the danger was not great, and the rewards were considerable. Those on Ward's "special squad" got paid in gold out of Ward's own pockets—none of that worthless Confederate paper for the special squad. Still, he pondered, maybe it was time to take French leave, filter up into the north, and lose himself in one of the big cities there.

Everything about the special squad was beginning to get on his nerves. Even the gold wasn't quite right—always Spanish pieces at least two hundred years old. And the things the special squad had to do from time to time! It was not that he minded killing nigger-loving Union sympathizers, he told himself. They deserved all that they got. It was the *way* the major insisted they be killed sometimes that bothered him. It was all right to kill those Yankee-lovers at that farm last month—maybe even all right to put out the traitor's eyes. However, to make him watch what was done to his boy first was too far—never mind what was done to the boy himself. The man regarded himself as a free thinker who had left Christian superstitions far behind. Still, he shuddered at the mere thought of nailing the poor little bastard upside-down on the cross—and of what had been done to the tyke's heart.

In its own way, he thought the girl was even worse. To his surprise, he had not actually been able to participate in the . . . enjoyment of the girl. The man knew he was not the only one in the special squad that was becoming unnerved at some of Ward's actions. No, he thought, it was about time to go—perhaps this very night. He had saved most of the Spanish gold Ward had given him. With a good horse and a few rations, he could be clean up to Kentucky before . . .

Swift as lighting, a blue-clad arm snaked around the tree against which the rebel lounged. The arm ended in a bright piece of metal, which sliced once. His life's blood gushed out in powerful squirts. The man was only able to gurgle softly once, before he fell to the soft forest floor and died. Alphonso Clay stepped quietly from behind the tree and looked expressionlessly at the man he had just killed. He leaned down and wiped the blade of his Bowie knife clean on the man's clothes, just like he had done a few minutes before, after having snuffed out one of the dead man's comrades.

He then looked down the slope at the rude cabin near the stream, just where Sanders' map had indicated that it would be. Six horses were tethered to various nearby trees, which implied Ward and three troopers, assuming there had been a separate horse for each of the two women. Clay had dispatched the two who had been assigned as sentries. That left Ward and one other armed man inside the cabin, calculated Clay. Not impossibly long odds, since he had dispatched the sentries before they could give the alarm. His main concern was that Mrs. Sanders might be harmed if he did not approach this in just the correct fashion. He was also apprehensive about whether Duval was inside and what role she would play. He did not underestimate the danger she could pose but felt additional motivation from the opportunity to deal with her. Clay always believed in killing two birds with one stone wherever possible.

Moving with the assured stealth of an Indian, Clay glided from tree to tree, angling his approach to avoid the door and the cabin's single window. It was true that the door was closed, the window covered with tarpaper, but Clay was determined to take no unnecessary risks. Having attained the cabin wall to the left of the door, Clay smoothly drew his Smith & Wesson Number 2, carefully cocking it. Drawing a deep breath, he surged into motion, kicking the door open and leaping into the cabin's one large room.

Ward was sitting at a plank table with Marjorie Sanders and Duval. The instant the door had flown open, Ward leapt to his feet, jerked the indignant widow in front of him with one arm while drawing his large LeMat revolver with the other, and held the massive weapon to her head. A surprised cavalryman stood frozen in the act of tending a kettle that hung over the fire that fitfully smoked on the hearth. Teresa Duval sat quietly at the table, to all appearances unconcerned.

Ward laughed heartily. "Well, well, Alphonso Clay, at last. I had begun to give up on my hopes that you would act on the map I left Sanders. I am relieved that my faith in you was not misplaced."

Clay frowned slightly in puzzlement, but the revolver in his hand was rock-steady. "Release Mrs. Sanders. If you and your man surrender without resistance, you will be taken prisoner according to the usages of war."

Ward laughed again. "My, my, a true barracks lawyer. Usages of war, indeed! Do you recognize the gun in my hand? It's a LeMat. A truly fearsome gun. Nine chambers containing .42-caliber balls, and a central barrel with a load of buckshot. I've set the trigger to fire the central barrel at the slightest touch. If you do not immediately drop your weapon, I will blow this woman's head apart. I know that you are capable of killing me at this range without harming Mrs. Sanders, but you know that you could not stop me from reflexively pulling the trigger."

"Don't listen to him! He'll never kill that bitch!" shouted Duval suddenly.

"On the count of three, then," said Ward. "One . . . two . . ."

Clay made his decision in an instant. In a smooth action, he uncocked the Smith & Wesson and allowed it to fall to the floor. He knew that he could kill Ward in a moment, but that in that moment, Ward could put a load of buckshot into the head of his hostage. He gave no thought to putting himself into Ward's power. He was a Clay and incapable of violating his promise to the dying General Sanders and allowing his wife to come to harm.

"Much better," responded Ward. "Now we can talk in a civilized manner like gentlemen. Please be so good as to sit in the chair I have just vacated."

As Clay walked around the table, eyes never leaving Ward's face, he said "I have done as you wish. Please unhand Mrs. Sanders." Clay sat in the empty chair ramrod straight, his spine never touching the back of the chair.

With a laugh, Ward released his hostage. "Please collect the good captain's weapon." A smile on her face, Marjorie Sanders stepped over to where Clay had been, bent over to retrieve the revolver, and brought it back to Ward, who responded, "Thank you, my dear."

Clay's eyes widened, the only outward sign of the stunning shock that he felt. Teresa Duval glared savagely at him, saying, "Stupid bastard. I warned you. They're in it together." Her New England twang was gone, replaced by a definite Irish brogue. Clay turned to look at her, and from his seated vantage, he could now see that her hands were tied together, while a stout rope around her middle secured her to the chair itself. He turned his attention back to Ward, who was now pointing his LeMat at Clay, while Mrs. Sanders took his arm possessively and smiled.

"I see," Clay said quietly to her. "How long have you and this animal been lovers?"

The smile left Marjorie Sander's face. "That comes ill from the man the newspapers still call '*The Beast of New Orleans*.'" She nodded to the trooper by the fire. "Pierce, please bind Captain Clay as securely as you did the white trash."

"More securely," added Ward. "He has abilities that might surprise you." Clay did not resist as the solder warily tied first his hands and then his feet, always taking care to stay out of Ward's line of fire. Finally, after gingerly relieving Clay of the Bowie knife, he fastened Clay to the chair, giving a vicious last jerk as he finished tightening the bonds. The soldier seemed mildly disappointed that Clay gave no sign of discomfort. He then said, "Major, want that I get Hopkins and Sweeney?"

"Oh, by all means find their remains; I expect our visitor has taken care of them very efficiently."

With a surly glance at Clay, the soldier left, closing the door behind him. With a flourish, Ward brought a chair over to Sanders, who daintily settled herself in it. Finally, he drew up the room's remaining chair to the table across from Clay, seated himself, and stared at the captain with bright-eyed satisfaction.

Clay shook his head slowly. "I should have suspected someone of your character would not normally travel with a Praetorian Guard of only three. You lured me here and did not want me warned off by impossible odds."

"A risk Clay, but an acceptable one, given that I expected you to be bold and energetic."

"So, how do you propose to deliver me to Richmond?"

With a laugh, Ward replied, "Who said anything about delivering you to Richmond?"

Clay seemed taken aback. "I assume the purpose of this trap was to secure me for a public trial over my actions in New

Orleans. A trial very embarrassing to Washington, here and in Europe."

Mrs. Sanders laughed softly. "We certainly do not wish to see you hang, Captain Clay. When the Confederate Congress passed an act requiring General Benjamin Butler to be executed upon capture rather than taken prisoner, as punishment for his crimes in Louisiana, did you never wonder why you were not included in its provisions as well?"

Reluctantly, Clay replied, "It had struck me as strange, madam."

"Wade Hampton and others of us worked quietly behind the scenes to have your name dropped from the legislation. President Davis was disturbed by that but had to accept it. Wade Hampton owns over one hundred thousand acres and twenty thousand slaves, and Davis simply does not have the power to run afoul of Wade and our other friends."

Teresa Duval could no longer stay silent. "And who are these 'friends' you keep talking about?" she rasped.

Ward laughed. "Captain Clay knows. Why don't you illuminate your scrub friend there?"

Clay said only two words. "Starry Wisdom."

Ward laughed again. "Oh, the newspapers! How they liked that name! So sensational! It was merely an alias given to our New England friends, a name that would make them seem at worst a collection of religious cranks. Our group is so old and far-flung, it has no common name. So hard to take a group calling itself 'Starry Wisdom' seriously—so hard to persuade officials to waste time looking deeper into its activities." The smile left his face. "Your late friend, John Brown of Providence, proved we were overconfident. Of course, Professor Slaughter was a fool and left evidence where none should have been left, but still, any large group has a few fools, and we should have taken that into account."

Frowning, Duval asked Clay, "What's this English-loving bastard talking about?"

Ward was laughing again. "Yes, by all means tell the slut, Clay."

Never taking his eyes off Ward, Clay said, "I have no idea to what this man refers."

"Why, he is referring to a small group that seek knowledge, and through that knowledge power, Miss Duval," responded Sanders in a sweet voice. "Power beyond the imaginings of most people—not just the power of superior people over slaves, not just the power of people of quality over white trash, not even power over a nation. For those who believe, for those who help, power literally beyond imagining."

Duval laughed harshly and turned her attention to Clay. "English-loving bitch must have the pox! Only someone with a softened brain could . . ." She trailed off.

Clay was not laughing. He stared at Ward and Sanders with an expression of disgust, but not mirth or disbelief. "You cannot. Too much is uncertain, the risks too high. You do not have the knowledge," he said.

Ward's expression sobered for a moment. "True enough. Starry Wisdom has built great influence and acquired great wealth, done in ways that would astonish your friend, but of course not you. However, the key to the ultimate eludes us. Oh, we've tried over the decades, we've tried. You might be surprised to know how many of Wade Hampton's twenty thousand slaves have disappeared in our efforts to find that key. And then we learned of your existence and deduced what your German grandfather must have done, realizing that you yourself might be the key. That's why it was so important to possess you alive. When we learned of your presence with the Union army, obtaining you intact became my principle assignment, although certain other duties also occupied my time."

"You are quite mad," responded Clay, the first hint of fear marking his placid features. "Friedrich von Juntz was nothing more than a scholar, about whom the ignorant rabble assembled outrageous stories."

"Tell me then, what was the name of your grandmother? What was the name of your mother's mother, von Juntz's mate? From whence did your mother spring?"

The bound Clay shrugged his shoulders. "My mother was a natural child of a Prussian Junker. There was undoubtedly shame, and the mother's name was hidden."

"We have been able to piece it together. Some from your grandfather's *Unausprechlichen Kulten,* which had hints of what we had already learned in other ways, and which revealed so much more: the unknown nature of your grandmother, the strange manner of your grandfather's death, torn literally to pieces while in a locked room. Furthermore, your father was at one time a member of our brotherhood, although he broke with us due to his lack of belly for the methods we were exploring. You of course knew of his association with us, did you not?"

The faintest spots of red appeared on Clay's cheeks. He did not reply.

Then Ward continued. "Cicero Clay was a hypocrite of the first water. He broke with us because he disapproved of doing what needed to be done, but when he learned of your mother's existence, he virtually flew across the Atlantic. I imagine he expected to set forth a whole brood of superior Clays on the world. He did not anticipate your mother's death in childbed. Still, he had you. It wasn't perfect; nothing ever is. Take your vision, for instance; it is a shame about the spectacles. However, all else worked as he had hoped."

"What is this bastard talking about?" growled Teresa Duval. Beneath the level of the table, out of sight of Ward and Sanders, with the tiniest of motions, she was flexing her wrists, the wrists that she had braced as hard as she had dared while she was being bound and had now relaxed, leaving slack. The amount of slack was tiny, but sweat was beginning to lubricate her efforts, and she was confident that she could discretely free her hands if given enough time.

"Tell her Clay," responded Ward with a laugh. "Tell her how you were always the number one student in every class you ever took, without exception. Tell her how you ranked number one at Miskatonic College and at Harvard, the finest universities in the Americas. Tell her just how fast you can be, just how strong you are, when the need arises. We know. We have been discretely checking ever since we realized what Cicero had done. Tell her the abilities your ancestry gives, what you can command—like calling to like, as it were. Tell her about the night at the Devereaux plantation, when you held your dead nigger whore in your arms, uttering the words, and the response you received. We had the story from a witness. If you had made certain preparations, the response would have been all you desired."

Clay turned to Duval. He gave no sign that from his angle he could see her patiently working on her bonds. "Miss Duval, I fear we have fallen into the hands of a 'monomaniac,' suffering from what some of the European alienists call a 'fixed delusion.' It is best to do what he says; such people are very dangerous when their delusions are contradicted."

Ward's mask of affability began to slip. "Tell the cracker what you like! You know I speak the truth. Well, you will be coming with us as a prisoner, with this woman as hostage for your good behavior. There is a place on one of Hampton's estates where we will have complete privacy. We hope that you will see the point of voluntary cooperation. Regardless, we will eventually have your cooperation, voluntary or no. Think of that on our journey because I assure you, we will stop at nothing, literally nothing, to shorten the way."

In a voice scarcely above a whisper, Clay said, "Was not owning human beings as chattels, treating them as objects, enough for your thirst for power? Do you realize what your success will mean for mankind?"

"Who cares about the white trash, much less niggers, chinks, and Indians?" replied Sanders. "The elite will rule as they should. I started to explain that to my husband, once Solomon had inducted me into the mysteries, but William was weak," she said thoughtfully, not a trace of sorrow or guilt in her voice. "I saw the look of growing horror on his face, and I realized that the same weakness that kept him enslaved to the pitiful democracy of the Union kept him blind to my love for Solomon. His weakness would never allow him to be free of conscience or delusions of morality—as a truly superior person should be. I convinced him that I was playing a joke—the poor fool, such putty in my hands. Later I came up with the idea of having Solomon pretend to threaten my life, in order to obtain William's cooperation. Poor, love-struck idiot! There was nothing he would not do to protect me."

"You are both quite mad," said Clay, a note of wonder creeping through his voice. He gave no sign that with his excellent peripheral vision he saw what the table prevented the lovers from seeing: that Duval had succeeded in slipping her hands free but continued to hold her arms as if still bound.

Teresa Duval was extremely glad that she had spent some time with that traveling magician some years ago, the one who had taught her his secrets of escaping from various kinds of knots. Now, however, came the hardest part. Willing herself to keep the rest of her body absolutely still, she inched her hand toward the cunningly concealed pocket in her dress. When Ward had first captured her, he had relieved her of the Sharp's pepperbox but had not detected the slim, specially sharpened razor. With tiny movements, she edged the implement into her hand, opened the blade, and began to cut with delicate motions the rope that held her to the chair. She was confident that she would be free in moments. She only hoped that Clay did not notice what she was doing and give the game away with his reaction. Luckily, Clay appeared to be oblivious, keeping his eyes focused on Solomon Ward.

"With all of your delusions, I am surprised you had the time to try to assassinate Captain Larson," commented Clay sarcastically. "With such power within your grasp, why should you fear any tale he might tell about Fort Pillow?"

A genuinely uneasy look flitted across Ward's face. "I have always been aware that chance might thwart our goals. If any other policeman but John Brown had looked into the child disappearances in Providence, I am sure Professor Slaughter would have been able to throw dust in his eyes, and success would have ours without your assistance. Chance thwarted our carefully nurtured plans *then*. And *now*, I need to assure that there is no credible witness to what happened at Fort Pillow. I do not underestimate how dangerous a man Nathan Bedford Forrest could be. I would not want him as a complication as we move toward our goal."

Clay looked genuinely confused. "Why on Earth would you fear Forrest? You implemented his obscene order—and did it very well."

Ward laughed, but now his laugh was somewhat forced, and he replied with anger in his voice. "Damn low-born scrub, placed in a position to give me orders! That demonstrates why there is no more hope for the Confederacy than for the Union. I knew how to deal with niggers who dared to take up arms against their betters, and told him so, but the money-grubbing scrub told me to take the darkies for sale and the white officers as prisoners. Imagine, telling me what to do with property in rebellion! Well, as soon as he was out of earshot, I gave the order to kill everyone."

Clay looked stunned. "That is not possible," he said in a voice so low as to be almost a whisper. "The massacre must have been Forrest's doing. It must have been."

"When Forrest found out what happened, he was almost out of his mind with rage," responded Ward. "Not about the dead Yankees, he could not have cared less about them. I had made an error. I did not realize just how seriously he took someone defying his orders. He threatened to kill me on the spot, and I knew that he meant it. That kind of threat is to be respected from Forrest, illiterate scrub that he is."

A trace of a smile flitted across Clay's face. "I can well understand your concerns. People in both North and South are still talking about the little disagreement he had with one of his staff officers a few months back."

"What is that? I don't believe I heard of it," said Duval, her rigid posture giving not the slightest sign of the tiny back-and-forth sawing movements of her hands as she delicately attacked the rope that bound her to the chair.

"The account I read was hardly credible," explained Clay. "The story went that the argument escalated until the young officer drew his Colt and shot Forrest in the belly. Instead of falling, Forrest grabbed the man's gun arm, drew a small clasp knife from his pocket, and eviscerated his assailant. What's even more unbelievable is that Forrest recovered within weeks from being gut-shot, which frankly seems impossible."

"You can believe it," said Ward grimly. "I came on the scene moments after it happened. So you see, it's not cowardice but healthy respect that makes it necessary for me to hide my responsibility for doing what needed to be done at Fort Pillow. Of course, in time, I will be in a position to render Forrest harmless to myself, or anyone else, but I must be circumspect until then. In any event . . ."

The door was flung open. Ward's soldier strode into the room, murderous fury on his face. "Hopkins and Sweeney are dead all right," the soldier grated. "He slaughtered them like sheep! I'll have the Yankee bastard beggin' for death."

"You will do no such thing," interrupted Ward. "Fortunes of war, and all that. Captain Clay will be our guest on a very long ride. You will be extremely cautious about him, but his life must never be put at risk. Now go prepare the horses. After they're ready, we will very carefully secure the captain and his lady-friend so that they will not be able to make a break, and then start immediately."

"But Major, ain't we gonna bury . . ."

"No time for that Pierce. However, what I intended to pay them will fall to your portion; I presume that will sooth your grief over your late comrades."

"Well, all right," responded the soldier, somewhat mollified. He turned and left the cabin.

Ward then spoke to his paramour. "My dear, it is best for us to answer the calls of nature before we set out. Of course, one of us should stay with our guests at all times. Please keep them entertained for a few moments. When I return, I will perform the same service for you." He handed Sanders the LeMat. Despite her delicate appearance and the massiveness of the weapon, she took the gun and held it with familiarity, barrel aimed between Clay and Duval. Ward left the cabin. Holding the pistol rock steady, Sanders smiled sweetly at the two captives. Clay ignored the blonde woman and addressed his fellow captive. "Miss Duval, I believe I owe you something of an apology. I could tell from the moment I met you that you were up-from-the-gutter Irish and were aping the manners of your betters to conceal something unsavory."

"Captain Clay, if that is your apology, I dread your insults," responded Duval with a cynical laugh. She had finished severing the rope around her belly but kept it from falling by holding the severed ends with her fingertips; the table continued to block

Marjorie Sanders' view. Duval now realized that from his angle Clay could see perfectly well what she had done, but had not given the slightest sign. She decided that the next few moments would be interesting indeed.

"I am curious as to why you struck Sergeant Lot."

"The stupid darky was going to start another brawl, in which I feared I would be killed. It was the purest of self-preservation, Captain."

Clay stared steadily at her for a moment, then said, "It is very lucky for you that you did not kill him. I have obligations to the sergeant that would have required me to take certain actions, actions that would be distasteful to me, should he have died. This is over and above what I owe you for an extremely unpleasant evening. What did you use, digitalis in the tea?"

Duval emitted one of her silvery, heartless laughs. "Luck had nothing to do with the sergeant. I have had some experience with the cosh in my earlier life, and I know just how much force will stun a man and just how much will break his skull. If he lived, it's because I didn't want him to die." She paused, then spoke with a note of genuine regret in her voice. "As for the . . . other thing, I felt that you were a threat to me and needed to be put out of the way. Believe me or don't, I am somewhat pleased that I was unsuccessful."

Clay looked appraisingly at her, then replied, "You're a very remarkable woman, Miss Duval. It was obvious from the first that you were playing a very deep, sinister game. I still believe that you are, although I now see it is not on behalf of the Confederacy, or of Major Ward's friends. To my shame, I allowed the deference I automatically feel toward a well-born woman to lull my suspicions concerning Mrs. Sanders. With hindsight I can see that she yields nothing to you in the arts of deception and concealment."

Sanders frowned and said "That is very ungallant, Captain."

However, Clay ignored her and continued to speak to Duval. "I am curious about a few things. Now that it seems that the proper authorities will not ever be hearing what we discuss, I hope you will satisfy my curiosity. It was you who killed the three wounded Rebels, was it not?"

Duval hesitated, then just nodded her head once.

"That puzzles me. Why did you do it? You are clearly not a Union irregular."

Duval frowned, as if something unpleasant had crossed her mind. "I have no love for the English; why is something I will keep to myself. But when I see the damned Rebels trying to bring in the English aristocracy, setting up class distinctions, aping aristocratic manners, giving them airs over those in the dust, it causes me no love for anyone who follows the stars and bars." She hesitated, then added, "It was stupid of me to take the risk; it did not aid me in my . . . job. But that little surgeon from the 27th Ohio is a good man—a fool and an idealist, but a good man. God knows there are precious few of them. When I heard him say he would stay with those bastards even if it meant Andersonville . . . well, it just didn't seem that I should let that happen, if I could prevent it without risk to myself. It wasn't too difficult, after all."

Clay shifted his gaze to Mrs. Sanders. "Madam, you can see that there is indeed a large difference between yourself and Miss Duval, but it is not one of class and breeding. I am certain that there are many dark corners in her background, but unlike you, she will occasional give consideration to something beyond her own wants and desires. Certainly she would never lower herself to betraying a good man who loved her, for an animal lust after a creature such as Ward, rendering herself lower than the grimiest Louisville whore."

Marjorie Sanders was not accustomed to being addressed in such a manner. A hard, angry look on her face, her attention completely on Clay, she leveled the revolver directly at the center of his chest and said "How dare you! If you were not so vital . . ."

Duval took instant advantage of the distraction Clay had provided her. She hurled herself across the table, razor in hand. The impact knocked the surprised Sanders backwards out of her chair. The two women landed hard on the floor in a confused tangle. With one hand, Duval held the arm that possessed the gun away, while she slashed at the other woman's throat. At the last instant, Sanders ducked her head to protect her neck, and the blade instead inflicted a deep wound on her cheek. Crying out and reflexively dropping the gun, Sanders shoved Duval violently away and rolled to the far wall, clutching her wounded face and screaming. Swiftly pocketing her razor, Duval quickly scooped up the LeMat and pointed it at Sanders.

"Don't kill her!" bellowed Clay. "We may need her to negotiate our escape. Come cut me loose before Ward and his man return."

Glancing at Sanders and seeing the woman was rolling back and forth on the floor, unlikely to be a threat for the moment, Duval turned and walked toward Clay, reaching into her pocket with her free hand, removing the razor and flipping it open with a casual movement of her wrist. She thought to herself that she would have no need of Clay in effecting her escape and that Clay suspected far too much about her to be allowed to live. As Clay looked steadily at her through his wire-rimmed spectacles, she reflected that all that was needed was a quick slashing of his throat; then using Marjorie Sanders as a shield she could easily kill Ward and Pierce. After that, she would dispatch the woman, and no one would be left who could tell tales.

She reached Clay, bent over, and to her immense surprise, severed the bindings on his wrists with a few strokes. A few more freed him from the rope around his body. Clay stood up, massaging his hands to restore circulation, while Duval stood immobile, marveling how her body had rebelled against her conscious plans, and searching her mind for some explanation.

Hurried steps were heard approaching the door; Sanders' cries had attracted attention. With an impossibly quick movement, Clay plucked the revolver from Duval's hand, cocked it, and swiveled it toward the door just as Pierce burst into the cabin, Colt in hand. Clay fired, and Pierce's head jerked; the cavalryman fell backward into Ward, who reflexively grabbed the dying man. Clay pointed the revolver at Ward's head, cocked it, and said, "Please raise your hands, Major, and join your paramour in the corner."

Casting a venomous look at Clay, Ward let the soldier's body slide heavily to the ground, and he went to the corner where Sanders now lay softly weeping, clutching her wounded face, blood oozing between her fingers. "What have you done to her?" he snarled.

"Silence. She had a disagreement with Miss Duval. Miss Duval seems to have had the better of the argument. I believe the wound is rather superficial, although unpleasant to view. You may tend to her as best you can, but do not utter a word." Clay then turned to Duval. "Take one of the horses and ride like the wind for Knoxville. Explain the situation there, and immediately return with a cavalry squad. These are very dangerous people, and it is just possible that there are more of Forrest's men around. It would be unwise for us to transport these prisoners to Knoxville by ourselves. Pushing the horse as fast as you can, it should take half an hour for you to attain Knoxville. To explain the situation, obtain an escort, then return should take about an hour. I will therefore see you in about an hour and a half. Alas, there is one thing that I want from you before you go."

"Really?" said Duval as she restored her weapon to its hiding place.

"I am certain that if I inquire deeply into your background, I would discover a number of criminal, unsavory matters. However,

I am all too aware that you could discover the same in my background, and I am not a hypocrite. Therefore, as a condition of my not making further inquiries, I want your word of honor that you have not in the past and will not in the future take any actions against the Government of the United States, or in favor of the so-called Confederacy. Oh, and that you will make no more attempts upon my life."

Duval laughed her silvery laugh. "My word of honor? Honor is a fiction, a meaningless concept used by aristocrats to justify their pride and greed. You would not seriously put store in any such assurance from me, would you?"

"Do I have it?" replied Clay.

Duval started to laugh again but checked herself. Looking strangely at Clay, she said, "I will not phrase it 'terms of honor,' but you can wager the farm that I will never help English-loving bastards like those two in the corner. As for the other matter, it would seem there is no longer a need for me to take such . . . decisive action."

Nodding his head, Clay replied, "Very well. Now make haste. Take whichever of the horses outside seems the strongest. I will see you in ninety minutes." Duval strode out of the cabin, banging the flimsy door behind her. Clay turned to his prisoners. Ward had helped Sanders to her feet. She was holding her lover's handkerchief to her wounded cheek; the bleeding had slowed with the pressure, proving Clay's assertion that the wound was relatively superficial.

Holding his arm around Sanders, Ward looked at Clay with a weird mixture of rage, fear, and plaintiveness in his features. "Clay, it is still not too late," he said urgently. "We can be gone long before the bitch returns with soldiers. It's still not too late for you to join. It is still not too late for you to gain power unimaginable, to view wonders incredible."

Clay was silent for several moments, seeming to consider

what Ward said. "I am not immune to attraction of power and of wonders," he said finally. "However, as a Clay, I can never disregard the demands of honor and decency. To throw in with you would be to abandon the United States, the country my family helped to build. Furthermore, it would be to forget your murder of a number of excellent people—Corporal Samson and Major Price, to name just two. It would be to forget your unpardonable slur against the woman I loved, a woman superior to you in every respect. Finally, it would be to forget what is owed to that farmer whom you blinded, his obscenely slaughtered son, and his defiled daughter. No cause, no goal would justify these actions. The depravity of your Starry Wisdom is limitless."

"Those people did not signify," responded Ward desperately. "Peasants and slaves, of no worth to a superior person such as yourself."

Clay shook his head slightly. "There was no chance you could tempt me into your ranks. I had intended to let you live, to testify against Forrest, but unfortunately for you, you revealed that the massacre of the prisoners at Fort Pillow was not directly his fault. He has committed many crimes, and someday I will see him destroyed for them, but much to my surprise, it would appear that Fort Pillow is not among those crimes. In that case, your usefulness to me is at an end."

True fear finally shown on the faces of both Ward and Sanders. "You are going to kill us both?" quavered the wounded, teary Sanders.

"Madam, I promised your late husband that I would do what I could to preserve your life. I will not go back on such a promise, even after learning how little you deserved his devotion. However, the two of you seem interested in mysteries. You will be witness to a mystery, and Major Ward will experience it."

Clay began to tremble all over, and the expression on his face began to change.

Ward and Sanders began to scream. Ward's screams stopped after a while, but Sanders' went on and on and on.

It was almost exactly ninety minutes later that a party of fifteen horsemen approached the cabin. Leading them was Teresa Duval. Riding astride rather than side-saddle, her assured handling of her mount made some of the riders behind her seem clumsy by comparison. The three horsemen directly behind her were Sergeant Lot, Lieutenant Bierce, and General John Turchin.

When Duval had galloped up to Burnside's headquarters, she was just in time to see Turchin's brigade enter Knoxville, the advance guard to Sherman's army. Interrupting Burnside's formal greeting of Turchin, she explained the situation briefly. Turchin remembered Clay and cheerfully volunteered himself and his head-quarters guard to follow her to the cabin. As the tired, grumbling troopers obeyed their general and prepared their mounts to hit the road again, Duval quickly informed Bierce and Lot of what had happened. Larson was gone on some errand, and Duval was not inclined to waste time tracking him down. Against the advice of a concerned Bierce, Lot insisted on joining the posse. Less than ten minutes after first addressing Burnside, Duval was leading the small party out of Knoxville.

As they approached the cabin, the wild, hysteric screams of a woman became audible. Most of the horsemen frowned, but strangely, the Russian general smiled broadly and said, "Ho! Sounds like Clay enjoy fruits of victory. Women of an enemy can expect nothing less." Lot looked shocked at the comment; even the cynical Bierce struggled to keep a look of disgust from his face.

The horsemen reached the front of the cabin and dismounted. As the others loosely tethered their mounts to nearby trees, Turchin strode up to the cabin door. However, before he could open it, it opened of its own accord, and a screaming Marjorie Sanders erupted from the cabin, the clotted slash on her cheek and her wide, crazed eyes making the beautiful woman a horrific sight. Turchin frowned with puzzlement as the woman staggered blindly past him, screaming over and over. As several of his men gingerly attempted to restrain and calm the crazed woman, Turchin turned to the cabin and stepped inside. Before any of the others could reach the door, Turchin staggered out, leaned forward, and vomited the contents of his stomach onto the ground.

As the general retched, Alphonso Clay stepped calmly from the cabin. He was spattered with blood; some droplets even appeared on his spectacles, which had slipped crookedly down on his nose. Slowly, he adjusted the stems on his ears so that the glasses rested levelly on his face. He walked a few steps, slowly, as if in a trance; then his gaze rested on Jeremiah Lot, who was rushing forward to him.

"Alphonso! Are you hurt? Where are you hurt?"

As the black sergeant seized his shoulders, Clay looked uneasily at his friend. "Jeremiah, I fear you will be disappointed in me. I seem to have rather . . . let myself go."

Turchin had finished emptying the contents of his stomach. He turned to face Clay, loathing warring with fear in his expression. "*Upir*," he said obscurely in his native tongue. "No man could do what you did. This was not punishing of traitors. This was . . . *upir*. I put you down like mad dog." He loosened the flap of his holster and began to draw his Colt. Seeing what was about to happen, Lot released Clay's shoulders and resolutely stepped between his friend and the general.

"Out of my way, Sergeant. This man an animal, worse than animal. I end him here."

Lot swayed slightly; he was still woozy from his head wound. "I will not do so, sir. If there is a charge to make, then it will be made before a court martial."

"You not see what happen in there. No point in court. If you make me, I shoot through you."

"You will have to do so, but think how the Radical Republicans in the Senate will react, what Sumner and Sherman will feel when they hear you have killed a black man wearing the blue. Their influence saved you once before, after the Athens business because they believed you devoted to Negro rights. I doubt they will save you again."

While the enraged general and resolute sergeant argued, Marjorie Sanders continued to cry and moan. Several soldiers tried ineffectively to calm her.

Bierce took the liberty of quietly stepping up to the door and looked inside the cabin. For a few moments, his eyes refused to acknowledge what was before them. Then his mind processed the images, and he fully understood what had caused a Cossack to vomit.

Suddenly next to him he heard a soft, moaning sound. He turned to see that the sound came from Teresa Duval, who was looking over his shoulder, eyes bright, face slack, drinking in the horror inside the cabin. There was a sudden, sharp gasp from her. Bierce, who had extensive amorous experience, recognized what that gasp had meant. With a cry of revulsion and disgust, he shoved her backward from the cabin, entered, and slammed the door behind him.

Bierce thought with furious speed. He now perfectly understood Turchin's reaction. It would be the reaction of any court martial as well. They would hang Clay, and the hanging of Clay would devastate the devoted Lot, as would the mere knowledge of what Clay had done. He owed both of them his life, twice. Much as what had happened here horrified him; he could not forget that. However, he had only moments before other witnesses entered who could back up whatever Turchin would say. He spotted an oil lamp in the corner. Moving swiftly, trying not to focus on what was scattered around the room, he picked it up. It gurgled, showing itself to be nearly full. Quickly he emptied the oil onto the dried wooden floor, produced a friction match, and lit it. He dropped the match into the nearest puddle of oil, which ignited with a whoomp, streamers of blue flame spreading quickly to the other little puddles on the floor. Swiftly he opened the door and left the cabin, closing the door before anyone could notice the growing flames. Fortunately, the other soldiers' attention was utterly riveted on the spectacle of a sergeant defying a general. "Very well," growled Turchin at last. "We take this dog to Knoxville and have him hanged there. Anyone who see what he did will be glad to be hangman himself. And you, I have court-martialed for disrespect!"

"Excuse me, sir," said Bierce politely. "Just what charge would you levy against Captain Clay?"

"What charge? Look in that cabin, and tell me what difference it make! What charge!"

"I have looked in there, sir," replied Bierce in a respectful voice. "All I saw was a dead officer from Forrest's command, an officer known to have used Federal uniforms to spy upon us and to kill several excellent soldiers, including Major Dallas Price."

"Fool! Did you see what was done to him?"

Innocently, Bierce shrugged. "He appeared to have been shot. Of course, gunshot wounds can be ugly, sir, very ugly."

Teresa Duval glanced at the tarpaper that covered the one window of the cabin. She realized that so far she was the only one who had noticed the flickering, growing flames that shown faintly through the tarpaper. Turning to Turchin, resuming her New England twang, she said, "I too saw the body, sir. Messy gunshot wound, but I have seen poor souls with worse." Bierce turned to look at her with amazement.

Turchin looked with even greater amazement at Bierce and Duval. Then he gestured to his escort who had been nervous witnesses to all that transpired. "Come! I show you something that will haunt your dreams for years!" Followed by his men, Turchin strode up to the door and flung it open. The burst of fresh air caused the flames inside to roar into greater strength. Turchin only barely avoided serious burns by throwing himself backward as a blast of fire erupted from the doorway.

Turchin and his men retreated to a safe distance and watched the dry wooden structure become an enormous bonfire.

Teresa Duval walked up to him and said sweetly, "No matter what you tell a court martial now, Lieutenant Bierce and I are the only other people who can testify as to what was in that cabin, and we will testify that there was nothing untoward in there. Perhaps the long march to Knoxville has exhausted you. I have known many people to see strange things when exhausted." Leaving the furious Russian, she walked over to where Lot and Bierce had gathered around Clay, who seemed to be in something of a daze.

"I am truly sorry, Jeremiah," Clay muttered. "I did not intend for it to go so far. But all the blood, well the blood . . ."

"Do not speak on it," said Lot, then to Bierce and Duval, in a lowered voice said "He is in some kind of shock. We must get him to Knoxville and administer a sedative. Help me get him to a horse. We will have to take it very slowly, to avoid any further upset."

The three began to gently guide Clay to where the horses were tethered. As they passed the furious Turchin, Clay seemed to become more alert. Without stopping, he turned his head and said to the general, "I recall you once told me that you thought we were much alike. I suspect you no longer believe so." Clay giggled and turned his head forward as the party continued walking.

John Turchin stared after Clay for a long moment. Then crossing himself in the Orthodox style, something he had not done in many a year, he muttered "*upir.*"

CHAPTER 7

CHRISTMAS EVE, 1863

Headquarters, Army of the Cumberland, Chattanooga

General George Thomas lumbered carefully about the large hotel parlor that had been his personal office for some weeks, solemnly nodding to the various groups of chatting officers he had invited to his little party. Occasionally, gravely offering one a cup of whiskey punch from a large silver tureen that stood on his desk, he imagined that they looked knowingly at each other behind his back. '*Old Slow-Trot could not move fast even at his own Christmas Eve party*,' they must be thinking. They did not know that the pain in his lower back had once again flared up and that the slightest sudden movement could bring tears to his eyes. Setting his bearded jaw grimly, he redoubled his efforts to keep any sign of weakness from showing. He knew that the men laughed behind his back at his slow movements but admired his strength and determination. Already he was being called "*The Rock of Chickamauga*." He believed it vital to do nothing to qualify their faith in him. 1864 was likely to be even worse than 1863, and he would need their trust and confidence.

He looked over at a far corner and saw Ulysses Grant sitting, quietly smoking. Strange, Thomas thought, how his commander had a tendency to appear absolutely alone while in the midst of a crowd. He suddenly recalled that Julia Grant had gone with their children to Missouri for the holidays, to be with her beloved Copperhead father. It appeared that despite his love for his family, Grant had chosen not to subject himself to a week of pro-Rebel ranting from the unpleasant old slave-holder who had somehow managed to sire the love of his life. Thomas thought of his own wife in faraway New York, and an emotional pang every bit as painful as the ones in his back shot through him. Thomas strolled over to the sofa and gingerly sat next to Grant.

"Merry Christmas, sir."

"Merry Christmas," Grant replied shortly, sparing only a glance at Thomas before turning his attention back to his cigar, which he appeared to be trying to smoke as quickly as possible.

"I understand that there may be a significant Christmas gift for you from the nation," said Thomas. "The rumor is that Congress is reviving the rank of permanent lieutenant general and that there is no question as to who Lincoln will nominate for the post."

"Hasn't happened yet," said Grant, strangely unenthusiastic about his coming promotion.

"I believe it will, sir. You will be the only one to hold that rank since George Washington." As he said it, the incongruity suddenly struck Thomas with full force—the rumpled little man on the sofa beside him would hold the rank that only Washington had held before.

"Don't blame you for finding it passing strange," said Grant suddenly, seeming to read the surprised Thomas' mind. "No one finds it stranger than me. Mighty big shoes to fill." He took a final pull on the stub of his cigar and threw the smoldering remnant into the spittoon beside the sofa. Suddenly Grant turned to face him, a grim, searching expression on his face. "Assuming the rumor is true, I'll be going back east. Meade and the Army of the Potomac are not what they should be, and I'll need to be on the scene with them. I will be promoting Sherman to command the Military Division of the Mississippi and McPherson to take his place as commander of the Army of the Tennessee."

The proud Thomas felt as if he had been slapped in the face. He had ranked Sherman at every step from the academy onwards, but now the man who had nearly left the army two years ago because of a mental illness would be his superior. And McPherson . . . McPherson would be his equal; McPherson, only nine years out of the academy, two years ago a lieutenant colonel on Grant's staff. Anger began to build in Thomas' massive chest, but as it did, Grant spoke further.

"I know how you must feel; believe me George, I know. You have served your country ably and well, at considerable cost, and I would not blame you if you resigned. But let me answer one question before you asked it: no, I am not doing this to humiliate you into leaving the service, and to make room for a crony. I have thought long and hard about this. Cump is a risk taker, and I need a commander here who can take risks. McPherson may not be the most experienced general in our service, but he shines in bringing out the best in the officers and the men, and the Army of the Tennessee has some hard cases that will respond to his touch. Both Sherman and McPherson need experience and ballast to hold them back from mistakes. That is your role. I am asking you to continue as commander of the Army of the Cumberland."

Thomas looked sternly at Grant, who did not flinch from the gaze. It suddenly struck Thomas as odd that anyone had ever considered Grant a weakling. He had not flinched at giving bad news himself, and although Thomas could now see it pained Grant to disappoint him so, it was not callousness but strength that led

Grant to personally let down a proud subordinate. Slowly, reluctantly, Thomas nodded. Anger only partly defused by Grant's obvious sincerity, Thomas forced himself to respond with dignity.

"Yes, sir, I will serve the United States in any position that you designate for me. Any officer who would put his own feelings on rank before service to his country, is unfit to wear the blue."

"I knew you would say something like that," said Grant with a shrug. "But you are just about the only man I know who could say it and mean it."

Thomas had an image of himself creating a dramatic, ill-tempered scene; the image was so implausible that the tension broke, and the "*Rock of Chickamauga*" actually smiled. "No, sir, there has been too much temper and pride. We must all lay aside out personal feelings and work to end this awful struggle as soon as may be."

Seemingly out of nowhere, Ambrose Bierce materialized in front of the two generals, a brimming cup of punch in each hand, a silly grin on his face. "Merry Christmas, sirs! Allow me to present you each with some of this excellent libation, with which we may toast the destruction of the Confederacy!" The glassy-eyed Bierce seemed completely unintimidated at being the lowest-ranking officer in the room. Thomas smiled at the sight of the young officer, while Grant frowned.

"I think I will pass on that, Bierce," said Grant, looking at Bierce like the muzzle of a cannon.

"Thank you, Captain," said Thomas as he took one of the cups.

"Captain?" blurted Bierce, midway in raising the other cup to his lips.

"Yes, Captain," replied Thomas, actually chuckling that he had surprised the normally unflappable Bierce. "In the morning, you will have your commission, promoting you to captain in the United States Volunteers. Merry Christmas!" For a moment Thomas was afraid that Bierce would begin to cry and realized that Bierce had already drank enough to reach the maudlin stage.

"Sir, this is unexpected," stammered the suddenly solemn Bierce. "It is really a very thoughtful Christmas gift. I hardly know how to repay it."

"Repayment is not the issue, Captain. You have earned it. Your service at Chickamauga, along with what Clay told me of your jaunt to Knoxville, demonstrates it's long overdue."

At the mention of Clay's name, Grant joined the conversation. "That reminds me, Bierce. Major Clay and Lieutenant Lot left a small package with me to give to you, before setting off on Christmas leave."

Bierce suddenly seemed completely sober. Carefully, he placed the drink on a small end table before saying "Well, the world is indeed turned upside down, sir. I saw the promotion for Clay coming, but not for Lot."

"You disapprove?" asked Grant, who was busy lighting another cigar.

"Far from it, sir. It's just that I thought the law forbade commissioning a Negro."

"I knew that," said Grant between puffs. "Told Clay when he told me he would not accept promotion unless his sergeant was commissioned. He then pointed out that the prohibition applied to the Regular Army and that there was no such rule as to the Volunteers."

For a moment Thomas' mind wandered back three decades to a dusty road and a frightened boy facing a powerful, dignified slave who was saying, 'Here we stand, little George.' Thomas shook his head slightly to bring himself back to the present; the world turned upside down indeed.

Grant was continuing to speak. "Clay also insisted that feller Larson be promoted to major and sent to one of McPherson's new colored regiments. Anyway, you weren't around when they had to catch the boat, so they asked me to give this to you." Grant reached beside him to where an oblong package had been wedged between his leg and the arm of the sofa. He handed the package to Bierce. With a puzzled frown, he removed the butcher-paper with which it was wrapped. Once the paper was removed, he was faced with a wooden box emblazoned with the logo of Messrs Smith and Wesson. Clumsily, he opened it up to find a gleaming new Model 2 revolver, with two packages of metallic cartridges. Bierce threw his head back and emitted a series of his barking, unlovely laughs. After he brought himself under control, he obviously felt he should explain his reaction.

"Pardon me, sirs, but this is priceless! You see, during our . . . travels my Colt failed me twice. Apparently Major Clay and Lieutenant Lot feel I will be safer with a weapon whose ammunition is less likely to go awry." The humor left his face, and Bierce turned serious. "I hate to think what they must have paid to get one of these on short notice. Even with no Government orders, the factory will have to work a year at full capacity just to fill the civilian orders they've already got. This is such a thoughtful gift. And I got them nothing." With sudden decisiveness, Bierce said, "Excuse me, sirs, I must go to my quarters immediately and write my thanks." Saluting clumsily, Bierce turned and wended his way through the knots of gossiping officers.

As Grant watched Bierce go, he commented to Thomas, "Strange man. Good soldier, but strange man."

Thomas nodded solemnly. "Cut him some slack, sir. He was wounded long before he joined the army, if you know what I mean."

Grant sighed, taking another puff on his cigar. "He's not the only one who is strange, Thomas. Even Turchin's gone a little soft in the head. Came to me with wild accusations about Clay. When

I told him I didn't care to hear such things, he began to curse in Russian; kept calling Clay *upir*."

Thomas frowned. "What's that? I don't know Russian."

Grant shrugged. "Picked up a few phrases when I was stationed in the Northwest in the early 50's; there were still a few Russian trappers around. If I remember right, it's monster, vampire, some such nonsense. I know Clay makes a lot of folks nervous, but Turchin is about the last officer I would expect to be spooked like that."

Thomas saw that the other officers were keeping a respectful distance from their commanders and would not be likely to overhear their conversation over the low buzz of voices that filled the room. "So tell me, sir, how will we handle the aftermath of the Sanders affair?"

Grant took a long pull on his cigar and slowly expelled the smoke toward the ceiling before answering. "Things are settling out better than we could have hoped. Only a handful of people know of his treason. The official story is that General Sanders died a hero's death. In a way, it's even true. Generals Schurz and Sigel will be privately informed that the murderer of their friend Joachim von Lindau is dead; I expect they will be satisfied with that."

"What about Mrs. Sanders?"

"Well, we were lucky there. It seems her craziness was an act. Burnside wired me that one evening she just disappeared from the hospital where she was being kept; must be well beyond the Confederate lines by now. Shame to let her go, but I imagine she'll keep her mouth shut, at least until the war is over and it no longer matters. It all ended well enough."

"Except for Sanders, and of course von Lindau," said Thomas solemnly.

Grant nodded. "That reminds me. Clay insisted that I wire to Prussia to request that von Lindau's grandson be granted permission to undertake officer training in their army. Seems he was being kept out because of the same political trouble that caused von Lindau to come here in '48. Clay told me that their king's minister, a fellow named Bismarck, would only put the request to his monarch if accompanied by a high-level request from an American. Clay thought I would be high enough. I wrote to Bismarck, and much to my surprise, I got a reply today; telegraphed to me directly once the Cunard packet boat docked in New York. Anyway, here it is." Grant fished a flimsy page from the side-pocket of his tunic and handed it to Thomas, who read the following:

"YOUR REQUEST PLACED BEFORE HIS MAJESTY STOP PLEASED TO BE OF SERVICE TO GREAT AMERICAN MILITARY HERO STOP WORD ALREADY SENT TO FRAU VON HINDENBERG THAT HER SON PAUL WILL BE PERMITTED TO PURSUE MILITARY CAREER STOP MAJESTY HOPES HIS SERVICE WILL REDEEM HIS FAMILY NAME STOP BISMARCK."

Thomas handed the telegram back to Grant, saying, "Well, I hope that wherever von Lindau is, he will have the satisfaction of knowing Paul von Hindenburg will be an officer in the Prussian army."

A private dining room, Delmonico's Restaurant, New York City

The boisterous group of four had just done justice to the world-famous cuisine of Delmonico's and was ready for the after-dinner toasting. The party consisted of Ambrose Burnside and his wife, and Generals Parke and Potter. Captain Poe had been invited but had archly informed Burnside that he had plans for his Christmas leave.

Burnside arose, wineglass in hand, and smiled down at his petite wife, a deathly pale woman with large, feverish eyes. "Gentlemen, a toast to Mrs. Burnside, the love of my life. Without her, my coming assignment in Virginia would be unbearable."

The cheerful Burnside drained his glass in a gulp, as did Parke, who promptly refilled both glasses. Potter took a careful sip, a shadow seeming to flit across his face for a moment. Mrs. Burnside started to drink but then seemed to gag on the wine. She began coughing, a deep, rasping series of coughs that went on for nearly a minute. While the fit continued, Potter watched the woman with deep concern, recognizing the early symptoms of consumption in his commander's wife.

Parke, instead, was focused on his commander's face and saw that although the smile was plastered in place, Burnside's eyes were grief-stricken and glistened with unshed tears.

Mrs. Burnside recovered herself. Then, acting as nothing untoward had happened, she toasted her husband. "To the hero of Knoxville! May he hang Jeff Davis from a sour apple tree!"

After Burnside had settled himself back into his chair, Robert Potter reached inside his tunic and came out with his silver hip flask. Handing it to his commander, Potter said, "Sir, I hope that you will accept this in token of your great victory." Burnside took the flask and peered at the fresh engraving that read "To Ambrose Burnside in memory of the victory at Knoxville, from Robert Potter and the boys of the 9th Corps."

Burnside looked at his subordinate and said, "Why Robert, this is the one you carried during the campaign. What a very thoughtful gift. I should get you a new one to replace it."

After a moment's hesitation, the balding general replied "There is no need, sir. I will not be needing a replacement."

"Are you sure?" asked Burnside in a bantering tone. "The campaign in Virginia is liable to last for months."

Swallowing the fear that would never leave him but that he now knew he could conquer, Potter quietly responded, "No sir. It will not matter how long."

Parke drained the remainder of his glass in a single gulp and said, "Well, that's it for me. My regrets, but I must turn in early tonight."

Disappointment plain on his face, Burnside asked, "Are you sure you won't come back to the hotel with Mrs. Burnside and me? We were planning on cards, or perhaps some music. She is a wonder on the piano."

"No, thank you, sir. All I would do is fall asleep on you, and that would be the height of rudeness."

"Well, let me at least escort you to the street. Dear, Robert, take your time. I will be right back."

The two generals left the banquet room and crossed the bustling main dining area to the front entrance. A smiling doorman, noticing the stars on their shoulders, hurriedly tipped his hat with one hand while he opened the door with the other. The two generals stepped out into the freezing night air, their only company on the sidewalk an occasional passerby and a vendor of roasted chestnuts who had positioned his wagon under a flaring gas streetlamp.

Burnside turned to face his chief of staff and took his hand, vigorously shaking it. "Thank you, John. Thank you for all you have done in the last year. Without you, I doubt I could face what is to come in Virginia. You know how many of those generals in the Army of the Potomac will be talking me down, blaming me for anything that goes wrong, whether it's my fault or not. I am a big boy, and I can take it, especially in the service of the country, but it will mean a lot to have a true friend at my side."

Parke took a deep breath and made one last attempt to help the man he adored. "It's not too late, Ambrose. Turn down an active command. Make some health excuse. Ask Lincoln to give you a district command in the North. Remember what it was like after Fredericksburg? Many of the same generals who stabbed you in the back then are still with the Army of the Potomac. One little setback, and they'll tear into you like starving wolves. I beg you. Don't go to Virginia."

Burnside's handsome features softened as he looked at his anguished chief of staff. "The President has asked me, John, and I have said yes. It's too late. However, I can't believe they'll be carrying grudges. They'll regard the good of the nation as foremost, especially now that the end is coming into view."

Parke bit his lip, realizing that it would be of no use to argue further. Ambrose Burnside was a fair-minded, trusting patriot; having no evil or vindictiveness inside him, he found it hard to imagine it in others. Well, reflected Parke, he would do his best to protect his simple commander against the maneuverings of less decent men in the coming year.

"There is one other thing, John," continued Burnside. "Should have done it sooner, but a good opportunity never seemed to come up." He reached inside his tunic and removed an envelope spotted with darkish stains. "Clay told me that before Sanders died, he gave this envelope to him. Asked him to give it to me; implied it had something scandalous about you. Clay delivered it to me unopened. I now deliver it to you unopened."

Parke felt like he had been punched in the stomach. When he had learned of Sanders' death, he had secretly celebrated not only the death of a traitor but the death of someone who could destroy him with a word. With a hand that shook slightly, Parke gingerly took the envelope, saying "Sir, should you not read this? It was intended for you."

From his great height, Burnside looked down indulgently at his chief of staff and smiled. "No, I do not care to. That God-damned traitor wanted me to doubt my best friend and most valued officer. I do not care what's in that letter; consider it a gift. Merry Christmas, John." With a smile and a wave, Burnside re-entered the warmth of Delmonico's.

Parke stared for a long moment at the envelope in his hand. Then, he slowly walked over to the streetlamp beside the chestnut-seller who was morosely tending the fire on his cart. With a sudden motion, he tore open the envelope, and with shaking hands, he unfolded the single piece of paper that it contained. By the flickering gas lamp he read what he had expected to read—about the evening an outraged Sanders had caught him with that beautiful young private from Illinois—about how Sanders refused to accept Parke's stammered excuses that it wasn't what it seemed. Finishing the letter, he suddenly hurled it and the envelope into the fire of the startled chestnut seller.

Tears began to fill his eyes. Ambrose Burnside had handed him back his career, his very life, with the simple trust that he so often displayed, to the point of foolishness. Parke swore he would do whatever he could to shield the beautiful, open man he loved more than he had ever loved the youths he encountered and used—the man so pure that that Parke knew there was not the slightest chance of his returning love in the way Parke dreamed. Parke began walking quickly toward the Bowery, where he knew of a house that catered to his tastes. With luck, they would have someone who would remind him of Ambrose Burnside.

Gramercy Park, New York City

"Good evening, Mr. Gould."

Jay Gould started so violently he nearly slipped on the frosty pavement. "Good God! You must teach me some day how you manage to appear like that."

Stepping from the deep shadows under the elm tree at the edge of the park, Teresa Duval uttered one of her silvery, chilling laughs. "I could Mr. Gould, but you might find the tuition expensive. In any event, isn't this somewhat early for one of our meetings?"

Gould gestured vaguely at the deserted streets. "You can see for yourself. Most everyone is home at some sort of celebration; we are safe enough from observation. Besides, I need to be with my own family shortly. In any event, my thanks for your messages. All the sheep expected Burnside and his army to be destroyed and were dumping their shares for anything they could get. Thanks to your information that there would be a Federal victory, I was able to pick up many good investments at pennies on the dollar. Our . . . arrangement worked out even better than I expected. So well, that I would like it to continue. I want you to return immediately to the Army of the Cumberland, in your guise of a nurse for the Sanitary Commission. Our terms will remain as before: $2,000 in advance, $2,000 upon completion of your mission. In addition, I have arranged for you to pick up a little extra. I have talked to Allan Pinkerton; used to be a railroad detective and is now setting up something he calls the Secret Service for Lincoln. You will now be carried as an agent on his books, at a salary of $600 per annum. You will report fully and officially on matters of interest to him. You will also informally report to me on those and any other matters that may impact my financial interests."

Duval frowned. "When do you want me to leave?"

"Immediately."

"On Christmas?"

"Come, Miss Duval, I know that you have no family or romantic attachments; the holiday should be of no interest to you," responded Gould brutally. Then reaching into the side pocket of his frock coat, he produced a thick envelope and tossed it casually to Duval, who deftly caught it in one hand. "The $2,000 for completion of your last assignment, the $2,000 advance on your new assignment, and a $1,000 bonus. $5,000 total."

Duval frowned. "Bonus?"

"I really did very well on the basis of your information. Very well indeed. Consider it a Christmas present."

"What a very thoughtful gift," responded Duval dryly.

"Well, our business is concluded. You know how to keep in touch. Merry Christmas." Gould nodded at Duval, turned, and walked away briskly.

Duval stared at the envelope in her hand with a frown, feeling dissatisfied for no reason she could explain. Then she made the envelope disappear, and with silent, gliding steps, she began to follow Jay Gould at a distance. Gould walked briskly and covered the distance to his mansion in less than a minute. Bounding up the steps, he entered his home without noticing Teresa Duval silently move into the deep shadows near the front parlor window.

Duval stared into the brightly-lit parlor, where she could make out an elaborately decorated Christmas tree. In a few moments, she saw Gould and a beautiful blonde woman enter the room. He was tenderly carrying a small infant. Gould suddenly lifted the child high above his head and gently moved it back and forth; this was apparently a familiar game, and Duval could see without hearing the child laugh with delight. Then lowering the infant and cradling it with one arm, he grabbed the blond woman around the shoulder and kissed her tenderly.

For reasons that she could not have easily explained, the sight enraged Teresa Duval. She felt a sudden urge to break into the parlor and slaughter the woman and child before Gould's eyes. However, she immediately realized that this was madness, and she forced the thought back into the dark corner of her mind where her demons raged. No, she decided. Far better to show the smug, self-satisfied Gould that Teresa Duval could have everything he had, and even more. After all, she had already set a plan in motion that would gain her more than mere wealth and independence. She smiled a smile that would have terrified anyone who could have seen it, turned, and silently went off into the frosty evening.

The Clay estate at Dignitas, Kentucky

Clay minutely inspected himself in the mirror that hung over the library's fireplace. He looked carefully at the trim of his long blond hair, swept back so that it fell almost but not quite to his shoulders. He gazed seriously at his new uniform, the double row of brass buttons on the front and oak leaves encased in the shoulder straps indicating his new rank of major. He nodded to himself, satisfied at the appearance.

"Giving in to vanity, are we?" came a familiar voice from behind him. Clay turned to see his cousin and friend, Jeremiah Lot, in a spanking new lieutenant's uniform, boots polished to a mirror shine.

For once, the tight grimace that usually served Clay for a smile was genuine. "It would seem that I am not the only one. You wear an officer's garb well."

"It's not the only thing I must do well," replied Lot seriously. "There are a great many who will be hoping for a black officer to fail. I intend to do everything better than any other lieutenant, so there will be no excuse for that."

Clay actually laughed. "I have no doubt that you will." Suddenly he sobered. "I need hardly tell you what a long and hard road it's going to be, for you and your people."

"There is no longer 'my people,'" Lot responded. "There will only be Americans. That is what this war is about, as much as it is about the Union. I was born to a much better place than most slaves—and given a much better start. Therefore, it's my duty to set the best example on the road to Zion."

Clay smiled again, but it was now tinged with melancholy. "Always 'the road to Zion' with you. I wish I could share your uncomplicated faith."

"Someday you will," said Lot with conviction. "God will not

permit you to dwell in darkness forever." Suddenly, he laughed merrily. "Listen to me preach. My apologies. Actually, I came in to ask you what in the world is wrong with Jacobson. I saw him scurrying out of here like he was fleeing the devil himself."

Clay moved to the ornate desk to the side of the fireplace, the desk his father had used, and which was now his. He picked up a sheaf of documents and turned his now expressionless gaze on Lot. "It would seem that our estate manager has been selling our horses to the Government for full twice what they cost. Furthermore, he's been selling the gunpowder from the mill we established at a full three times the cost of production."

Lot frowned. "Outrageous. What was he doing with such profits?"

"Oh, he carefully banked them to the estate's account. He was honest to that extent. When I had examined the accounts and confronted him with what I found, he seemed to expect my thanks. Thanks that a Clay was a war profiteer in his country's time of need!"

"He probably thought you expected him to get the maximum profit."

"Jacobson now knows better. I have instructed him to return all profits above ten percent to the Government and to never again charge such sums during this emergency."

"Why didn't you dismiss him?"

Clay shrugged his narrow shoulders. "The man has a family and was honest by his lights. Besides, it's Christmas Eve." Clay put the papers he was holding down on the desk and picked up another document. "Here is something of which you should know. While you were in town this afternoon, I executed my will. With a few small reservations, everything I have will be yours upon my death."

Lot could not keep the shock from his face. "Alphonso, that isn't right. I'm black, and a former slave. The estate will be in the millions. You know what people will think if I were to receive such a legacy. Besides, I'm not really comfortable with this talk of death."

"We must be realistic, Jeremiah; the next year could easily bring the end of either or both of us. As for what people will think, it's about time they get used to the idea of a wealthy, able American who happens to be black. You know better than anyone that it would be as much a burden as gift. The estate is complex and will get more so, especially if our investments with John Rockefeller develop as he claims." Clay paused, and a haunted look came to his normally placid features. "You will be a far better steward than I. What happened with Ward reminded me about how deeply, horribly . . . tainted I am."

"Would you like to talk about that?" asked Lot quietly. Clay had refused to share any details of what had transpired in the cabin.

Clay shook his head. "Please do not ask me again. I do not wish to burden you with something that should be borne by myself alone."

"Well, whatever you did, it was less than he deserved," responded Lot firmly. "What we saw at that farm alone was enough to ensure his damnation. Besides, you should know by now there's literally nothing that you could do that would affect my regard for you."

Clay shook his head as if to rid it of a troublesome thought. "These matters are inappropriate for Christmas Eve. Here, this is something I meant to give you tomorrow, but I might as well do it now." He took a wrapped package from the corner of the desk and handed it to his friend. Lot unwrapped it and then froze, shocked by wonder and awe. "A Guttenberg Bible! Can it be?" Gingerly he opened the worn cover and inspected the ornate Latin words that were printed in Gothic lettering on the first few pages. "It is! How did you come upon such a thing?"

"It wasn't easy," replied Clay. "I wrote to my German friend Wagner some time ago to make inquiries among his publishing friends. It's not a perfect copy; there is some damage to certain pages. Still, I knew that you would appreciate it."

Lot looked up; tears filled his eyes. "Alphonso, this is the most thoughtful gift I could imagine." He paused, then said, "Let me give you your present." Placing the precious Guttenberg carefully on the corner of the desk, he reached into his tunic's inner pocket, and extracted an unwrapped, smaller volume. "I didn't have the time to wrap it, but Merry Christmas!"

Clay accepted the volume. It was then his turn to freeze in surprise. "*On the Origin of Species*," he read aloud, and then turned to the title page. "Autographed by Charles Darwin himself. How did you manage that?"

"I have my own contacts. Anyway, with your interest in the natural sciences, I knew you would appreciate it."

Clay looked at his friend for a long moment, and then asked, "Do you not find the sentiments in this volume in conflict with your faith?"

Lot shook his head, smiling. "Not in the least. I believe in an all-powerful God, and He has chosen to implement many aspects of His will through natural laws, which the human mind can comprehend. Speaking of which, the colored church in town has asked me to address the Christmas Eve service. They feel that the example of a black officer who is a believing Christian would do much good. I would be honored if you would accompany me."

Clay looked pained, so pained that Lot immediately regretted extending the invitation. "I truly wish that I could accept your offer. I truly do," responded Clay in a strained voice. "However, for . . . certain reasons, I should not visit a church, on Christmas Eve or any other time. Perhaps in the future it would be appropriate, but not right now." With an obvious effort, Clay lightened his tone. "And in any event, there is much paperwork to clear up, matters that Jacobsen did not feel empowered to handle. I will spend the evening attending to that."

Reluctantly, Lot took up the precious Bible and said, "Well, then I must be on my way. In case you retire before I return, Merry Christmas."

"Merry Christmas, Jeremiah," Clay responded softly. He watched Lot leave the room, closing the door behind him. With a sigh, Clay settled himself into the leather chair behind the desk—the desk from which his father Cicero Clay had run the affairs of a great estate for so many years—the desk he had used the day he sold his niece, Jeremiah's sister and Alphonso's lover, to Nathan Bedford Forrest in order to break up an affair he regarded as destructive to his son's prospects.

Clay took a moment to wonder why he still loved the memory of his father, the father who had set Arabella on a path that would drive her to suicide, while he had nothing but blinding, burning hatred for Forrest himself. It was a matter of intent, he finally decided. As unnatural and unfeeling as his actions had seemed, as disastrously as they had turned out, Cicero Clay meant those actions for the best, feeling that the affair would destroy both of them, one way or another, in slave-owning Kentucky. He had after all demanded that Forrest see Arabella placed with a family who respected her gentile (for a slave) upbringing. And that was why Clay's hatred of Forrest would never die until the man himself was dead, Clay decided. Forrest had treated his beloved with less consideration than he would give to a horse or a mule and had indifferently placed her with a family that would hound her to self-destruction. Clay swore yet again to himself that he would never rest until he saw Forrest destroyed utterly and completely—not just his life, but everything he treasured or cared about.

Clay pondered for a moment his bloodthirstiness. His nameless grandmother had passed something terrible to Clay's mother— and through her passed to it to him. That gift was decidedly two-sided. He knew he had Grandpa von Juntz's mate to thank for his inhuman strength and intelligence; he also knew that he had her to thank for what had happened at the Devereaux plantation and in the small cabin outside Knoxville. If the legacy was to be positive on the whole, it was because of the stern devotion to honor America, a moral he had been given by his father. And that, Clay finally decided, was ultimately why he could not hate Cicero Clay.

Sighing again, he turned to the large pile of mail in the center of the desk. His attention was immediately drawn to a small parcel wrapped in butcher paper. The address was printed in careful block letters; no return destination was given. He unwrapped it to find a small wooden box within, the sort of box that women use to hold the cheaper kinds of jewelry. He opened the top, and after an instant, he hissed as he drew a surprised breath, dropping it to the desktop.

He stared at the contents of the box, rapidly considering what they signified. The contents were simple enough. The box was filled with salt, intended to act as a crude preservative. Half-embedded in the salt were two dried objects: a pair of human ears. As he stared at the dried objects, he realized that they were a woman's ears, and from the distinctive patterns of cartilage, he realized that he had known the woman to which they belonged. The ears were those of Marjorie Sanders.

The box contained no message. It did not need to; the ears were the message, as was the fact they had been sent to him. Although he knew there would be not the slightest clue to the sender's identity in the box, he was completely certain that the package had come from Teresa Duval. She must have realized how much it pained him that his sense of honor kept him from punishing the woman who had so shamelessly betrayed and ultimately destroyed William Sanders. Suddenly tears filled Clay's eyes. He hated such displays but realized he simply could not help himself.

It was such a terribly thoughtful gift.

AFTERWORD

This is a work of fiction. For entertainment purposes massive liberties have been taken with the historical record. For instance, the events surrounding the siege of Knoxville were compressed and simplified, although the construction of Orlando Poe's fort was indeed the key to the successful defense, and General Sanders really did give his life in a counterattack meant to give Poe time to complete his fortification. Another example is the massacre at Fort Pillow; although I changed the timing, it did indeed take place as described, and debate still rages as to whether Forrest explicitly ordered the mass murder or simply permitted it to happen. Where historical characters have appeared, I have tried to give a flavor of the real individual, even when he is placed in fictional situations. What follows are brief descriptions of the historical characters who appear in *Battle Cry of Freedom* and indications where some liberties have been taken, for which I beg the informed reader's forgiveness.

Ambrose G. Bierce (1842–1914?) Bierce was indeed a scout with the Army of the Cumberland and performed numerous acts of lunatic bravery. His commanders thought so highly of him that although he enlisted as a private, he ended the war as a major of volunteers by brevet. He miraculously survived being shot through the head during the Atlanta campaign. Within two months he had returned to combat, despite being plagued by blinding headaches and vertigo that would be with him on and off for the rest of his life. Some people attribute his black view of life to damage from this head wound, but the evidence was abundant that he was a strange and difficult personality long before a Confederate bullet injured his brain.

After the war he earned his living as a journalist, working much of the time for the young William Randolph Hearst. On the side, he wrote fiction on the supernatural and the all-too real horrors of the Civil War. His greatest moment of glory, aside from the Civil War, was when he directed for Hearst the public relations campaign against the Southern Pacific Railway's attempt to sneak through Congress a bill forgiving some $70 million in back taxes owed to the Federal Government. The then-head of Southern Pacific, the old robber baron Collis Huntington, was nothing if not direct. He personally accosted Bierce on a street, informing him that every man had his price, and bluntly asked what Bierce's price would be. Bierce's reply is reputed to have been: "A check for $70 million, made payable to my good friend, the Treasurer of the United States;" eventually, that check was written.

From this point, his life slid downhill, due as much to his own flawed character as anything else. By 1913, he was seventy-one years old, in constant pain, and divorced by a wife he had genuinely loved, who could no longer tolerate his repeated infidelities. One beloved son had murdered a friend in a sordid fight over a girl, before turning the weapon on himself. Another had quietly drank himself into an early grave. His daughter wanted nothing to do with him. Telling some people he intended to go to Mexico to join a revolution, and others that he intended to throw himself into the Grand Canyon, he disappeared. No trace of his fate has ever been found. He would have undoubtedly been amused by the mystery he left behind.

Ambrose E. Burnside (1824–1881) was one of those people to whom ill-luck clings. He was not an unintelligent man, having graduated in the middle of his class from West Point, but his judgment seemed sadly lacking at times.

On his way to his first frontier assignment, he was fleeced of all his traveling money by a riverboat gambler. In his first attempt at marriage, his prospective bride changed her mind, literally at the altar. His second attempt at matrimony was much more successful. Having left the peacetime army to market a breech-loading rifle of his own invention, he lost control of the company he founded just before large army orders began to roll in. Things like that happened to Ambrose Burnside.

Rejoining the army at the outbreak of the Civil War, he was rapidly promoted due to his successes in several small operations. When Lincoln offered him control of the Army of the Potomac, by far the largest of the Federal armies, he tried to turn it down. Only repeated arm-twisting by Lincoln finally persuaded him to accept the command. Sadly, his lack of confidence in his own abilities was justified. Knowing that he had been appointed to get the sluggish Athat. The result is that he fell into a trap at Fredericksburg, losing thousands of brave men; some of them lost because certain of Burnside's disgusted generals seemed determine to allow him to fail.

Removed from this command, Burnside was sent to command the Army of the Ohio where he did much better; perhaps because that army was scarcely a fifth the size of his prior command and hence easier to handle.

In 1864 he was sent to be a corps commander in the Army of the Potomac. Many of the generals there remembered him from his prior command and held him in contempt; blaming him for everything that went wrong during the Petersburg campaign, whether it was his fault or not. After his corps suffered a devastating defeat at the Battle of the Crater, a defeat for which army commander George Meade was as responsible as Burnside, Grant removed him from active duty.

It speaks well for both men that they remained personal friends for the rest of their lives. Burnside resigned from the army in April 1865, and pursued with some success various railroad ventures. His military failures had not affected his popularity in his home state of Rhode Island. He was governor from 1867 to 1870, and United States Senator from 1875 until his death. Because of his elaborate muttonchops whiskers, such facial hair came to be called "Burnsides" by the public; somehow in the ensuing years the syllables were reversed, giving rise to "sideburns."

In his memoirs, Ulysses Grant gave the fairest assessment of Burnside as a commander: "General Burnside was an officer who was generally liked and respected. He was not, however, fitted to command an army. No one knew that better than himself."

Jay Gould (1836–1892) was probably the most sinister character of the age of the robber barons, a man who was a model husband and father but completely devoid of honesty and decency when it came to business transactions.

He gained control of the Erie Railroad through bribery and fraud and shamelessly looted its assets to finance his further ventures. His supreme effort came in late 1869, when he embarked on a scheme to control all contracts for the future delivery of gold. As the United States was on the gold standard, this would have effectively given him control of America's currency supply. The only thing that could stop him would be a Presidential order to sell government reserves of gold on the open market. Thinking to cover this contingency, one of his henchmen wooed and married the spinster sister of President Grant. Disproving the charges of cronyism that then shorted that then and thereafter were levied against him, when Grant learned of the scheme he ordered the release of Government gold, destroying his beloved sister's husband. Gould managed to get out of the scheme with most of his fortune intact, and left insufficient evidence to support a prosecution.

In later years, Gould acquired control of the Union Pacific and Western Union, treating them as his personal piggy-banks. He died of tuberculosis, having spent his last years with his books and gardens, which, aside from his wife and children, seem to have been the only things he ever loved.

Ulysses S. Grant (1822–1885) was born Hiram Ulysses Grant; a clerk at West Point made an error in recording his name as Ulysses S. Grant, and he never bothered to have it corrected. His initials of U. S. Grant led to classmates calling him "Uncle Sam," later shorted to "Sam."

Throughout his career, everyone noted the absence of foul language in Grant, all the more puzzling in that he seems never to have formally joined a church. His foulest epithets really were "darn" and "doggone." Controversy over his political career has obscured the fact that most modern military historians rate him as one of the three greatest American generals (for those who are interested, Winfield Scott and Douglas Macarthur are usually considered the other two). It is clear that he was not happy with his military profession, the only career in which he was completely successful.

Although often denounced by political opponents as a mindless butcher, interested only in attrition, he in fact was supremely skilled; he lost fewer hands of the Confederates. His Presidency is usually considered a failure. However, recent historians have been revising his political reputation upward, although it will never equal his military reputation. The corruption of his administration was exaggerated by his political enemies. In fact, when he learned of illegal practices, he moved against them relentlessly, even if it involved his own relations.

The group called the "Liberal Republicans" criticized him as incompetent and dictatorial, and since many then-famous writers were members of that group, their hatred has tarnished his political reputation to this day. However, it should be noted that they meant to be "liberal" to the defeated Confederates, and were angry at Grant for using martial law to put down the Ku Klux Klan and to enforce the political rights of blacks. If Grant's successors had continued his policies, the civil rights struggles of the 20th Century would not have been necessary.

In 1884 his savings were completely wiped out by the failure of a fraudulent Wall Street firm in which he had been persuaded to invest. At the same time, he discovered he was dying of throat cancer; a 20-cigar-a-day habit had caught up with him. His family was still dependent on him for support, and he knew the only thing he had to sell was his memoirs. Racing death, unable to eat solid food, refusing more than low doses of pain killers in order to keep his mind clear, he finished the book the day before his death, gaining his family $500,000 and winning his last battle.

John G. Parke (1827–1900) was a skilled and loyal subordinate. Rapidly promoted early in the war, Burnside selected him to be his chief of staff, a position he fulfilled intelligently as long as Burnside was on active service. When Burnside was removed from command of the 9th Corps after the Battle of the Crater, Parke was given his command. He fulfilled his duties so well that for two brief periods he was given command of the entire Army of the Potomac. After the war, he held a number of engineering positions, ending his career as a colonel in the Regular Army and Commandant of West Point.

Orlando M. Poe (1832–1895) was a brilliant but cold military engineer; his foreboding personality perhaps kept him from advancing as far as he deserved. After the Knoxville Campaign General Sherman selected him to be his own chief engineer, a position he held during Sherman's famous campaigns in Georgia and the Carolinas. At the end of these campaigns he was given the brevet rank of brigadier general in the Volunteers. However, at the end of the war the Volunteers were completely disbanded and he reverted to his permanent rank of major in the regular army. In 1882 he was appointed lieutenant colonel, and retired not long afterward.

Robert B. Potter (1829–1887) was the son of an Episcopal Bishop. Serving primarily in the 9th Corps, he rose to command a division, and by the end of the war was brevetted major general in the Volunteers. In 1866 he left the army, and spent the rest of his life occupied in various railroad ventures.

William P. Sanders (1833–1863) was a Kentucky-born cavalry officer, whose loyalty was never in doubt, despite numerous ties to the Deep South. His traitorous wife Marjorie is completely fictional. Sanders was rapidly promoted due to his skill, daring, and complete disregard for personal risk. He died as was described, leading a spoiling counterattack designed to gain time for the completion of Knoxville's defenses.

George H. Thomas (1816–1870) was often described as have the appearance and dignity of proconsul. His devotion to duty was absolute; he did not give himself a single day of leave in the entire four years of the Civil War.

He had been a child living in the area of Nat Turner's slave rebellion when it occurred. His father died mysteriously about the time of that rebellion. Although there is no documentation indicating he was one of the scores of whites killed by the rebels, in this book I took the liberty of assuming that he was.

Despite his many ties to Virginia, Thomas did not hesitate in affirming his loyalty to the Union. He gained the first significant Union victory of the war at Mill Springs in January 1862, a victory that essentially ended Confederate hopes for taking Kentucky. He was a corps commander under Rosecrans at Chickamauga. His determined, resolute leadership of his men saved the army from complete destruction after Rosie fled the field.

When General Sherman set forth on his march through Georgia, he sent Thomas back (along with frankly second-rate units) to defend Tennessee from counterattacks by the elusive army of John Hood. Hood placed Thomas under siege in Nashville. Grant ordered Thomas to counterattack, but Thomas refused to do so until he had collected enough men and cavalry to make such a counterattack decisive. An impatient Grant set out for Nashville to personally relieve Thomas of command. However, before he got there Thomas finally moved; utterly smashing Hood's army and destroying it for good as on organized force. As a reward, Thomas was promoted to major general in the regular army.

After the war he was assigned to command several districts, ending up in San Francisco where among many things he directed the landscaping of the sand dunes of the Presidio which makes it such a beautiful place to this day.

Although he and his only brother were reconciled after the war, his two sisters (whom he had essentially raised) refused to have any contact with him, except for an insulting request that he change his name. His feelings can perhaps be guessed from the fact that before his death he destroyed all of his personal papers, and refused to utter a word about family matters. He never wrote his memoirs, saying only "*All that I did for my government are matters of history, but my private life is my own and I will not have it hawked about for the curious.*"

John B. Turchin (1822–1901) was born Ivan Turchinoff, but Americanized his name when he left the Russian army under a cloud to come to America. When the Civil War broke out, he volunteered; his skill and experience, leading to rapid promotion. However, in May 1862 while during a raid into Athens, Alabama two of his men were killed by civilian snipers. An outraged Turchin told his men, "For one hour I close my eyes," and an orgy of murder rape and arson took place, the extent of which is still debated by Civil War experts.

He was dismissed from the army, but reinstated under obscure circumstances. He served ably under General Sherman for the remainder of the war, earning from the grim Sherman the nickname "The Russian Thunderbolt." After the war he engaged in various business enterprises; he suffered from increasing mental disturbances as the years progressed, and died in an insane asylum.,

ABOUT THE AUTHOR

Tracing his Californian ancestry all the way back to the 1830s, Jack Martin developed a passion for American history and the mystery genre. With encouragement and support from his beloved wife Sonia, he began writing the Alphonso Clay Mysteries. Sonia passed away on Christmas Eve 2009. He promised her he would finish the books and become a published author. The series includes: *John Brown's Body, Battle Cry of Freedom, Marching Through Georgia, Battle Hymn of the Republic, and Hail, Columbia!* Martin is also the author of the Harry Bierce Mysteries.

ABOUT THE AUTHOR

ALPHONSO CLAY MYSTERIES OF THE CIVIL WAR

FROM OPEN ROAD MEDIA

INTEGRATED MEDIA

Find a full list of our authors and
titles at www.openroadmedia.com

FOLLOW US
@OpenRoadMedia

EARLY BIRD BOOKS

FRESH DEALS, DELIVERED DAILY

Love to read?
Love great sales?

Get fantastic deals on
bestselling ebooks delivered
to your inbox every day!

Sign up today at
earlybirdbooks.com/book

www.ingramcontent.com/pod-product-compliance
Lightning Source LLC
Chambersburg PA
CBHW030533030726
47495CB00004B/974